I0762109

FLEETING MEMORY

By Sherban Young

THE ENESCU FLEET SERIES

Fleeting Memory
Fleeting Glance
Fleeting Note
Fleeting Chance
Fleeting Promise

THE WARREN KINGSLEY SERIES

Five Star Detour
Double Cover

MORE BOOKS

Opportunity Slips
Dead Men Do Tell Tales

FLEETING MEMORY

An Enescu Fleet Mystery

Sherban Young

Columbia, MD

Copyright © 2011 Sherban Young
All rights reserved.

MysteryCaper hardcover edition first published in 2013

Cover and illustrations by Katerina Vamvasaki

Editing services by Katherine Richards from *The Reading Panda*

All characters in this book are fictitious.
Any resemblance to actual persons, living or dead, is purely coincidental.

ISBN-10: 0-9912324-3-7
EAN-13: 978-0-9912324-3-7

MysteryCaper Press
Columbia, Maryland

www.mysterycaper.com
www.sherbanyoung.com

Preface

Welcome to the world of Enescu Fleet, semiretired private investigator and master of the obscure-reference puzzle.

It has been exactly five years since the publication of the first Fleet mystery, and on this splendiferous, half-decade anniversary—I believe the recommended gift in most etiquette handbooks is a wad of cash sent to "Sherban Young"—I thought it only fitting that I say a few words, maybe several words, such as *splendiferous* and *wads of cash sent to Sherban*.

On this topic of puzzles, by the way, it's my sincere hope that as you amble through this first adventure…and the one after that…and the one after that…you have time to solve some of these conundrums yourself. Hopefully, in most cases, before Fleet does.

Beyond the pure pleasure of the thing, you'll be helping to preserve knowledge. In this breakneck world, where people almost never have time to discuss nineteenth-century poetry anymore, or little-known word origins, or Schubert lieder (not more than once or twice a week anyway), where else are you going to showcase your skills as a scholarly detective?

You are the crossword-puzzle solvers, the trivia-game purists, the *Jeopardy!* geniuses. This is your time to shine. Fleet is depending on you.

And if he ends up getting most of the accolades, because he's the world-renowned semiretired private detective and you're not, you just have to bear up, as I always do. Men like Enescu Fleet get the credit, while we do the heavy lifting.

It's okay. He usually slaps you on the back or gives you a hearty nod, and that's worth any number of names up in lights.

Sherban Young

1 — A Slight Lapse

I lifted my face from a rumpled sofa cushion and looked around the room. Morning. And a pretty rotten morning at that. Maybe it was the rain pounding on the window behind my head (or the tiny *1812 Overture* pounding between my ears), but I hadn't slept well. In fact, now that I really thought about it, I couldn't say for sure that I had slept at all. I felt like hell.

I think I must have rolled over on my other side at this point. I remember gazing up at my rustic living room ceiling…at my rustic living room walls and furniture…and finally at my rustic living room floor as I toppled off the sofa with a thud. A couple seconds later, someone started beating away at the front door, which rounded the thing out nicely.

By the time I stumbled to my feet, the rat-tat-tatting had reached a truly inspired level of racket. I opened the door and peered out into an uncertain world.

I was glad I did. On the threshold stood a striking young woman—in her late twenties I would have guessed—slim and fair, and very, very soaked. She had the most stirring color of green eyes I had ever seen in my life. Not hazel exactly but a bright and stunning green. She also had a smooth and peachy complexion and a cute little figure.

Mostly she was soaked.

"Could you please…" She hooked back a strand of golden blonde hair from her face and continued, "Could you please help me?"

I blinked at her once or twice. I didn't know what she needed, or how rain drenched I would become because of it, but whatever it was, I was the guy for her. "Come in, come in," I said, tucking in my shirt-tails, and she came in. "I'll start a fire," I remarked, stepping over to the wood-burning stove. It still felt warm to the touch.

She nodded blankly—and rather listlessly too. Heat, whatever its many merits, did not appear to be what she was after. She stood on the outskirts of the room, rubbing her hands together, while I fiddled with the poker. Once I had fanned the flame, nearly catching my sleeve on fire twice, she seemed to relax, and I felt better as well.

I offered her the sofa and asked her to start at the beginning.

"That's just it," she said, "I don't know where the beginning is!"

I blinked at her two or three times. I was intrigued. The girl was beautiful and mysterious, my favorite combination.

"Start anywhere," I suggested. "I'm not picky."

"I can't—"

"Here's a thought. What's your name?"

"I don't know!"

She couldn't have found me more sympathetic. "Did you have an accident?"

"I don't know."

"A fall? A bonk on the head?"

"I don't know."

"Have you eaten any bad shellfish lately?" I inquired, getting technical.

"I. Don't. Know," she told me.

I began to sense a certain annoyance from my beautiful guest. I couldn't blame her. I'd be pretty annoyed myself if I couldn't remember what I'd forgotten. I waited patiently while she collected her thoughts.

"All I can remember is standing outside, staring up at your cabin."

I looked at my cabin.

"And then the rain soaking through my sweater."

I looked at her sweater.

"And finally an icy shiver running up and down my spine."

I just let her finish her story.

"I don't know how I got here or where I came from. I can't remember anything."

I patted her hand. "The important thing is not to panic. We'll figure this out together. Let's start at my cabin. You were outside. It was raining."

"Yes?"

"Well, that's all I got so far," I admitted. "But bear with me. Are you hungry at all?"

She shook her head. "No, but please, don't let me keep you from your breakfast, Mr.—I'm sorry, I don't know your name either," she said, and then laughed at the absurdity of it all.

I laughed with her. (As it turned out, it would be my last truly carefree moment for some time to come.) "That's not surprising, my dear. My name—and we can forget all that 'Mr.' stuff—my name…"

I trailed off. An icy shiver had just run down my spine, and it had nothing to do with any rain. "Holy crap, I can't remember!"

And I couldn't. Really.

Perhaps that tumble off the couch had jostled my mind. Or maybe I was just such a princely host that I would do anything to put my more amnesiac guests at their ease. I didn't know. All I knew for certain was, when it came to my identity, I didn't know a damn thing for certain. Apparently I was the sort of guy who called hot young chicks "my dear," but other than that, a complete blank.

It suddenly dawned on me that I didn't recognize this rustic cabin. It was news to me that I even had a rustic cabin. The worn tapestries on the floor, the woodstove, the row of knickknacks along the mantelpiece with the truly grotesque porcelain elephant at the far end—you could file these all under "Duh."

And this girl, this fantastic girl, had the same problem as I had—this fantastic girl who was no longer on the sofa. I spun around to see her heading for the door.

"I suppose you think you're real funny," she said, and swept out into the rain again.

I reached the covered porch—evidently I had a covered porch—in time to watch her hurrying down the garden path and into the woods.

I lived near the woods apparently.

2 — A Total Haze

I stood there in a haze. It had to be the liquor. That was the answer, surely. I had obviously overindulged the night before and as a result my mind had come temporarily unstuck. That had to be it. Any second now I would sober up. My memory would kick in, and I would be my old, unforgettable self once again. Any second now. Just needed to give these things time. Any minute.

It wasn't kicking in. What's more, I didn't feel hungover. My head still had that nice, musical thumping sensation, but I was pretty sure the timpani wasn't due to alcohol. This was something else.

I drifted down the steps of the porch and onto the garden path. The air felt cold and wet, and it wasn't long before I was jamming my hands into the pockets of my jeans, trying to keep warm. On the upside, the rain had started to let up.

I continued to drift down to the edge of the forest. There's a problem with drifting, however, or so I quickly discovered. If you have no idea where you're going, you're apt to get there pretty fast. That's what I did. I paused about ten feet in and evaluated my progress.

I had no idea where my visitor had gone. I wanted to call out her name, but of course I didn't know her name. I didn't know anything about her. I considered yelling "Woman!" but somehow yelling "Woman!" didn't seem quite right. I had already had my fill of "My dear," and "Yo, blondie" wasn't me either. "Lady" had potential, but upon reflection, it sounded a bit too Jerry Lewis for my tastes, and I was pretty sure I hated Jerry Lewis.

I decided to compromise—

"Honey!"

It sounded too awful for words. I might as well have shouted "My dear." It didn't help that my voice cracked under the strain. I had been hoping for a passionate wail, the sort of searing cry that sends the birds flapping out from their trees. What came out sounded more like the reedy piping of a lovesick muskrat. I sounded like a dork.

I was starting to freeze. Minutes passed—cold, icy minutes—and still no answer. I removed my hands from my pockets and began rubbing my shoulders in a futile attempt to get some heat going. On about the sixth pass, I paused, partly because I was looking down at my feet and realized I had no shoes on and partly because I thought I could hear something. I listened closer and was able to make it out clearly now—the sound of twigs distinctly snapping.

Everything went quiet again. I couldn't shake the feeling that it was a sort of artificial quiet, though. The sort of quiet that is almost too quiet. I started to walk back to the cabin. I could hear the snapping noise revving up in time with my movements. I halted, and the noise shut off at the source. Someone was definitely dogging my footsteps. I don't know why I suspected it. It could have easily been my beautiful blonde friend keeping a thoughtful distance or some particularly inquisitive woodland creature intrigued by my presence. But I did suspect it. I suspected the crap out of it. Maybe it was the memory loss. Perhaps I was suspicious of snapping noises by nature. Whatever the reason, I distrusted it.

I picked up my tread again, gradually as before, and then suddenly broke out into a full gallop. Moments later, I was bursting through that familiar entranceway, on a line for my old pal, the wood-burning stove.

The fire felt nice and warm. In fact—not to overdo it on a theme—it almost felt too warm. Someone else had been stoking the fire. And if not me, then who?

I shook my head. Obviously I hadn't been gone as long as I had thought. Either that, or I was just a really brilliant fire-starter—a man who, when he lit a fire, it stayed lit.

The fire no longer intrigued me. I gazed around at the cabin, hoping for some kind of sensory recall.

I started at the mantel. An old brass clock, indicating five past eight. Never seen it before in my life. Toy roadster, wooden, painted yellow and green. Nada. Porcelain elephant, tiny chip in trunk, glossy coating. "Made in Bingham" stamped on bottom. God bless Bingham, thought I, and placed it back on the shelf.

I turned away and surveyed the rest of the living room. There was a folded newspaper on the coffee table, complete with pen, suggesting that someone, perhaps me, had been giving the crossword a try.

I picked it up and stared at it. The scrawled notes in the margins gave me an idea. Finding a clean space, I began to take stock. "What I Know," I wrote.

I paused, tapping the pen to my lips.

"Lives in cabin," I began. It was a start. I looked at my ring finger. "Not married," I listed. Again I paused, and I suspect my face clouded over here. I pictured my recent guest and felt better. "Likes women," I continued. I glanced out the window at the trees. "Likes trees," I wrote. I focused on the mantelpiece. "Hates elephants."

I took a mental step back here, wondering if I was making any actual headway. I started a new list. "What I Can Remember—In General." Much better.

Except it wasn't. It's pretty hard remembering what you can remember without any cue or starting point. It's like someone asking you to be witty and charming. You need a lead-in. I soldiered on. I wrote down "Eggs." I could remember eggs. Also bacon. Steak. Pretty much all food. I was hungry. I tried a few more items, eventually returning to the steak-and-eggs motif, and soon grew tired of this activity as well.

It was around this point that another of those curious noises, a sort of faint snuffling sound, began to lean on my subconscious, as if to say, "Psst, buddy, down here."

It started as a mere suggestion of sound, like a noise in a daydream. Then it became louder, then more noticeable, and I soon realized that it was in the room with me. I revolved around, all ready to enjoy my next bewildering encounter of the morning.

It was a dog. A small furry dog at my feet. I was pretty sure it was a Maltese, though with shorter hair than you usually see. (Dog breeds

I could remember fine. Everything else…) At the sight of me, it gave a little bound of excitement, barked uncontrollably for perhaps three tenths of a second, and then squatted on the floor and piddled.

This done, it scurried off, and I returned to my list.

"Owns incontinent Maltese," I noted. It didn't occur to me to wonder why I hadn't seen the miniature wombat before then. I had too much on my mind to delve into the movements of any roving fluff-balls.

It wasn't long after the introduction of the resident pee-pot that a certain amount of growling could be heard manifesting itself from the far reaches of the cabin. I tracked the Maltese's *grrs* down a short hallway.

I carried the paper along with me, although I had pretty much given up on my list making by now. I didn't need lists; I needed answers. I needed that girl, and very possibly a dog trainer.

I reached the end of the hall and saw there were two bedrooms here and a bathroom.

I went with the bedroom straight ahead. It was a pretty typical bedroom. Bed, bureau, smattering of art. It did nothing for me. There was a generic feel about this place. Too neat and plain. It seemed to me that if this was my home, I must not be a very dynamic personality.

Pausing to peer about for a wallet or cell phone or anything else that could tell me who the frig I was, I was about to move on when I noticed a standing mirror in the corner. I sidled up and gave it the once-over.

I hadn't expected to recognize the face staring back at me, and I wasn't disappointed. I didn't recognize it at all. Properly considered, it wasn't a bad face. Plain, honest. A pleasant face. I mean, it was nothing special. For one thing, it needed a shave; for another, I could have sworn my right eyebrow was an eighth of an inch higher than the left one. But, all in all, not bad. If I had been slotted to appear on some exciting new TV show called *This Is Your Face,* I wouldn't have minded getting stuck with it.

I was about to take a stab at my age—thirty perhaps, call it twenty-nine—when the Hound of the Baskervilles came online again. It was making a nuisance of itself in the other bedroom.

Well, you know how it is with us guys with faces. Stick us in front of a mirror, and it takes us a while to pull ourselves away.

I finally turned from my reflection and proceeded across the hall to investigate. My furry friend was there, wrestling with a shoe on the other side of the bed. Its tiny fangs were grinding away rapidly, as it bravely attempted to get a toehold on its subject.

I wondered whose footwear it was. I was still walking around in my socks—for all I knew it could have been my shoe the creature was devouring.

I rolled up my newspaper, only to find that I needn't have worried. The shoe wasn't mine. It was already attached to a foot, this attached to a leg, this attached to a corpse, this corpse shot in the chest with a crossbow bolt.

That cleared that up.

3 — A Complete Blank

I knelt by the remains. The figure was male, kind of a fireplug in shape, and totally dead. He was wearing a brown wool sweater damp with blood, tan wool trousers and a black scarf, also wool. I put him down as a wool fan. The way his head was cocked had covered his cheek with the scarf and pushed his glasses askew (thick black frames bedewed with tiny droplets of rainwater).

Then, of course, there was the crossbow bolt in his chest.

Careful not to add my fingerprints to the evidence—I wasn't a complete moron—I poked his glasses into place with my trusty pen and slid the scarf down. His face was mustached, ruddy in complexion and quite rough, like burgundy sandpaper. I liked mine better. I didn't recognize him (no shocker there), and for a minute I sat back on my heels, wondering who could have killed him and why. He seemed like a decent sort, for a corpse.

Suddenly the corpse spoke, and I sprang back from it, ramming my not entirely unpleasant face into a solid wood dresser in my path—teak, if I remember correctly.

The Maltese, pausing to squat and tinkle again, darted from the room, no doubt feeling its presence was no longer required here.

It was just me and the dead guy now: apparently not as totally dead as I had figured him. I scooched over and tilted my ear to listen.

"Heat," I thought I heard him say.

I nodded sympathetically. If I had been a corpse, I probably would have found it pretty nippy in there too. "I'll call for help," I whispered.

He shook his head and said, "No time," softly.

Unfortunately I didn't quite make this out, and replied, equally softly, "Half past eight."

He glared at me. "Not *the* time, you ignoramus. *No* time."

I had nettled the poor guy. Even still, I didn't see why he had to get personal about it. He drew me in closer. He might have called me an ignoramus again; I can't be sure.

"Ka—" he began. "Ka—"

"Ka—" I said with him. *Ka. Ka.* Was he trying to pronounce *ka-ching*? First *Heat*, then sound effects? It didn't make any sense.

"K-eat-s," he concluded. *Keats!* He had been saying *Keats*, not *Heat*. He had sort of muffled the *s*, you see, and well, it had really sounded like *Heat*.

"Keats," he said more clearly.

I was totally with him now. He was enunciating beautifully. *Keats*. A man named Keats had evidently shot him or knew who had shot him. "Keats who?" I asked.

He reached up and gripped my shirt.

"The answer...lies...with...Keats," he told me.

The line was said with such emphasis, with such a resounding weight to the words, that I had no choice but to lean back and consider it in the spirit in which it had been uttered.

The answer lies with Keats. I took it all in.

"What answer?" I asked.

He shook his head again. "Cretin," he remarked, and was gone.

He was really dead this time. Really dead and kind of rude.

I must have gone out into the living room after that.

I sat down on the sofa, shot a withering look at the Maltese (now running in circles at my feet) and tried to concentrate. I probably kept at this for a good twelve seconds or so before a voice behind me spoke.

"I must apologize," it said.

I bounded up, creeped out to no small degree. Expecting to see my plucky houseguest again, coming out to say how sorry he was for speaking crossly, I shivered from head to toe.

The speaker was not the corpse. This was a totally new visitor. (I might not have known my identity, but whomever I was, I was Mr. Popularity today.)

The new guy was older than my other guest—midsixties, gray haired, with twinkling blue eyes and a full though well-cropped salt-and-pepper beard. He was robustly built, pretty brawny for a man his age, and while his manner was undoubtedly perceptive, even a tad piercing, he managed to convey a sort of cheery indifference as well. He seemed friendly.

Seeing me jump, he took a cautious step forward. "And I've startled you to boot. I must learn not to sneak up on the people I'm trespassing on. Please excuse me for barging in."

I said "Um, sure," or something equally brilliant, and he smiled and looked relieved.

For some reason, I focused on his attire more than anything. He was casual but not too casual: open-collared shirt (plaid), V-neck sweater (dark green) and an old yet richly appointed tweed sport jacket, which looked like it could tell a tale or two. I think it was the blazer that mesmerized me the most. I stood by, transfixed by it, wondering what kind of tweed you called that and whether it itched or not.

"You see, I'm here for my dog," he said.

The word awoke a vague recollection on my part. Dog. Dog. There was something about dogs that I knew.

At my feet the growling Maltese tugged gently at my pant leg.

My guest's twinkling blue eyes twinkled even further at the display. "I can only assume she got in through the front door, which is ajar by the way. She's constantly on the lookout for someone to rub her belly."

He pointed down, and I saw that, indeed, the pup had curled over on her back, exposing her rose-colored stomach.

Declining to give her more than a cursory tickle, I scooped up the pooch and handed her over, explaining, somewhat incoherently, that I thought the dog was mine.

My guest appeared confused but affable. He asked me if I had a Maltese too, to which I replied that I wasn't sure.

Uncertain what to do with this comment, he opted to introduce himself instead.

"Enescu Fleet," he declared, pronouncing the first name beautifully—which, of course, he would. It was his name. "Perhaps you've heard of me?"

I was forced to let him down.

"It's no matter. If the Enescu is too much of a mouthful, most of my friends call me by my initials—*E F*—spoken together phonetically, like the letter *F*. *Ef*."

I nodded. F. Quaint.

"Are you here for the hootenanny this weekend?" he asked.

I replied that it was entirely possible that I was (whatever this hootenanny may be), and he took this partial answer for what it was worth.

Silence. Nearby, the woodstove had dwindled down to its last few embers.

You would have thought my inability/reluctance to reciprocate in the introductions would have put my new friend off. Nothing of the sort.

Turning toward the stove, he offered to stoke the fire for me. I said it wasn't necessary but found myself discussing the issue with his broad, tweed-covered back. Apparently the offer, presented in the form of a question, had been merely rhetorical.

Watching him build the flame back up with an expert hand, not burning himself even once, I realized that my earlier paranoia might have had some foundation, after all. He very well could have been the person who had attended to the woodstove while I was outside searching for befuddled blondes. And if he had attended to it, then how long had he been here? And if he had been here, what had he seen?

"Wow, that's great," I said, once he had finished. "Looks like you've done that before."

"Nothing to it. We have one in our cabin too. Very cozy."

This tidbit didn't help me at all. Or did it?

"Your cabin?"

"Yes. Across the way. Much more homey than you would expect from a hotel."

Hotel! It made perfect sense. I was in a hotel-room cabin. No wonder it was utterly devoid of any personality.

Back to the inquisition. "Been here long?" I inquired, meaning my cabin.

"Oh, only a day or so," he answered, and I frowned. That wasn't what I meant, and he knew it.

"What's your dog called?" I asked. It was my considered opinion that no one could talk idly about dog names if they had recently witnessed a crossbowed corpse in the back bedroom. I eyed him carefully as he answered.

"Don't think less of me," he smiled, dusting off his trouser legs, "but her name is Pixie. My poor late wife, you see—Oh, you little fathead!"

Having already been called worse that morning, I hardly even noticed the comment. It was just as well. The fathead remark was not directed at me. The dog, Pixie, finding the door still ajar, had somehow managed to paw it open. Before we could react, she had scrambled out through the egress. All the girls were doing that to me today.

By the time we caught up to her, she had scooted around the back of the house and was in the process of bouncing up in the air in a haphazard fashion. Using an overturned canoe as her springboard, she was trying to take a chomp out of one of the back windowsills.

Personally, I welcomed the change of venue. Outside was good. Cold but good. I was now almost certain that Mr. Enescu Fleet had not seen the corpse in the back bedroom. This would buy me time to work out what to do.

I didn't know what to do.

On one hand, I had come to like old F. He seemed like a good 'un, and I could use all the good 'uns in my corner I could stand. On the other, could I trust him? Could I trust myself? I had no idea who I was, who anybody was, and no clue who had shot the man in my cabin.

My cabin. I couldn't be sure that I hadn't—I didn't want to go there.

Fleet was busily concluding the legacy of the dog, Pixie: "My late wife, you see, named her. It was her dog, not mine. But with her gone, well, you understand—"

I said I understood.

"It's been a pleasure meeting you," said Enescu Fleet, after another prolonged silence. He shook my hand. "Speaking of names," he asked, releasing his grip, "I don't think I caught yours?"

I'm ashamed to say I chickened out.

Half of me wanted to reveal everything I knew—granted not much—sobbing on his tweedy shoulder if the feeling so moved me. The other half, the half that won out, decided silence was best. Until I had things figured out, I would do well to remain a lone wolf. Go solo. I just needed to give this guy a name, and he would leave me to it.

I like to think that I would have come up with something better than "John." In fact, I'm pretty sure I had settled on "Rex"—I don't know why—when Fleet cut me off before I could answer.

"Oh, for goodness sake, she's off again!" he said, nodding toward the furry white blur.

Together he and I scurried back around the side of the cabin. Pixie easily outdistanced us, darting back in through the open door. I really had to start shutting that.

Inside, Fleet announced himself stymied. "She must have gone into one of the bedrooms. Hold on, I'll check."

With these words, I had a sudden change of thought on the whole reveal-nothing premise. Going solo was overrated. I needed to explain everything before my elderly neighbor saw all for himself. (It never occurred to me to go back and grab the mutt myself.)

"Wait!" I shouted, and crumpled down on the sofa as I said it. "I can't keep up this facade any longer. I'm in a tough spot here."

I told my story pretty well, I think. I told him about waking up on the couch, the girl, the mutual memory loss, everything. Happy to get this off my chest, I prepared to give him the most important tid-bit of all.

"Back here," I told him.

I led the way down the hall and pushed open the bedroom door on the right.

On the bed lay Pixie, tummy up as usual. On the floor there was no corpse to be found, sweatered or otherwise.

Typical.

4 — Merely a Memory

I wasn't having a very good morning.

I looked at the floor again, under the bed, in the closet and in the chest of drawers in the bedroom across the hall. Baffled beyond repair, I returned to the living room sofa, sat down and slowly shook my head. Fleet, who had spent my entire outburst standing by, stroking Pixie on her belly, followed.

He chose a leather ottoman for his seat, his air helpful and concerned. Pixie, in turn, jumped onto the cushion next to mine and put her paw on my leg.

Her owner took the initiative. "Trouble?" he asked.

I made a funny gurgle. I couldn't bring myself to mention the body; I just couldn't. It was like telling a woman you adore her on the first date. It didn't matter how much you believed it; the words just sounded too damn silly.

"You look like you could use a drink," he said. He stood and went to the kitchenette. "How does cold coffee strike you?" he wondered, twiddling a black-and-gold pitcher.

I shook my head, but Fleet paid me no heed. He rinsed out a cup, poured me a tepid mugful and set it on the table beside me. In the same motion, he reached down and handed me a pair of leather shoes he had spotted stuffed under the sofa. My shoes.

I sighed. Shoes were better than nothing, I supposed.

He didn't confine himself to footwear. He went to earth again, poking about on the floor around the couch. A few seconds later, he returned to the surface with the fruits of his labor.

A very tiny fruit.

He held it in the palm of his hand, studying it. It was small and white, a little sliver of ivory. He peered around, and his gaze settled on the mantel. "I believe this chip came from that sculpture."

I nodded. I remembered the elephant had a chip in its trunk. The man would make a good detective.

"You expected to find something back there," he said, as I laced up my shoes. It was more of a statement than a question. I shook my head again, his signal to completely ignore me. "The girl perhaps?"

I said no, not the girl.

"Tell me about the young lady."

I reminded him that I had already told him about the young lady, assuming she was ever even here. I wasn't putting too much stock in my recollections right now.

"You told me about her, yes. But not every detail. Tell me everything, everything that happened before she arrived and after she left. Everything you can remember."

I found it an ironic request but complied. Fleet listened. When I reached the part with my useless lists and the arrival of the amazing piddling Pixie, he made a face, clearly resenting my indictment of the pup. I'm sure if I had asked him, he would have concluded that the piddle had been there the whole time, placed there by her enemies.

We moved past the piddle. I wrapped up my saga (again), once more skipping the detail of the harpooned body in the back room. He nodded. He told me I had an excellent short-term memory. Well organized and to the point. No doubt it came in handy at times. He may have been right. I couldn't remember.

These niceties concluded, he produced the paper I had been carrying around with me. I must have left it in the bedroom after my fictional meeting with the non-corpse. I watched as he studied the page, poring over the crossword and my list of remembered objects.

"You hate elephants?" he asked.

I don't want to say that I was growing weary of my visitor. He was only trying to help, I could see that. But I couldn't abide any more questions. I stood up and to my surprise he immediately joined me, reaching out and taking my hands in his. For an instant, I thought he was going to read my palm. Life line good, long-term-memory line total crap.

He didn't read my palm. After a quick inspection of each hand, he returned them to me. "Funny you couldn't find a wallet," he pondered aloud.

"Very amusing."

"You searched the whole cabin?"

"The whole cabin."

"And no cell phone either. Nothing like that?"

I agreed no cell phone or anything like that.

"Strange. People your age always have their phones."

I sniffed. I might have argued against this stereotype had I known my actual age.

"There's nothing you're forgetting, then?"

"I'm sure there are lots of things I'm forgetting!" I protested.

"Of course. But what I was wondering is if there is anything that you forgot to say that you know, and know that you forgot to say that you know it?"

"Say that again."

"Let me put it this way—"

I held up a hand. I told him that I understood his meaning alright and had told him everything I could. He seemed strangely unsatisfied. He wanted information, information I was no longer prepared to give. Was it possible that he knew anyway? I decided to test him.

"What do you make of the phrase *The answer lies with Keats*?" I asked.

He considered this a moment and then replied, "It sounds like the answer to some question has a connection to the poet John Keats."

"Poet," I whispered, mentally slapping my forehead. I knew that.

"Why do you ask?"

"No reason."

Fleet gave me a look.

"Just something someone said to me," I explained.

"The girl?"

"It's always about girls with you!"

"If not she, then who? You said you couldn't remember talking to anyone else."

"Okay, it was her," I said.

"She said it? She told you *The answer lies with Keats*, without any explanation?"

I said sure, why not, and he frowned. "When was this?"

"Oh, you know, just before she left."

The frown deepened. "Why is it that I feel you're not being entirely frank with me?"

Frank. I hoped my name wasn't Frank.

"I've told you everything I can."

My guest snorted. "You keep saying that. As if you're the only one who realizes that *Everything I can* can have more than one meaning. *Everything I can* because that's all you remember, or *Everything I can* because something is holding you back? Or someone?"

"No one is holding me back," I argued. Not anymore anyway.

Fleet placed a friendly hand on my shoulder. "I'm only here to help."

"I thought you were only here for your dog?"

His friendly grip tightened. Not for the first time I noticed how well put together this old geezer was. I had the feeling that if he wanted to help you, *he was going to help you.*

Seeing me cringe, he loosened his grasp. "You mustn't overexcite yourself. Granted, I have never encountered a case precisely like yours, but I am no stranger to abnormal behavior. The best thing is not to struggle against it."

His words filled me with a cold, dead feeling. I couldn't have felt colder or deader if I had been lying on a bedroom floor with a crossbow bolt in my chest. "Who *are* you?"

"I am just a friend."

"A friend or a head shrinker?"

"I have never found that a very apt phrase."

"Then you are a psychologist!"

"I suppose I am something of one, yes. In my line, knowledge of human nature—"

In a flash, it all became clear. The visit, the puppy pretext. The body that wasn't a body. All tests, experiments to see what I did, how I reacted.

Who was to say that I hadn't been down this path a hundred times already? A thousand! Perhaps this so-called Enescu Fleet was here to crack the nut that refused to be cracked.

"Your face has gone very peculiar," said the so-called Fleet. "We mustn't overexcite ourselves, really."

I glared at him hotly. "Don't keep telling me not to excite myself!"

"*Over*excite. And no. No, of course not. I wouldn't dream of it." The salt-and-pepper had softened into another soothing smile. The twinkling was a soothing twinkling, almost hypnotic. "I think you could use a rest. A nice rest. Perhaps I can find you an edition of the poet Keats—"

I jerked away. I wasn't ready for the butterfly net just yet. I spun to my right and gasped. "Pixie, don't!"

It worked. He twirled away from me, scanning the horizon for his phantom pup, while I bolted for the door. A twist of the handle, a whoosh of oak, and I was out in the fresh air, scrambling down the garden path. It was the choice of beautiful blonde babes, why not the likes of me?

Take that, Mr. Enescu Fleet! (If that was, indeed, your real name.)

5 — A Vague Detour

I charged headlong into the forest. I charged hard. I charged far. The whole time, I kept expecting someone to spring out at me. I didn't know who. Orderlies with straightjackets. Sneering men with clipboards and pointed goatee beards. But no. There was nothing but trees and more trees. (And the occasional startled squirrel.)

At last I held up. I hunched over with my hands on my knees, panting slightly. I had made it. I was alone. I was free.

I was lost. I straightened up and surveyed my surroundings. Pine, lots and lots of pine.

I was happy to have my shoes. That was one of the Fleet man's only slip-ups. Never give your patient footwear—he will only use it. Shoes notwithstanding, I was still in pretty bad shape. It was probably only in the lower fifties, but after all the storms there was a dampness in the air, and it chilled me to the bone. I was also starving and a little thirsty. I should have drunk that coffee after all, tepid or not.

I don't know how long I ran about in the woods, surviving on nothing but my wits. Not very long, probably. My wits weren't all that dependable. I had no direction in mind. I only wanted to avoid the direction I had come from, and I managed this quite easily by minding the shadows. The shadows from the trees were pointing to the right. As long as I kept them that way, I was okay. I was making progress.

At some point, I came to a clearing. There was a hill there and a large rock. Behind the rock there was an old tree stump. I sat on the stump and looked at the rock. I thought about the poet Keats.

The answer lies with Keats.

What could it mean? Why had the man gasped it out with his last breath—and if it had been his last breath, where had he gone? These were the questions I asked myself.

"What's your name?" was the question somebody else asked me.

It showed how far I had come in my mental state—hardened, maybe even a bit jaded—that I no longer whirled about at sudden noises. With nothing more than a brief, choking gasp, I wheeled to my right and saw a pleasant little girl in designer, child-sized overalls and a long-sleeved shirt. She was no more than four, with large, expressive eyes. She clearly found the huffing man on the stump a cheerful diversion with which she could pass an idle moment.

"What's your name?" she repeated.

I found her question in poor taste. "I don't know," I told her.

"My name is Emilia," she said, happy enough with her own name for the both of us. "I'm named for a region. Are you named for a region?"

"I don't know."

"Mommy's sister Aunt Sarah—" She pointed to a sullen woman sitting on a bench about fifteen yards away. I nodded wearily; Aunt Sarah returned my weary nod with topspin. "Mommy's sister Aunt Sarah," the little girl continued, "says that Emilia is the name of a lady called Earhart who disappeared in the air but Daddy says that that Amelia is spelled with an *A* and I'm named for a region and Aunt Sarah is an old *scone*. Do you like frogs?"

Bored with my standard straight line, I replied that I could take frogs or leave them alone.

"Aunt Sarah and I were looking for frogs," explained Emilia. "In that stump." She pointed.

No sooner had I looked than I felt a sharp rap on my left ankle. Not a frog.

I glanced down and saw a small boy of about three, maybe a hard-living two. He had just kicked me in the ankle and proceeded to kick me again.

"That's my brother," Emilia sighed. "He likes kicking things."

I could see that. "And what's his name? Tuscany?"

"Sam. His name is Sam. Aunt Sarah says he is going through a *face* and that he only kicks because he wants attention and that it's his face." Sam, who seemed to agree with this assessment, kicked me in the right ankle. From the bench, Aunt Sarah grumbled something about not kicking. "Aunt Sarah says that if you kiss a frog it might become a prince but that I shouldn't kiss frogs because they are filthy. Are you a prince?"

I answered that it was very unlikely I was a prince. Some kind of lost duke or viscount perhaps, but not a prince.

"Why is he on our stump?" asked Sam, no longer content to play the strong silent type. I had a feeling that little Sam doubted my royal lineage.

Emilia rolled her eyes. "He is sitting there, Sam, because he was sent away by the Pine Tree Emperor and must sit and guard the forest from the Cricket Men."

Sam looked dubious of this explanation and stood by stoically, considering other theories. Thirty seconds later: "Why is he on our stump?"

Emilia shook her head. She had no patience for little brothers and their lack of folklore knowledge. "Have you been to the castle?" she asked me.

I said no, no I hadn't, to which Emilia replied that I should, and it was a very pretty castle, the prettiest castle she had ever seen. Sam, kicking me, asked why I was on their stump.

"Aunt Sarah says that many people end up out in the cold because they lose their shirts at the castle. Have you lost your shirt at the castle?"

I peered down at my Oxford broadcloth and frowned. As anyone could see, I *had* my shirt, one of the few things I did have. Why she should ask if I had lost it, I couldn't fathom. I was beginning to find the little one's dialogue a bit hard to follow, like some enigmatic child in a pastoral poem by Wordsworth. Sam's conversational method I could also do without.

"This is my shirt," I informed her. She no longer seemed concerned with shirts.

"Why did you say that the answer lies with eats?"

I told her it was not eats. It was Keats. She asked me what Keats was.

"A romantic-era poet."

"What's a romantic-era poet?"

"It's not important."

Little Emilia frowned. "Did he lie about the answer? Aunt Sarah says most men lie because—"

I explained that it was not that kind of lie. It was the other kind of lie, the kind that means to rest. The answer rests with him. "He has the answer," I explained.

"Is the answer tired? Because it needs to rest. Is it tired?"

My head was starting to hurt. Emilia, seeming to spot this, whispered, "Maybe the answer will tell you where the Pine Tree Emperor lives."

"Very possibly," I agreed.

"And if you find the Pine Tree Emperor, he could tell you your name."

"I would expect nothing less."

"He might make you solve a puzzle first, though. Emperors always ask people to solve puzzles in stories. Sam and I are good at puzzles."

This opened up a new line of thought. Not the part about the Pine Tree Emperor, that was all applesauce, but the puzzle bit. The Keats line, it sounded like a puzzle. But why a puzzle? I mean, why be complicated? And with a crossbow bolt in the chest, no less. If it really had been a crossbow bolt.

"Do you think it's a puzzle?" I asked her.

"I like crickets," said Emilia. "Even more than frogs. Do you like crickets?"

Our interview wrapped up soon after. Aunt Sarah called, "Em, Sam, breakfast," and the future star punter of the NFL toddled off.

His sister lingered behind. "Did your mommy and daddy make you your breakfast?"

I shook my head.

"You could have breakfast with us except Mommy says we can only fit five at the table and Daddy says Aunt Sarah is a leech."

I waved aside the offer. As much as I wanted to continue my nodding acquaintance with Aunt Sarah, I said I wasn't really hungry.

Besides, I told Emilia, I had matters to take up with the Pine Tree Emperor.

The child wasn't buying it. Despite Aunt Sarah's opinion of most men, I wasn't very good at lying.

Emilia removed a chocolate bar from her center pocket. "Aunt Sarah gave Sam and me this for after breakfast but we want you to have it." She handed it to me in the wrapper.

"Shouldn't you confer with Sam on this?" I asked, touched by her generous act.

"Mommy says that kids eat too much chocolate and Daddy says that chocolate promotes tooth decay. Daddy is a—is a—" She struggled with the term. "An *ornithologist*," said Emilia.

And, with another quick word to watch out for the Cricket Men, she sped off toward Sam.

I'm not sure I have ever enjoyed a meal more. I had no way of knowing the last time I had eaten, but from the way I gobbled down that chocolate bar, it might have been weeks. Even if it had only been a day, it seemed to me that the little overall-wearing angel (which is how I will always view her) had saved my life, and if it turned out that I was a duke or viscount, I would make sure she had all the frogs and crickets she wanted in my fiefdom.

Sam, I wasn't so sure about.

As soon as I had finished eating, I began to think more clearly, and the first thing I considered was how to solve that puzzle. If it was a puzzle. *The answer lies with Keats.* I could only figure the solution must have something to do with my memory.

It must.

I stood up, a new man. My legs were still pretty wonky under me, but I could walk. I headed toward the hill. And what do you think I saw as I came up over the ridge, but a giant ivory-colored castle.

The little tyke had all the answers.

6 — Bluffing

She was right. It was a very pretty castle. Viewing it from half a mile away, I could see it was comprised of long white bricks and white stone tiers. It had several hundred windows, one of these gigantic and star shaped, gleaming out from the center in a bright mosaic design. There were six battlements in all, each ten stories high, sleek and tapered as they rose.

Oh yes, there were also slews of people milling about in resort sweatshirts; banners heralding blackjack, poker, the loosest slots in New England and the most uproarious nightclub acts around; and a short distance beyond all that, an azure sign with silver letters that read: "The Wolf Valley Casino." I was beginning to think it was some kind of casino.

As I approached, the hub of humanity became more condensed. Man, woman and child weaved to and fro, some talking into phones, a few to each other. They talked of food, shows, pots they had scooped in and hands that hadn't gone their way. Many, I suspected, had misplaced their shirts during these activities.

I reached the enormous chrome doors and nodded in bewilderment at the security guard in attendance there. I went in.

The lobby was dominated almost entirely by the mosaic. I could see it better now: a wolf in a valley. Made sense. The rest had a definite shopping mall feel: long, cavernous corridors shooting off in every direction like spokes in a wheel. It was well lit but not overly lit. And noisy. The rattle of slots—the loosest in New England—competed alongside the hum of voices: cheering, yelling, laughing and shouting.

I was pretty sure this wasn't my first visit to a casino. I felt comfortable and at home here, as if I belonged. There was something different about this casino, though, something that distinguished it from other ones I might have been in. A moment's reflection and I had it. Most casinos I could picture had few or no windows—as little reminder of time or space outside its walls as possible. The Wolf Valley had tons. Huge, hulking things.

Observing a skylight overhead, I stepped back to take a gander through it and almost immediately barged into a pair of men talking.

Even with their backs to me, I could see they were in uniform. Security guards or maybe local police. Officer A, who looked like he was about nineteen, was stating to Officer B, who looked even younger, "He's about six foot, medium build and coloring. Jeans. Oxford broadcloth shirt, blue. Oh, and he's got no wallet or cell phone, so he couldn't have gotten far."

I inched away discreetly. I needed to be elsewhere, *far* away elsewhere.

I returned to the main entrance and peered back at the men talking about me. They appeared to be looking my way now. I jerked out of view, this motion attracting the notice of the guard at the door.

It's hard to say what brought me to the set of doors at the far end of the lobby. They just seemed to beckon me. Through the panel of windows I could see a bus, and outside that bus, a bunch of people were queueing up. I didn't know where they were going but I wanted to be among their number. I nipped through the doors and got in the back of the line.

There were two problems with this maneuver as far as I could make out. As the guards had pointed out, I had no wallet and therefore no money for a ticket. That was Problem One. Problem Two revolved around the cops themselves. They were outside now, approaching the front of the bus.

I managed to stay out of view. For the time being. It was too late to run: to make a break for it now would sink me for sure. The junior rent-a-cops had paused at the door of the bus, peering up and down the queue. I endeavored to merge deeper into the mob.

I had to think. Think! Slowly I began to form an idea. A casino employee was strolling past the line, idly clicking a ballpoint pen. I asked her if I could borrow it.

I needed one more item. Something, anything—

I saw my chance. Directly in front of me was a man, younger looking than me and well lit on casino firewater. He had started early. He stood unsteadily in line and twice in the last minute had tried to answer a cell phone that hadn't rung. He must have found all this drink warming to the body, for a Wolf Valley sweatshirt was slung over his shoulder, unworn. I crept up and woke him with a finger to the rib cage.

"Dude, I like your sweatshirt."

He rolled to his right along the stone pillar supporting him and grinned at me. "Thanks, dude, I like yours too."

My invisible garment thanked him. "Mind if I see yours for a second? I was thinking of buying one."

He waved his hand extravagantly. "Go right ahead," he said. As long as he could see mine when I was done.

I had only seconds to assume my clever disguise before the cops passed along. The sweatshirt helped conceal my outfit, but it was the performance that sold it.

Holding up a hand to the small plastic clip in my ear, I did my best obnoxious townie. "Yes," I said. "I don't know. Ask Fitch what he thinks. I know that, but don't forget about Abercrombie. Yeah. Sure. Water chestnuts. Yeah. No. Lettuce, tomato, mayonnaise. Exactly."

The guards walked past without even looking at me. I might as well have been painted on the backdrop.

I sighed in relief and tried to still my beating pulse.

It actually worked! I was amazed. I couldn't tell you what sort of gambler I was normally, but it was nice to see that I had the bluffing part down.

I reached up and pulled the object from my ear, rubbing the area softly. If you've ever clipped a pen cap to your lobe, you know it's not something you care to leave there indefinitely. I slipped it into my shirt pocket. (Oxford broadcloth. Blue.)

We began to shuffle forward onto the bus now. I slung the sweatshirt back over the hunch of my sleepwalking accomplice and took a deep breath. I had solved Problem Two.

Problem One presented itself as I took my seat.

"You must be freezing," said the elderly bus attendant, as I slid across the vinyl. He had a gravelly voice and tiny shrewd eyes. "No jacket?" he asked. I explained that I had naturally warm blood, and the attendant laughed and said, "You should try one of those Polar Bear Swims. Guys like you enjoy freezing their balls off." He chuckled again and then added, somewhat abruptly, "Ticket please." He was no longer chuckling.

The spotlight was back on me. With a casual nod, I fumbled in my right jeans pocket. I fumbled in my left jeans pocket. I fumbled in my rear jeans pockets, in my shirt pocket and then back to my jeans pockets. I rolled my eyes. I had left the ticket in my bag!

"The thick blue one," I explained, remembering a hefty-looking specimen. It had gone in first in the compartment underneath the bus, with the rest of the bags piled in around it. "Guess someone will have to pull it out again," I sighed.

The bus attendant scowled. "That won't be necessary," he whispered. "We'll get it when we get to Boston." He slid back down the aisle, and I felt the bus shimmy as it slipped roughly into gear.

The issue of Problem One, Subsection ii—what to do when we arrived at our destination—I declined to bother myself with now. I would deal with that when we arrived in Boston.

Boston. I wondered if I had ever visited Boston.

I closed my eyes. I slept.

7 — Taken for a Ride

I awoke sometime later to a hand shaking me. The bus attendant was leaning over me, his hat pushed back from his forehead.

I felt a sudden panic. I had thought of nothing! I hadn't even begun to think about thinking of something. I had slept, and now we were in Boston, where the authorities were not so easily taken in. And I had no ticket. Or money. And no notion of how to deal with Problem One, Subsection ii. I hadn't even stretched properly.

"Easy does it," said the attendant, observing my agitation.

I popped up in my seat and peered around. The bus was completely deserted. Through the smudgy window I could see the familiar line of taxis and shuttles scattered alongside the flank of the Wolf Valley Casino.

"What's going on?" I demanded.

"Engine trouble. Crapped out about five miles out. Had to turn around and come back so we could change buses."

"And you didn't wake me?"

The attendant pushed the brim of his hat farther up his forehead. It looked like it was going to slide down the other side. "I'm sorry about that. But the other bus has a different staff, see, and they wouldn't have taken so kindly to that ruse of yours."

"What ruse of mine?"

"The ruse with the ticket." He held up a gnarled hand. "I know your ticket isn't in the blue bag. The bag isn't yours at all, is it?"

"You knew that?"

"I haven't been working the lines forty years not to notice whose bag is whose, especially when it weighs an earthly ton. That's where the tips are. It was clever of you to try, though. Pretty clever how you hid from them guards too."

I thanked him. But not effusively.

"Having a bit of bad luck?" he asked, glancing back at the casino. I figured he asked that a lot.

"You could say that," I said—but it wasn't cards or slots that had brought me to this sorry state, I explained.

"Ah. Roulette," remarked the attendant knowingly.

I leaned back in my seat and worked out the various kinks in my body. I felt strangely at ease around this man identified by his name tag as Roy. I felt Roy was on my side, a friend. (He hadn't called the cops back in anyway, and that was all I required of my friends at this point.)

"What's the trouble?" asked my friend Roy.

I shook my head. Where did I begin? "What time is it?" (Among other things lacking in my life, I had no watch.)

"Ten of noon. Lunchtime."

Lunch. I wondered how I would scrounge *that* up.

"Ever feel like you don't know who you are, Roy?"

"Can't say that I have," said Roy. "Then again," he reflected, "there's times when you feel like you don't have much say in who you are. That's all your boss and your wife and your kids—all of them telling you who you are and who you aren't, and then you look in the mirror one day and realize they're right."

"I think you're a philosopher at heart, Roy."

Roy smiled at the compliment. "But I'm past trying to find myself," he said. "Too late for me to worry about all that malarkey. I am who I am, and that's all that I am," spoke the philosopher attendant proudly.

I thought he sounded a touch like Popeye there, but the sentiment was healthy enough. I wished it were that easy for me.

"Can I ask if it's women troubles you've been having?"

I brooded a moment. I said yes, in a way, it was women troubles. One woman anyway. "You see, she says she doesn't know who she is either."

"I've been there."

"Then she left. Before I could even talk to her."

"That's what they do. Flap off like little birds. But they always come back if you say the right things."

"I can't say the right things if I don't know where to find her."

"That's true enough. You try her mother's?"

"I don't know where her mother is."

"I wish I could say that," said Roy, shivering. "My wife's lives with us. Ninety years young she is and as outspoken as ever." He shivered again. "How about your lady's friends? Could she have gone there?"

"I don't know who her friends are."

"They probably wouldn't help you anyway. Women stick together, always have. How about your friends? They have any ideas for you?"

I told him that I didn't know who my friends were.

"It is tough sometimes," Roy agreed. "Hey, have you considered having one of them songs dedicated to her on the radio?" he asked suddenly. "Friend of mine did that once. Called up the station and had them play his lady's favorite song over and over again, by way of saying he was sorry he broke her brother's collarbone. You see?"

I said I saw. "Except I don't know her favorite song."

"That's too bad."

"I don't know her name either," I pointed out.

For the first time, I felt Roy could appreciate the obstacles I had to overcome. "You don't know—*her name*?"

"Nope."

"But I…you…don't…"

"—know anything about her. That's right. Except that she's blonde and doesn't know who she is and has the carriage of a goddess."

"When you say she doesn't know who she is—"

"I mean she doesn't know who she is. It's like I told you. She doesn't know who she is; I don't know who she is. I don't know who I am either."

"You don't—"

"Know anything about myself—that's right. All I know is a cabin, a girl, and some guy covered in blood who keeps babbling about Keats."

"Covered in blood—"

"Well, there wasn't that much blood, actually. And I'm not too worried about him. The blood didn't seem to keep him from disappearing again. It's the Keats I'm curious about. *The answer lies with Keats.* That's what he told me."

Roy looked quite rattled now. "This Keats—he dead too?"

"Well yeah. For some time."

"Oh my Lord."

"No, it's fine—"

Roy had begun to back away. "Fine?"

"No, I mean, he died a long time ago. Natural causes. Well, actually, somebody—Byron I think it was—said he died from a bad review, but that was only poet humor."

"Poet—"

"—humor. It was just a joke."

"And this man covered in blood? That some kind of joke too?"

"I don't know. It could have been a joke, yes," I conceded. "Some kind of crazy prank."

"And the answer to this prank," said Roy, his voice shaking with emotion, "it's with this Keats fellow, lying in his grave?"

I hadn't thought about it like that before. In his grave. *The answer lies with Keats.* He took it with him to the grave. It made sense.

"Do you think that might be it?" I asked, excitedly snatching at the fabric of Roy's uniform. "The grave? You think we might find it there?"

"I don't know nothing about no graves!" spouted Roy, wrenching himself free. His hat had tipped off his forehead, but he trampled right over it, a casualty of retreat. "Your lady is best free of your likes," he said, hastening out the door of the bus.

I followed sometime after. I couldn't help feeling that things with my friend Roy hadn't gone as well as they might have.

As I alighted, I noticed a young woman standing in the shadows, watching. She must have thought the attendant mad, dashing out like that, muttering to himself. I didn't know what she thought of me.

She was attractive in a minimalist way. Olive skin with long, black hair. A small, round face above a long and slinky figure.

"Looking for a lady?" she asked.

I felt my cheeks flush. I might not have known who my mother was, but I suspected she had warned me about girls like this. I knew ladies of the evening liked to work the casinos, but I never would have guessed they worked them so strong in New England, and in broad daylight no less. I quickened my pace.

"A lady," this purposeful young professional repeated, following me. "A nice blonde perhaps?"

I was a little surprised that she had shifted gears so readily—a blonde she was offering now, in contrast to her raven locks. (These ladies would do anything to satisfy.) Feeling the rest of my face color in shyness and embarrassment, I walked faster.

The woman trailed behind, honing her sales pitch. "A nice young blonde with green eyes and without a name?"

I froze. This put a new complexion on the matter. I jerked around and asked her what she knew about my blonde.

The brunette's lips had parted in a glossy smile. Her dark eyes continued to bore through me—a piercing stare I had felt on me before. "I know you're looking," was all she said.

"You know where she is?"

She tilted her head toward a small shuttle bus idling in the lane. "This way."

I don't know what compelled me to believe her. I guess the strain of not knowing what she knew was too great. And it wasn't like I had anything better to do. I followed her up the steps and inside.

We sat midway up the aisle, her on the outside, me on the inside. It was only then that I saw the dignified old gent in the seat to our immediate left. He wore a natty tweed jacket and had a small Maltese dog in his lap.

Enescu Fleet greeted me with a nod. Pixie confined herself to a short, sharp "Woof!"

8 — Finding Oneself

"You're a difficult man to pin down," said Enescu Fleet, steadying Pixie on his legs.

I made no attempt to flee. For one thing, it would have meant shoving his slinky brunette accomplice to the floor, and somehow, I felt that wouldn't have befitted my upbringing. For another, I had no place to flee. I was tired, and the shoes I had thought so highly of this morning were giving me a blister. I wasn't going anywhere.

"You've been having some adventure this morning," he remarked, as if reading the tribulations of the last few hours in my tousled appearance. I wasn't about to contradict him.

"What now?" I asked.

"That depends entirely on you," said my tweedy captor.

"Does it?"

"Absolutely. I admit I've spent the better part of the morning searching for you, calling in favors at the casino and getting a little unofficial help from the hotel staff. But now that I got you, I don't know what to do with you."

"I assumed you'd be hauling me back to the booby hatch by now."

"Pardon?"

"You are a loony doc, aren't you?"

Fleet made a disagreeable face. He shook his head. "I did imply that to you, didn't I?"

"You said it!"

He frowned, shaking his head a second time. "Let this be a lesson to me: never put on the dog!"

"Woof!"

"Not you, you little pinhead." He tickled Pixie behind the ear.

Once again, I was utterly baffled. "Are you a shrink or aren't you?"

"Aren't. Not officially, at any rate. You might say I'm a student of human psychology. In a way, I'm more of a psychologist than most psychologists. But only informally."

"What are you formally?"

Enescu Fleet puffed out his vest. "You will be relieved to learn that I am nothing more than a simple, run-of-the-mill detective. And a happily retired run-of-the-mill detective, at that."

"Hah!" laughed his accomplice.

I also felt like laughing, and did. Sardonically.

If this Fleet thought having a shamus on my trail would somehow ease my anxiety, then he wasn't as well versed in human psychology as he thought he was. The notion of how near I came to unveiling an inexplicable corpse to him gave me the heebie-jeebies, and from those jeebies came the derisive chuckle. (I guess I did have my carefree moments, after all.)

"That was fun," said Enescu Fleet, once I had finished. "I don't think anyone has ever reacted to my profession that way. You are amused?"

"Let's just say tickled."

"You think I'm too refined for the job? Too dignified? You may be right. I *am* urbane. It has often come in handy in my profession, especially at the start of my career. Refinement can be an effective smoke screen. It can be helpful in one's later years as well. I refer to those occasional moments when I step out from retirement and lend my modest expertise to an investigation."

"Occasional moments! Hah!" said the brunette.

Fleet cast an indulgent glance at the one-woman peanut gallery. He smiled. "My daughter thinks I'm too old to play the PI. The word she utters, in case you missed it, is 'Hah!' " He looked back and forth between us. "You two made your introductions outside, I presume?"

"Oh hi!" said Miss Fleet to me, in sarcastic exuberance. Her exaggerated smile quickly faded.

"I asked her to assist me in ensnaring you. She works at the casino, you see, so it was no trouble for her to come out and play." (I felt another "Hah!" coming on.) "My friends on the staff at the hotel weren't giving satisfaction. I figured if she mentioned your disappearing blonde, you would come running."

I had come running alright. "Then she hasn't seen her? The blonde?"

"Oh, I saw her," said Miss Fleet, irritated not to be addressed directly. "I bumped into her this morning, while I was out walking Pixie."

"Woof!"

"She was darting up the path from one of the cabins and nearly piled into me. I asked her if there was anything the matter, and she broke down and told me that she didn't know who she was or how she had gotten there. She said there was no one around who could help."

I liked that! No one around who could help! Women!

"I would have invited her back to my cabin, but Pixie slipped her collar. I instructed your chick to stay put while I chased the dog, but by the time I returned, she had already stridden off again."

She does that, I explained.

"I looked for her, but it was no good. I had to get back to tell Dad Pixie was on the prowl, and to be absolutely honest, I totally forgot about the wench after that. Sorry."

I told her not to be. It was somehow appropriate, that.

"She's gorgeous, isn't she?" I asked.

"She seemed nice."

I nodded. Nice and gorgeous, that was her alright. I turned Fleet's way. "You believe what the blonde said, don't you? About her memory?"

"I do. Beyond that, I believe what *you* said, and that's the important thing."

I didn't get it. What did I have to do with it?

"You see, unlike myself, my daughter is one of the least curious people in the world. Whereas I see your problem as something that can and must be solved, she can, and did, block it from her mind entirely. It's a gift. After she met the baffled blonde on the path, she truly did forget about her. I couldn't do that. Nor could I coolly stroll off, as she did, and go spend the morning clicking emails to people, or whatever it is she does here. As a result of her indifference, I didn't hear about the meeting on the path until now. If I had learned about it before we met, I would have believed your story immediately."

"Didn't you?"

"Of course not. Losing your memory? It's ridiculous. Granted, I could see being a little hazy after a late night out. But a total blank? Not likely. I figured you must be lying to hide something and had made up the story as a sort of decoy."

I would have looked offended, but the fact was, I *was* hiding something: a certain mustached something, possibly dead. I tried to look casual.

"But the whole time you were telling the truth about your memory. I see that now. The blonde proved it. And you helped that proof along with your behavior this morning. No one would have acted as fatheaded as you have if they *had* their memory."

I didn't know what to say. I felt insulted and vindicated in one neat bundle.

I started to speak, hesitantly, but it wasn't necessary. Fleet continued. I had the feeling that it didn't take much to keep him talking. "The fascinating thing is, the one detail that reinforces your story, the dashing blonde, also confounds it. Two individuals have lost their memory at the same time and place. How? Why? It can't be an accident."

I agreed with him there. "I—"

"But let's not waste breath now. Now, you will come back with us to our cabin—"

"*My* cabin," said his daughter.

"—we will lunch, we will talk, and in no time you will see the mystery unraveling for us. That is, if we can ever get this bucket moving."

Throughout his monologue, guests of the casino had been filling in around us, looking for a ride back to their accommodations. They poured in, choosing their spots, and with each new arrival, Pixie would growl or snap at the seat selection, a ferocious canine usher.

The last had settled in when the shuttle driver appeared in our midst. Pixie snarled.

"No dogs," he said.

Fleet begged to differ. He held up the Maltese, by way of Exhibit A, and said, simply, "Dog."

"No dogs allowed," clarified the driver.

Call it petty, but I secretly hoped for a physical confrontation here. As I have mentioned, Fleet was a remarkably well-knit duffer, more like a retired light heavyweight than a detective. The sneering shuttle driver, meanwhile, had the appearance of a lazy young twerp. For the older man to stand up and quietly pluck the youth's head from his body would have been a simple task. In some way, I think, it would have applied balm to my sense of frustration and persecution. (Even Pixie removing a chomp of flesh from his ankle would have capped off the morning on a brighter note.) Alas, it was not to be.

"Come," said Enescu Fleet to me. "It's a lovely day. We will walk. Honey?"

His daughter, having stood to let me by, sat back down again. "I'm good," she said.

Fleet and I exited, along with a very vocal Pixie, anxious to ascertain whether anybody on the shuttle would like a piece of her.

Evidently nobody did.

9 — Out of Context

"I forgot to ask—" began Fleet, as we strolled the path to the cabins.

The woods looked a lot more friendly now that I knew (sort of) where we were.

"—any luck remembering anything yet? Your identity? Your address? Some cryptic clue that springs to mind in dramatic flashback?"

I shook my head.

"Funny. I'm familiar with many types of amnesia but none as comprehensive as yours. It makes me sorry that I'm *not* a psychologist. I see a series of brilliantly written papers bound in pale card stock emerging out of this. Ah well. You appear okay on basic knowledge. You remember how to walk, how to eat, who the poet Keats is. But no flashes of experience of any kind? Odd. Have you considered the possibility that you're really just a very dull person?"

I told him that the thought had not crossed my mind, no. But then again, if I were a very dull person, I supposed it wouldn't.

"And no inkling whatsoever of a name?"

"None."

"Bizarre. Well, if I'm going to help you, I'm going to have to call you something. How does the name Chester strike you?"

"Like a sock full of wet sand."

He took this criticism in stride. "Walter, then? Or Harold? How about Lance?"

"How about no."

"Fenton. Nobody could hate the name Fenton. Apparently you can. Okay. I think I have it. Sylvester."

"No."

"Perhaps we're going about this the wrong way," he said, pausing to allow Pixie a snuffle at a passing pinecone. "Sometimes plain is best. Tom. No, I was once lured into a duel to the death in Guatemala by a Tom. John?"

"I don't like the name John."

"What's wrong with John?"

"Too boring."

"I suppose it is a little on the nose," he agreed. "John. John Doe. You're right; we can do better. Wilfred?"

"I don't think so."

Fleet shook his head. "You're a hard man to please, Mr. Sylvester Lance. I suppose you realize that most men don't have the luxury you have. They're given a name, and they're stuck with it. You should look on the bright side. You could be called Enescu."

We walked along in silence, save the sound of squirrels scampering in the trees above and Pixie snorting over the occasional chunk of forest.

I decided to ask a question of my own: "Why Enescu?"

"Excuse me?"

"It seems a funny sort of name," I remarked, and yes, I could see I was one to talk.

Fleet didn't seem to mind. "It's Romanian, a fine Romanian name."

"Are you Romanian?"

"Not as far as I know."

We crested a hill with a view of some of the cabins, and I asked him how he had ended up with a fine Romanian name if he wasn't Romanian. He smiled and told me it was a funny story. I suspected he said that a lot.

"I was born in a pickup truck on the Maine-Canadian border," began Enescu Fleet. "My mother, torn between calling me Pierre after the Canadian mounted police officer who assisted in my birth or her well-to-do American brother William, went with the obvious choice and called me Enescu."

"Are you American or Canadian?"

"Yes."

It was my turn to shake my head. "And she just picked a name from Romania?"

"I think she liked the sound of it. I'm amazed she knew how to spell it, bless her soul. Bucharest isn't exactly well represented in the backwoods of Maine. Of course, there was a story circulated about a Romanian fiddle player who passed through town a year before I was born. I could never get a straight answer from my mother on that. In fact, I think that was the start of my unnatural curiosity about things." He awoke from his reminiscences. "We're here," he informed me.

I looked around. There was a cabin straight ahead.

"Yours," said Fleet. "I brought us back here to see if it jogged your memory at all."

I responded with a noncommittal stare.

"I also thought this would be a good place for you to open up. Explain what it is that you're holding back from me."

In honor of the locale we had just left, I gave him my best poker face. "I don't know what you mean. I've told you—"

"—everything you can. Yes, I thought as much. Come. Our place is through here."

I thought it best, as we tramped past my cabin and down to the woods, to change the subject as quickly as possible. "Can you tell me where we are exactly? I know this is the Wolf Valley Casino. But where is the Wolf Valley Casino?"

I'm pretty sure Fleet would have given a full and complete history—no doubt playing up the funny parts—but at this point he diverged from the garden trail completely and beat a path across the grass.

Stepping carefully across the soggy turf, I followed.

Behind us was a hill with my cabin at the top. All around us on the other side was forest, and prickly looking forest to boot.

"I hadn't noticed that before," he said to himself.

"Noticed what?"

He was standing adjacent to a weatherworn gazebo, the last semi-comfortable spot before you reached all the pricklies. He looked at the structure and then to me and then turned and looked up at the cabin. Pixie, always one to assist, jogged around in circles, wrapping her leash around his legs.

Once he had disentangled himself, he entered the gazebo. He leaned over, abruptly disappearing from view. Seconds later he reappeared, holding a few shards of white crockery in the palm of his leather glove. What was it with this guy and porcelain?

"What do you make of this?" he asked me. Observing my blank stare, he said, "You're not at your best. I can appreciate that. Come, step inside here."

Slowly—hesitantly—I stepped inside. "Now what do you see?" he asked.

I looked around. More white shards. Various stains, which I preferred not to dwell on. Perhaps some wood rot in the back?

"Not *in* here," he said. "*From* here. What do you see *out there*, from this angle?"

I looked around again. I could see the cabin up on the hill, some firewood piled up against it, Pixie running up and down on the wet lawn, doing sprints. I shook my head.

"It's not important that you understand yet," he said, thumping me lightly on the back. "The important thing is that I understand."

"And do you?"

He smiled broadly. "Not yet, but I always do in the end." He paused. "This missing blonde of yours—"

"Yes?"

"What she said to you this morning—you reported it to me exactly?"

I said yes. Exactly.

"Cool beans," said Enescu Fleet, and we continued back along the garden path.

I followed at a more cautious distance. I couldn't figure what he was playing at, and thought it better not to get too close to him until I could.

10 — The Man

"In reply to your earlier question," he said, "we are on the Penobscot Tribal Reservation in Maine, home of the world's largest wildlife-named resort, the Wolf Valley Casino. It's late October, there is a distinct nip of autumn in the air, and the baseball playoffs have begun, with a view to completing the World Series sometime around Christmas. The other World Series—of Poker—is just wrapping up in Las Vegas, and presently we will crown a new Hold'em champion: some stony-faced young gunslinger whose mother still does his laundry.

"Let's see, what else? The fall TV schedule features several new reality shows. I've not viewed any of these myself, but I'm sure they're all delightful. In other watercooler topics, some celebrity somewhere has posted bail relating to drug charges; an economist has spent the better part of the day talking and saying nothing; and a politician has been caught in an untruth. I think that brings you up to speed."

"What about you? Why are you here?"

"Assuming you don't mean that philosophically, I am here to be a special guest contestant on an exciting new TV show."

"*This Is Your Face?*" I asked.

"Pardon?"

"What exciting new TV show?"

"It's called *Deadly Allusions*, and it's a game show based on the puzzle book and series of iPhone apps. It's going to be filmed up at the casino, a sort-of blend of trivia match and variety sketch show."

"How do you blend trivia and sketch show?"

"From what I understand, performers come out on stage and act out various comical vignettes depicting a murder scene."

"Comical murder scenes?"

"From what I understand, yes. In each case, the dead man leaves behind some vital clue fingering his killer. This clue always has some literary or cultural significance. An allusion. The contestants then have to play detective and figure out how the allusion relates to the suspects assembled—their names, their jobs, etc. It's a sort of elaborate riddle we all have to solve live. Think of it as a murder-filled crossword puzzle without the squares."

I was. I was also thinking of it as a bizarre experience I had recently had in the bedroom of my hotel cabin. "The dead man in the game tells the contestants the clue? The allusion?"

"In a way. He leaves the clue behind, scrawled in his own blood or clutched in his hand. I guess sometimes he might speak it—"

"With his dying breath?"

"Something like that. Why?"

"No reason," I said, walking faster now.

I could see Fleet squinting after me. An instant later his face brightened. "You're thinking of the Keats."

"What?"

"The line the girl told you. *The answer lies*—"

"Oh yeah. Right. *The girl.*"

"You think she might have something to do with the game show?"

"Maybe," I said, noncommittally.

Fleet had matched my speed and surpassed it. "We should look into it."

I agreed with him. "You said you're going to be a contestant?"

"Special guest contestant. In episode one, tomorrow. I have a minor background in the area," he explained without explaining.

He finally slowed his stride, but only because we had arrived at another cabin, his daughter's. Bungalow Three. He opened the door and showed me in.

Miss Fleet greeted us almost before we could enter. "Took you long enough," she said, looking flushed and severe. "There's beans and rice warming on the stove, if you want any. I gotta run. Got a day date."

She paused at the door, looking back at me. It was the kind of look she might have given a dead squirrel brought in and presented on the mat by the dog Pixie.

"Has he been telling you tales?" she wondered.

I replied that Fleet had told me a few, particularly how he got his name. She sniffed.

"Get him to tell you how I got mine while you're at it. Still trying to work that one out for myself. It's Ate, by the way," she said, giving my hand an efficient shake.

"Ah-tee?"

"That's right. Ate, named for the goddess Atë, the Greek personification of reckless impulse. And if that doesn't give a young girl a complex, nothing will. Mine's spelled like hers—*A-t-e*—minus the little bing-bongs over the *e*."

"Little bing-bongs?" I asked.

"Yup. Little bing-bongs," she agreed, pausing. "He's not much of a talker, is he?"

I resented this. "So it's spelled like 'ate,' " I said, dispelling this notion of not talking, "like someone 'ate' a sandwich?"

Ate frowned. "Like I didn't hear that one as a kid fifty times a week. *Ate ate the whole thing. Ate ate my homework. Ate eats worms.* I've heard them all. It's Ah-tee, buster, *Ah-tee!*"

I agreed with her. Names could be a real sore spot with some people. Not much of a problem for me at the moment. "Are you Greek?"

"No. My mother was from Madrid. And Dad—well, Dad, as you probably already know by now, is from Jupiter. Most people around here seem to think I'm Penobscot, and I don't bother to correct them. Having native ties, real or perceived, isn't bad for business, especially when dealing with the Tribal Council."

"Ate is a huge noise at the local network," inserted Fleet, "and by extension, the TV show I mentioned to you earlier. The network is owned by Sprightly Sports Drinks, with their main offices located here on the reservation. It was Ate who helped develop the show. She was also instrumental in getting me invited as a special guest contestant for the inaugural episode."

"More like instrumental in trying to get you *not* invited," said his daughter. "It didn't matter. It was Croker—Wilson Croker, the host," she explained to me—"who wanted you all along, and now he's gotten his wish."

"But you had to approve the selection."

"No. He had his mind made up about you, regardless of what I said, and the network always listens to talent. I suppose you do have some vague credentials."

"Please, dear, you're gushing."

I still didn't get this. "What credentials?"

Ate's eyes widened. "You mean you haven't regaled him with your entire life story, Dad? I'm amazed."

"You know I hate talking about myself," said her father.

"Don't you believe it," she whispered to me. "Well, I guess I should give you the short version. Enescu Fleet," she began, pausing somewhat stagily. "The quintessential man's man. Could out-Hemingway Hemingway. Has met kings, romanced princesses and climbed every mountain, both literal and figurative. In his early forties, he was marooned on a deserted island after a yachting accident. Not only did he flourish there all by himself for three months, but he single-handedly built two hurricane-proof tree forts, one for each side of the island. When not fighting off native hordes or sketching out his eventual rescue, he spent the time reading the entire *Collier's Encyclopedia*, which had washed up from the boat with him. It was thanks to this that he was able to win *mucho dinero* on the game show circuit when he got back to the States."

"As you well know," said Fleet, "there were no native hordes on the island, just a handful of cannibals. And it was Oxford not Collier."

"My mistake. At any rate, after stashing away his modest nest egg, he applied his many talents to the field of criminal investigation—spending the next two decades out–Hercule Poiroting Hercule Poirot. He is a widower and has one child—*yo*."

My head was spinning. Other than the widower part, and the one child, I was finding this difficult to absorb. "Did any of this really happen?"

The network goddess laid a hand on my shoulder. “The only thing more annoying than my father’s anecdotes is the fact that the majority of them are true.”

“Majority?” asked Fleet.

“The only ones I have ever doubted are how he asked my mother, a ravishing Spanish spokesmodel, to marry him the day he met her—”

“Call it the second date.”

“—and how he is the originator of the phrase ‘cool beans.’ ”

“I *am* the originator of the phrase ‘cool beans,’ ” said the quintessential man’s man with dignity.

“But, beyond that, you can take him at face value. He’s a fascinating, fascinating man,” she sighed, gathering up her purse. “Well, I’m off.”

“Did I hear something about a date?” asked Fleet, as she reached for the knob.

Ate turned and smiled. “I do date, you know.”

“Of course you do, honey. Who is this man, if you don’t mind my asking? Some nice, upstanding fellow? Should I get my horse whip handy?”

“Maybe save it for the second date. Look, not that it’s any of your business, but I don’t even know the guy.”

“That makes me feel a lot better, dear, thank you.”

“What I mean is it’s a semibusiness thing. His name’s John Hathaway, and his uncle is this congressman.”

“That must be Congressman George Hathaway. I met him at a charity function once,” said Fleet. “Typical politico. His nephew, I gather, is a total layabout, although there was something else about him in the news recently.” He frowned. “No, I can’t think of it. So you’re playing honorary tour guide of a sort?”

“Something like that. John is making a quick stay here and doesn’t know anyone. Contrary to your layabout comments, he is actually a very successful freelance courier—”

“What exactly *is* a successful freelance courier?”

“—and is bringing Mr. Lockhart, the CEO of Sprightly Sports Drinks, some kind of parcel on behalf of his Uncle George. I was supposed to meet John yesterday afternoon, but he couldn’t make it, so we’re doing it now. Anything else?”

Enescu Fleet had gone strangely silent. "Young Hathaway just arrived?"

"I guess?"

"And he doesn't know anyone?"

"No."

"And he has already missed an appointment with you?"

"Yes, yes. So? Where are you going with this, Dad?"

Fleet was soliloquizing now. "A stranger in these parts. Disoriented. Probably a little funny in the head, related to an old ass like George Hathaway." He glanced at me and nodded. He had made up his mind.

"I give you John Hathaway," he said with triumph.

11 — What's in a Name?

His daughter didn't seem very impressed. I wasn't sure if this had to do with the goods themselves—*yo*—or her father's interpretation of them.

She stared at me. She soon transferred this stare to the old man. "What are you talking about?"

"It makes perfect sense, darling. The clues, the hints. This must be John Hathaway."

Once again, I enjoyed two pairs of Fleet eyes running over me, searching me.

"I don't think so," said the female half, piercing me a little more than the male.

Her father smiled. "I grant you, you haven't had much occasion to see me at work lately, now that you've become a big noise at your TV network—"

"Quit calling me a noise."

"But if you recall watching my methods when you were a little girl, I usually gave the customers what they asked for. Instinct supported on a bedrock of outwardly unimportant facts. It never fails to give satisfaction."

"I don't know about the instinct," she said, "but the fact is, this isn't Hathaway."

"What makes you say that?"

"Let me see. For one thing, John Hathaway is taller."

"Is he?"

"And he doesn't have an accent."

"How do you know?"

"I've met him."

Fleet gave his mustache a downward twist. "You've met?"

"Didn't I say that? Well, I have—met him, I mean. We bumped into each other in the lobby yesterday and hit it off. I explained that I had been assigned to show him around, and he asked me to breakfast. I think he had a different meaning in mind by that, but for now we'll stick with the breakfast. Oh jeez, more like a late brunch," she said, glancing at the clock on her phone.

And with that, she left us. But not before pecking her father on the cheek, happy to have scored one off the man of the world for once.

I couldn't say whether Fleet's silence over the next fifteen minutes was due to his daughter's friendly mockery or because his little girl had begun socializing with a total layabout who routinely invited young ladies he had just met to "breakfast." In either event, it made the walk back to the casino a lot less bright. Although this could have had something to do with the drizzle starting up again.

Before we left, my host gave me a windbreaker to borrow, not tweed, so I was okay on the accoutrements. All I needed now was a hot meal—we had left the beans and rice untouched on the stove—and an explanation of why we were going back to the casino.

"Why are we going back to the casino?" I asked.

Fleet answered brightly enough. He reeled in Pixie on her leash and said, "I thought we'd pay a visit to the *Deadly Allusions* studio, see if anyone knows your young lady. While we're there, we can see if anyone recognizes you."

It was an idea, even if I had pretty much given up on anyone anywhere ever recognizing me.

"What did Ate mean about the accent?" I asked, changing the subject. I hated to bring up his daughter again, but her comment had really bugged me.

Fleet continued to speak good-naturedly. These ex-detectives don't wear their hearts on their sleeves (probably has something to do with the leather patches on the elbows). "She meant that you have an accent."

"Who does?"

"You do. You have a slight, though unmistakable, British accent."

"What rubbish," I said.

Truth be told, I had noticed a slight difference in our manners of speech. I had assumed they were the ones with the accent. "You know, come to think of it, my visitor had one too."

"The vanishing blonde?"

"Yes. That's probably why I hadn't noticed mine. Seemed natural."

"This could be an important detail," said Enescu Fleet.

I didn't see how, but let the matter rest.

A few minutes later, we hove up alongside the elaborate main door of the Wolf Valley. Fleet handed off Pixie to the security guard, and in we went.

Other than the occasional gambler or staff person giving Fleet a friendly wave or gun-shaped finger point, the journey through the casino went without incident. It wasn't until we had arrived in the lobby of the Ivory Buffalo—the nicest of the six hotels within the Wolf Valley—that anything worth noting occurred.

It was Ate. Head down and hands clenched, she swept past us across the marble tile as if she didn't know us. Her Latin-Jupiter blood had evidently been steamed up over some matter, and I remember thinking it wasn't necessarily a bad thing that she hadn't stayed to talk.

Fleet would have none of it. "Is there something the matter, honey?" he called after her.

She turned and gazed at us for a good ten seconds. "Oh, it's you, Dad," she said, coming out of her fog. She stepped closer, still fuming to an obvious degree.

"Trouble?"

"Oh nothing. It's just when you described John Hathaway as a total bum and layabout, you forgot to mention that he's also an utter rat bastard."

"Brunch not good?"

"Brunch not happening. When he didn't show, I asked a girl in reception if she knew where he was, and she said she had seen him in the company of some floozy early this morning. Looks like he's been cavorting with a different woman every hour on the hour since he arrived, including some slut last night. The current one is something special, though. He left a note for me saying he's checked out and won't be able to meet Jack Lockhart for dinner, after all."

"Perhaps it's not what it looks like."

Too weary for her customary *hah*, she asked us what we were doing here. Her father explained that we were on our way to meet the host of the show, Wilson Croker, and this time she did say hah.

"He won't see anyone. I tried to stop in at his dressing room to ask him something, and one of his bosomy interns sent me away. Apparently—like certain rat-bastard nephews of congressmen who shall remain nameless—he's not receiving visitors. Men," she scoffed, and stalked out.

Her father watched her exit with a kindly smile. "Just like her mother," he muttered solemnly. "Shall we go?"

"I thought she said What's-His-Name wouldn't see us?"

"Oh, I think Croker will make an exception for us. You have to know how to ask."

I nodded, wondering if this Croker would greet us with a friendly wave or a gun-shaped finger point. "Who is he again?"

"Wilson Croker? He's co-owner of the casino. He's also host of the game show."

"Ah," I said, nodding. "Did someone say something about bosomy interns?" I wondered, as we went.

Sadly, we encountered no interns on our way to the studio, bosomy or not. After a trek through a web of industrial hallways, we came to a heavy metal stage door. I had probably only gone about ten steps inside, when Fleet's hand lashed out and gripped my shoulder, holding me in place. Shocking developments greeted our entrance.

About twenty yards away, we could see a brightly lit room, surrounded in darkness. It looked like an extract from a hunting lodge. Pelts and club chairs and all the usual fixings adorned the area. There was a chessboard set up in the center of the room and three bottles of wine on the sideboard. Slightly to the right of these furnishings stood a man and a woman, both fairly aged (or so they appeared from that distance). They were both dressed as old-fashioned servants. The woman looked like a quintessential housekeeper, the man in his flannels and hunting cap, like some sort of gamekeeper. I didn't bother to wonder who they were or why the Wolf Valley had suddenly been transported back in time to merry old England. My attention was riveted on the hardwood floor between the two servants, currently occupied by a well-dressed gentleman lying at their feet. His form was rigid, lifeless, and in his chest, standing upright in the spotlight, was the bolt from a crossbow.

Before I could wrap my mind around what we were seeing—it was so obvious, really—someone shouted, "Cut," from the darkness, the lights went up and a stage was revealed. The game show stage. "That's lunch, everybody," said the voice.

I could see the row of contestant chairs now, the audience (almost entirely empty) and about ninety-six different studio employees, milling to and fro.

They were having a rehearsal.

The three actors from the stage, including the dead man, strolled off in various directions. The woman was much younger than she appeared, made up to be twenty years older at least. The gamekeeper I didn't get a good look at, but I suspected he wasn't a grizzled old coot. The third man could have been playing his own age; I couldn't decide. Average in size, with gray hair and a bony frame, he looked nothing like my woolen visitor from the cabin.

"I was sure you guys were going to blow it," he laughed, crossbow bolt jutting this way and that as he spoke. "Another few steps and you would have blundered right out into the cameras."

Fleet assured him that we would never dream of crossing the shot. "I'm surprised you could see us from your angle."

"Dead men see more than you think," smiled the corpse, scratching his crossbow wound. "Not that there is much else to do when you're the one stuck playing the stiff. As long as you don't open your eyes too wide, you're fine. It can be pretty fun too, especially when the interns don't wear underwear." He moved to nudge me, but I was too quick for him. "So, you guys contestants or something?"

"I am," said Fleet, and made the introductions. I was identified as "friend."

"Cool," said the corpse agreeably. Behind him, stagehands bustled about, adjusting the set and diddling with props. They were a noisy bunch, all grunts and growls and "Anybody seen Nick anywhere?" I noticed one of them was taking special attention with the bottles of wine and the chessboard. These were soon sealed up in a lockbox and shoved over to the side.

"Clues for the first puzzle," explained the dead guy. "All hush-hush. Can't have anyone getting a leg up on the other contestants. Well, I gotta run. Nice meeting ya."

Fleet bowed graciously. "Any objection to us wandering about?"

"None from me," said the walking cadaver. "I don't think you're supposed to be back here, but it's not like anyone is checking up on you. Just don't break anything. Some klutz already smashed up the grandfather clock prop this morning. The director was pissed."

We agreed to be extra special careful, especially around antique timepieces.

"One last thing," asked Fleet, as the cheerful murder victim turned to leave. "Do you have any blonde actresses working on the show?"

"We have a few, why? You like blondes? I can find you blondes."

"It's one blonde in particular. Did any of the young ladies fail to come to work today?"

"Not any of the ladies, no. Definitely not any of the blondes. If you're thinking of whisking one away for an afternoon's delight, I'm sure no one would notice. Although you might want to wait until after we rehearse the centerfold-party sketch. We need all the chicks we got for that one."

Fleet told him he would bear it in mind.

We spent the next ten minutes browsing the stage. There was an enormous bookshelf on the left of the set, more or less decorative, although probably helpful for some last-minute cramming.

Enescu Fleet poked about studiously. I noticed he spent an inordinately long session with the Keats.

"They definitely have a little of everything," he announced. "According to the guidelines for the game, every puzzle on the show can be solved from the knowledge contained in these simple volumes. Contestants don't have access to them during game play, but it's nice to know the producers have standards."

I said yup.

"There's a good deal of fiction mixed in here as well. P. G. Wodehouse, Agatha Christie, Rex Stout. All the basic necessities."

I nodded vaguely. One of the stagehands had shouted, "Lunch is here," and I was wondering if this invitation included gatecrashers.

Fleet was still speaking. "You seemed agitated by the hunting-lodge sketch. Didn't you realize it was fake?"

I said I had. It was just—"Nothing," I muttered.

"You've told me everything you can?"

I nodded again. I turned and looked at the ever-growing buffet line. Surely anyone could partake? I decided to risk it.

I must say, the spread put out by the game show folks was a notch above. Entirely satisfactory. I could have done with more bosomy interns—one caught a glimpse of one here or there, flitting on and off the set—but the food was top drawer. And I was starving. (Candy bars, however touching, only go so far.)

They had laid out a full buffet, hot and cold, and my first move was to camp out at the steam table and dig in.

I continued to ponder the crossbow theme as I ate. I began by contrasting the scene we had just viewed to the private performance I had received in my cabin. I tried to reconcile it in my mind. Could it have had any connection to the show? Some kind of PR stunt perhaps? It didn't feel like a PR stunt, and yet all the indicators were there. The vanishing body, the cryptic clue. Maybe I wasn't the only one to have a visit today. But if that were so, surely Fleet or his daughter would have mentioned something. And besides, the encounter in the cabin had felt so—genuine.

I turned these ideas over and over in my mind while I chewed. Mostly I just chewed.

In time, Fleet got the message, and anyone he thought I should meet he brought to the buffet table. "This is the director," he said, as I sampled some pastry things with meat and potato inside.

I waved a friendly meat-and-potato pie at him. He nodded back sans sustenance. He was thin boned but baby faced, with a Beatles haircut and one of those perpetual five o'clock shadows. You know the kind I mean—stubble that never seems to grow into a full beard and yet is never shaven clean either. "Pleasure to meet you," I lied.

"Dean," he remarked, identifying himself.

I was surprised. I would have pictured a Dean as much cooler.

He didn't seem to recognize my face, which was fine by me.

"Nice buffet," I said.

He frowned down at it, as if buffets, nice or not, meant nothing to him.

"This is Director Dean's first show," said Fleet, paving the way for additional dialogue, which I could have done without.

I just nodded.

"Prior to this, Dean had focused his talents on TV commercials. You did the one with the talking ketchup bottle, did you not?"

"Yeah."

"Stirring piece of work. I seldom reach for the condiments now without instinctively pausing for the ketchup to say a few words."

"Thanks," said Dean. It struck me that I had known ketchup bottles more talkative than this shaggy director.

"Well-deserved tribute," insisted Fleet. "And you mustn't fret about the naysayers. I think the show will be a huge success."

As something of a novice in the game show milieu—and somewhat busy with the selection of hot wings (in three different sauces!)—I couldn't appreciate all the ins and outs of Director Dean's languor. I gathered from his remarks, however, that the show wasn't well thought of among the network muckety-mucks and might only last a few episodes.

"People aren't into knowledge anymore. They want combatants skirmishing in whipped cream or reality shows where celebrities try to act normal. Trivia just isn't hip."

Fleet pointed out that this wasn't just trivia, it was *Deadly Allusions*. It had danger, excitement, comedy. And I seconded this view with a hearty *yeah*. Although, I had to say, that whipped-cream skirmish thing sounded kind of cool.

"It's not enough. If the show's going to make it to sweeps week, we're going to need something bold. Thrilling."

What this test study from a Prozac focus group considered sufficiently thrilling, we weren't privileged to learn. Before he could elaborate, a new party arrived. (After the depressive Dean, anyone else would feel like an actual Mardi Gras.)

I thought a lot more of this arrival. He commanded respect. He was a good deal taller than I was and more barrel-chested than Fleet. He had a presence, this one, the air of a practiced politician, but he was all business too—a man who routinely created wealth and knew what to do with it. Perfect reddish-blond hair, perfectly parted, perfect shirt and tie, the smile across the firm-but-not-too-chiseled jaw. I put his age at about fifty, and when he shook hands, it was with the suggestion that he knew he was better than you, but he was okay with it as long as you were.

Like everyone else we met, he knew Fleet.

"Enescu, wonderful to see you again."

Fleet looked up from a book he had selected from the stage library. He placed it beside the steam table and smiled. "Jack."

"Keeping busy in retirement, I trust?"

Fleet replied that there was usually something to keep an old rascal like himself busy, and topics soon turned to old times, which didn't come across as especially in-depth or personal in nature. The two men were just old acquaintances.

Eventually Fleet continued the introductions.

"This is Jack Lockhart," he told me, "CEO of Sprightly Sports Drinks, and co-owner of the Wolf Valley Casino, along with Wilson Croker." I nodded and consumed another hot wing. "Jack, this is John Hathaway."

12 — That is the Question

I forget what transpired after that. Nothing to do with my memory loss. My head was just swimming to such an extent that I didn't retain any of it.

John Hathaway. That's what he said. *This is John Hathaway.*

Lockhart seemed pleased. He was glad I could stick around after all, he said (going so far as to offer me a complimentary bottle of Bounding Berry sports drink to wash down the hot wing I was choking on). Then he invited us to a dinner party that night.

Director Dean said something about reading about me, John Hathaway, in the paper a while back, and the rest is all a fog. It was all I could do to sample dessert.

I came to again somewhere outside the studio, on the way to the dressing rooms.

"What the hell?" I said.

Fleet blinked at me, unable to catch the gist.

"John Hathaway! John Hathaway!"

He smiled knowingly. "Yes, I thought you'd wonder about that. Look, I know you have this unnatural aversion to the name John, but as I said before, you could do worse. Besides, we can dress it up. I was thinking of calling you Johnny."

"That's not the point! Didn't you hear what Ate said? I'm not John Hathaway."

"Of course you're not. John Hathaway is taller and able to keep a woman in the same room as him for more than five minutes."

I huffed. "And what happens when he comes into Lockhart's room? I'll be slung out."

"What makes you think he will come into Jack's room?"

"People do come into rooms."

"Not Hathaway. Not Lockhart's room. I know Hathaway's type. He falls for a girl, thankfully not my daughter, and whisks her away—"

"For an afternoon's delight?"

"More than that. Remember the note he left for Ate? He has no intention of schmoozing with the likes of Sprightly Sports Drinks, even if his uncle told him he must. He's made a bolt. It's like his trip to Rangeley Manor."

"What trip to Rangeley Manor?"

"The last time his uncle gave him an assignment, delivery of an ancient dagger called the Azure Star to Rangeley Manor, not only did he make a hash of the entire enterprise, but he skipped off in the middle of the night with the visiting daughter of a prominent publisher. He didn't come up for air again till the following summer."

"How do you know?"

"I remembered the article I'd read about him. It came back to me when Director Dean mentioned hearing something about you."

"Not me!"

"The fake you, then. Your Hathaway persona. It's a good persona, Johnny."

"Don't call me that!"

"But it fits so well. The girls, the gambling, the misadventures. He's quite a card, that Johnny Hathaway."

"I'll try to keep that in mind when I'm being hauled in for impersonating him."

"My dear boy, nobody has ever been arrested for impersonating a congressman's nephew. If anything, you should be admired for it. Admitting you're related to a politician is bad enough. Saddling yourself with it when there is ample evidence to the contrary—it's almost noble."

"Really."

Fleet smiled, lending a warmth to his argument by placing a kindly hand on my shoulder. I felt like shaking it off. "Have you ever read the works of P. G. Wodehouse?" he asked.

My head was swimming again. I was reminded of my interview with little Emilia, needing only sibling Sam booting my kneecap to complete the illusion.

"What's that got to do with anything?"

"I was only wondering. You seem to remember things like that."

"I remember reading P. G. Wodehouse at some point in my life, yes."

"Good. I was refreshing myself earlier with an installment from the game show library. If you've read Wodehouse, then you know the characters in his books are always introducing their friends into households under false names and pretenses. I had come upon such a passage in the book when Jack wandered over. I took it as a sign."

"Do you think we're in an English drawing room comedy?!"

"Why not? Reality is what you make it. You of all people should appreciate that. You're a blank slate."

"I'm nothing of the sort!"

"Call it semiblank, then." And back with the hand to the shoulder. "You have to see what you're up against. I can't keep introducing you as Nameless Ned. People will start asking questions. These questions will lead to the police. Clearly a cover is needed while we figure out who you are. It's already earned a dinner invitation, and who knows who we might meet there. Maybe somebody who can identify you."

This kind of help I didn't need. "Are you forgetting," I asked, "that John Hathaway is supposed to be bringing Lockhart some kind of package from Hathaway's uncle, and *that*, no doubt, is the real reason behind the dinner invitation?"

Fleet chewed his mustache thoughtfully. "I had forgotten that, yes."

I threw up my hands. And I was the one with the goofy memory. "So if you think I'm still going to dinner tonight—"

Fleet raised a hand. This time he held it in status quo and didn't reach for my shoulder. "It's fine."

"Fine?"

"He didn't ask for the parcel, did he? That means the real Hathaway already left it for him, at his office or something, before checking out. There, feel better?"

I would have answered this, but Fleet had already turned to face a dressing room door. He knocked.

"Who is it?" snapped the occupant.

"Enescu Fleet."

There was a hesitation. "A moment please."

Fleet assumed a confident smile. "He'll see us."

"But why do we want to see him?" I asked. I looked at the door. *Wilson Croker*. The show's host. What good did he do us?

"Wilson Croker is the best-connected man in Wolf Valley. He knows everybody. If he knows everybody, he might know you. And besides, he requested me for his show. It's always nice to give the people what they want."

I sneered. A couple more seconds passed, and Wilson Croker asked us to enter.

"Don't be overly awed by the man," Fleet advised me in a whisper. "I hear he's a sort of modern-day Orson Welles, this Croker. Brilliant but a true egotist."

I scoffed. Talk about the pot calling the kettle egocentric.

"In fact, better let me do most of the talking."

I sneered and scoffed in one breath. We entered.

A small, thickset man, heavily mustached and ruddy of complexion, nodded to us as we came in. He pushed back a pair of black-framed glasses on his nose and asked us to sit down.

I didn't. I didn't do anything. I stood there transfixed. The seated man, now regarding us with a strange and welcoming conceit, was my old pal from the cabin.

The dead one with the bolt in his chest.

13 — Walking Shadow

He didn't have a crossbow bolt in his chest now. As a matter of fact, he looked pretty good for a dead guy. He set down the book he had been reading—not Wodehouse—and gave us his finest supercilious smile.

Fleet took a seat opposite him. If he had noticed my agitation, he was concealing it beautifully.

"I'm Enescu Fleet and this—Or perhaps you know each other?"

The dead guy said he hadn't had the pleasure, no.

"Ah. This is John Hathaway, nephew of Congressman George Hathaway. He asks you not to hold this against him, however."

Croker nodded. I noticed his eyes fixated on the chair on Fleet's immediate left. I had been asked to sit, and I should sit.

I sat. "Have we met?" I asked him.

Fleet shot me a discouraging glare, reminding me that we had been over all that already. One should not be tedious.

"It's a pleasure to finally meet you, Mr. Fleet," said Croker, declining to reply to my tedium.

He was dressed much as he had been this morning. Always with the sweaters. The overall presentation was more polished, of course—the lack of blood helped that.

As requested, I let Fleet do the talking. I couldn't think of anything to say anyhow.

"It should be an exciting new venue," continued Croker, leaning back in his leather club chair. I felt he wasn't completely at ease. "We've been rehearsing for months. It's an unusual format, but I think we will be up to it."

"I suppose you have most of the questions all worked out?"

"Most of them, yes. The questions and answers for tomorrow's episode are locked in my safe, shut away from prying eyes."

"As well they should be," said Fleet. "Surely the skit actors know the solutions, though?"

Wilson Croker did not immediately answer. His eyes had strayed to the bookshelf. Suddenly he stiffened. "Did you say Hathaway?"

I stared blankly at him.

"John Hathaway?" he asked.

I nodded. "Yes. I mean, sure. Yeah."

Our host's manner had changed. He looked at Fleet and replied sharply, "These are not *skits*, Mr. Fleet. They are performance art. We take basic trivia, turn it into a compact mystery, and then bring it all to life."

"I know. Sounds great."

"And no, the actors do not know the answers. They are hardly actors at all. They are nothing more than semianimated objects shifted around the stage at my discretion. Their only role is to speak the lines given them, and on occasion, when truly challenged, to lay there and play dead. And even that is sometimes beyond their capabilities. They have knowledge of the subject matter but look to me for direction. The rest is improvised."

"Impressive. But I understood Dean to be the director?"

"Dean is a ninny. I direct. Dean would do well to accept that. So would you."

These struck me as fighting words, but Fleet turned the other cheek. "I'm sure your background on the stage has been of great assistance to you," he said, glancing up at some framed newspaper clippings on the wall. They depicted our host in Elizabethan garb, frozen in a variety of dramatic poses. (Apparently, he had won great acclaim performing Hamlet as a teenager and had moved on to all the major Shakespearean roles from there. Good for him.)

"My training has not gone for naught," Croker replied.

"You were swell in *Macbeth* last year."

"I thank you."

"I especially enjoyed your 'Life is but a waking shadow' speech. Excellent."

"I believe you mean 'Life is but a *walking* shadow.' "

"Do I? So I do. My apologies."

"Think nothing of it." His surliness kicked in again. "Now if you will excuse me, I have a great deal of work to do. Already much of my morning has been taken up with Jack Lockhart and discussion of advertising revenue for the show."

His eyes rested on the exit as he said this.

Fleet appeared to observe this too. He stood, but rather than moving to the door, he stepped to the dressing table and toyed with an emery board on the counter. He frowned. "We've taken up enough of your time. Johnny—"

I wasn't accepting direction very well that day. When people desired me to sit, I stood. When they desired me to stand, I sat. Wilson Croker, for his part, was no doubt wishing I was some mere stage prop he could shift around at his discretion.

"Johnny," said Fleet.

I stood. Feeling I should say something else before we left—the pride of the Hathaways was at stake—I asked, "Are you sure we haven't met?"

Again, our host did not answer.

Nodding vaguely, I joined Fleet at the door.

"You have to excuse Hathaway," he said. "He's recently had a young lady run out on him. But you know what Alfred Tennyson used to say about the fairer sex? 'Better to have loved and lost than never to have loved at all.' "

Smiling, Croker replied that it was usually the women in his life who lamented over having loved and lost *him*.

And on that strangely disturbing note, we left.

"I can't decide if that was a success or not," said Enescu Fleet, once we were back outside in the corridor. "Is it just me, or was that a man who couldn't care less whether his special guest did his show or not? I'm beginning to wonder if my daughter had more to do with my invitation than she cared to let on."

"Erf," I agreed.

"This Croker, meanwhile, is a fascinating study. In a life where we all play many parts, he plays the part of the giant dick-weed very well. The question is, does he play it too well?"

"Erf," said I.

Fleet gazed at me. "Why are you looking like a bloated corpse?"

"Heh," I whispered. Perfect choice of words. "No reason," I added. "I think I wouldn't mind laying down awhile, that's all."

He gave a cordial nod. His sofa was my sofa. We walked along, both immersed in thought. We arrived at an exit.

"And the word you want," he said, holding the door open, "is lying."

It took me a minute to realize he meant the sofa.

14 — The Company

I think, next to the food, the highlight of my day had to be the shower I got at Ate Fleet's cabin that evening (even if I did have to tiptoe around several hundred bottles of shampoo and lotion as I spritzed). It was shortly before our dinner at Jack Lockhart's, and not only did it wash off about an inch of grime, it gave me a chance to reflect. I still had no memory, not even a hint of one, but at least I could arrange my mind around the details we had collected thus far.

My head clear and the rest of me warm and steamy, I could state unequivocally that these details didn't make the slightest bit of sense. The only solution that seemed to fit was an elaborate prank. But why? I couldn't explain it, but I kept feeling like someone was tinkering with my reality.

I finished my shower, shaved and dressed, and strolled out from the master bedroom in time to witness the world's most fascinating man in the concluding laps of combing through his beard. He had on another tweed jacket, his dress tweed, pressed trousers and a tie. His daughter had left for the party without us. "She cool down any yet?" I asked.

"You mustn't take her comments too seriously," he told the mirror. "Ate will play ball. She always does."

Just to bring everyone up to speed, Miss Fleet didn't relish me and Dad joining her at Lockhart's dinner tonight. And when she learned I'd be posing as J. Hathaway at this soiree, her comments really flowed.

Fleet had left it to me to explain the Hathaway angle. Even though I stressed the deception wasn't my idea, I still felt like one of those brave sergeants who throw themselves on live grenades for the good of the platoon. Only here, the general had thrown me on the grenade for the good of—well, I didn't know what. All I did know was he possessed a professional singing baritone, just barely drowned out by the running shower and his daughter's stream of speech.

Replaying her remarks in my mind now, I tended to agree with her. It seemed to me that my impersonation would accomplish very little, if that, and could come unstuck a million different ways. I mentioned this to Fleet now, but he insisted that he had budgeted for these contingencies, and off we went to the party. (We only had to wait a few minutes extra for someone from the hotel to arrive to watch Pixie.)

Already I wasn't feeling at my best. Fleet had asked that I wear a tie, which he gladly lent me, but he also suggested a jacket to complete the look. None of his fit me—I wasn't brawny enough—and despite his insistence, I wasn't about to try on any of his daughter's blazers. We compromised by borrowing the dog watcher's, who worked as a concierge.

On the trousers I stood firm. I don't wear another man's slacks. Fleet made his arguments there as well, but I wouldn't budge, and eventually we left without any bared thighs between us. He later confessed that I pulled off the dressy-blue-jeans look pretty well.

"Who's likely to be at this get-together?" I asked on the shuttle bus—thinking of all the people who could unmask me: tall people, short people, people who hated blue jeans.

"No idea. Quite a few, if I know Jack. He always goes all out. Even before the money."

"Did he make it all on the sports drinks?"

"Not at all. Sprightly's a new endeavor. Everybody wants to be the next Vitaminwater. If anyone can make a go of it, Jack can. He has that knack. I've never known anyone so adept at finding and securing profit."

The party had more than a few guests: it was bursting at the seams. People, people everywhere, and none of them especially interested in my jeans. I began to feel more confident in my false identity. I felt even better once we had gotten past the hulking bouncer in the private foyer, also bursting at the seams. He looked like an Eskimo quarterback. After we had supplied the proper passphrase—if I heard this correctly, it was "Easy does it, big boy; we're on the invitation list"—Fleet explained that the tree trunk in question was Lockhart's personal driver, Neptune.

"Did you say 'Neptune'?"

"That's right. A fine old Penobscot name."

"He's a driver?"

"That's what I understand. I don't know how much driving he does, really."

Dinner was served on passing trays, offered up to only the most agile of customers by waiters who appeared to have a pressing engagement elsewhere.

Everybody seemed to be having a good time.

Familiar with several of the residents by now, I spotted Jack Lockhart talking to a few of his guests. Director Dean, listening. Several interns, busty. Fleet's daughter, still playing ball (or at least she hadn't denounced me as an impostor). And a slew of other people I had seen around the studio that day but hadn't met personally. One person I had met personally but didn't notice was Wilson Croker, and I was okay with that.

Fleet had settled in comfortably among a bevy of showgirls and was answering a question posed by one of them about what it was like to live on a deserted island for three years. Knowing the time to have actually been three months, I noticed Fleet didn't bother to correct her. When he had given his answer, speaking in a low, somber voice, we were all left with a palpable sense of the thriving infrastructure he had built. He didn't say it, but I have the feeling that, if pressed, he would have hinted that you might know the place today as Jamaica.

"You must have had some wonderful seafood while you were there!" one girl gushed.

Fleet agreed that the fish and crustaceans were very good, and always fresh, but pointed out that anything becomes old after a while. "Keep in mind that here in New England, where I was born and raised, lobster was once so plentiful that it used to be fed to prisoners. I doubt any of them considered it much of a treat."

"Did they have any oysters on your island?" asked the showgirl. "I love oysters," she explained, unable to wrap her mind around the concept of monotony.

I edged away from the gathering shortly thereafter.

The topic had shifted to Fleet's visits to the Arctic, his legendary ability to appease wild animals with nothing more than a gesture, and whether or not some beer commercial was really based on him.

Antsy that I would be trampled in the swarm of his ever-growing audience, I went over and stood by the mantel.

Lockhart's place was certainly very nice, but to be absolutely honest, the atmosphere of the penthouse apartment, with its cathedral ceilings and hand-carved fireplace, was starting to pale like overabundant lobster.

It didn't help that the cocktails were few and far between. Lockhart offered as his beverage of choice—wait for it—Sprightly Sports Drinks, straight out of the bottle. He had every flavor on the market, including Bounding Berry and Melon Madness, and not one of them with a drop of alcohol. You would think he owned a sports-drink company or something. The labels, I noticed, all had riddles on them, very literary, but I didn't give any much consideration. I'd had enough brainteasers for one day.

As was my wont (apparently), I began fingering knickknacks on the mantel. I started with a couple of wooden boxes that looked expensive, then moved on to a porcelain yak reminiscent of the elephant in my cabin. I flipped this over and, sure enough, saw the "Made in Bingham" label. Always with the Bingham, I said to myself, and stuck it back on the shelf.

That's when I saw it. Sitting a little to the left on a tiny table—an urn. But not just any old urn, mind you, a Grecian Urn.

I reached out and fingered it wantonly.

"You look like a man who's had an epiphany."

I turned and saw Ate, significantly chilled since our talk at her cabin.

She looked amused. "John Hathaway, I presume?"

I had no time for foolishness. "The poem," I said.

"Looks like a vase to me."

"No, I mean, the poem 'Ode on a Grecian Urn.' This looks like a Grecian urn."

"Is that important?"

"It could be very important," I said. "It could be Keats's answer."

I don't know why Croker's words still haunted me. I suppose we all have the impulse for solving a puzzle—even when this puzzle is posed by an egotistical jerk-off who has nothing better to do than play death pranks on unsuspecting guests of the casino.

Ate seemed less enthralled. "You've been hanging around Dad too much. He's always speaking in riddles."

I would have explained to her that I wasn't speaking in riddles, I was speaking in puzzles, but I wasn't given the opportunity. I had attracted the attention of Neptune. He was glaring over at me, two forceful black eyes peering out from under the heavy Penobscot brow. I figured he didn't like me fondling the art. I set the piece back on the stand and gave a little nod of acknowledgment.

My long-distance relationship with the hired muscle had not gone unnoticed. Across the room, a peculiar man was staring my way. I turned to Ate and inquired after my fellow guest.

"Who's the twit by the ice sculpture?"

He was on the stubby side, a bit paunchy around the belly. His arms were covered in tattoos, the area below his bottom lip in a tiny soul patch. He wore colorful, goggle-like glasses, and even from that distance you could see his blazingly bright teeth, shining out through a flamboyant grin that didn't seem to have any real reason behind it. Add to that a pair of baggy cargo pants and a T-shirt depicting a scantily dressed biker chick, and I suddenly didn't feel all that chagrined about my blue jeans.

"That's Todd Parnell," Ate answered. "He's one of the contestants on the show tomorrow with Dad."

I nodded uncertainly.

He appeared to be looking for someone (or maybe he was trying to remember where he had parked his Harley). Having swept from one side of the room to the other, his gaze rested on me again, continuing on a few seconds later. He didn't seem to know me.

"Has he ever been on a game show before?"

"You might say that."

"A lot of game shows?"

"Think of him as a younger, more tattooed version of Dad."

"I'd rather not."

"He holds the overall record for game show winnings, undefeated in every major venue but one. This will be his first public appearance in six months."

"Sounds like it was a coup getting him."

"Not really. He's from this area. He was happy to do it."

"Croker must have been tickled to get both him and your dad."

"I don't know. He wanted Dad. I kind of think he didn't actually want Parnell for some reason."

My estimation of Wilson Croker's taste went up slightly. "So how did this Parnell meet his Waterloo?"

"His what?"

I rolled my eyes. "You said he was undefeated on every game show but one. What was that one?"

"Oh. It was some kind of tournament of champions for one of the big shows. I can't remember which. Earlier in the season he had utterly blown everyone away in the regular match. Hardly anyone else got an answer in the whole week he was on. Then came this tournament at the end of the year, and he was totally off. Not awful, but not great either, if you know what I mean. He was leading going into the final category, and then missed the last question. He's never appeared on TV again after that."

I made a silent whistle. "And now the battered champion returns."

"I guess. He's Dad's only real competition on the show. The other guy—"

I didn't let her finish. I pushed past her, staring at the wall beyond the ice sculpture. Behind one of the ten-foot-high Sprightly placards stood a striking woman dressed in green silk, a blonde.

My blonde.

15 — Follow the Girl

She slipped out onto the balcony. I sprang after her, only to be blocked in my exit by the awe-inspiring form of Jack Lockhart.

"Good evening, Mr. Hathaway. Having a good time?"

I assured him that I was. I think my exact words were "You bet."

"I've been meaning to ask you about your accent. It's always nice meeting a fellow Brit in these parts. Odd your uncle never mentioning you were English. Or perhaps you picked up the accent in your travels. Tell me, where did you acquire it?"

"Oh, you know," I said, "here and there"—and then faking left, darted to my right. Right into his Grecian urn. It sailed off the table and careened into the fireplace. But it was okay.

Until it hit the floor. Then it shattered into about sixteen uniquely sized pieces, and that was all I knew or needed to know. I felt a grizzly bear grip on my person and, turning to my right, saw that this grip belonged to the "driver" Neptune. Our ruckus had silenced a handful of guests to our left and brought Enescu Fleet to the spot in a whoosh of dignified tweed.

"Problem?" he asked.

I had a feeling that Neptune, a true strong, silent type, would have answered by twisting my arm into some kind of tribal folk art. Thankfully, Jack Lockhart didn't allow that sort of thing on his inlaid stone tile. "It's fine," he said, holding up a well-manicured hand.

Neptune didn't look fine. He stood down, but he didn't look like he liked standing down.

"I'm awfully sorry." This came from me. Neptune continued to look like he regretted not yanking my arm off when he had the chance. "Kiwi Kraze—" I offered him.

"Don't worry about it, Mr. Hathaway." Lockhart was all class. "It was a replica, ironically a gift from your uncle."

"Really?

"Absolutely—a several-hundred-year-old replica, but a replica nonetheless."

There was a pause here, during which I apologized again and Lockhart looked bluff and magnanimous. In the interim, Fleet put his arm around Neptune's shoulder, which I wouldn't have attempted on a bet. He began to ask him about his tribal background (as stirring a testament to his ability to calm beasts with a gesture as anyone could hope to see). The latter might not know it, he said, leading him away from the fracas, but his daughter was part Penobscot. Ate said something under her breath and went off in the direction of the elusive martini shaker. That just left me and Jack Lockhart and a few several-hundred-year-old fragments.

"Thought I saw a girl I know," I said. I don't know why I said this. I thought it might explain my erratic behavior, but then again maybe it wouldn't. Most men don't bust up the place simply because a pretty woman has walked by.

The comment went over fair to middling. Lockhart didn't ask me to give him full and complete details, but he didn't punch me in the throat either (or have Neptune do it).

"Speaking of your uncle," he said, "I believe we have something to discuss?"

"Uh?"

"I understand there is a matter of a package?"

I probably would have panicked, given the chance. As it was, I was so wrapped up in chasing after blondes in green silk that I barely paused. I said unfortunately I didn't have it on me, which was perfectly true, and Lockhart said he understood and perhaps we could make arrangements for tomorrow. I said sure, why not, and made a dash for the balcony.

I would have liked to have known how Fleet would have handled it—him and his contingencies, hah!—but all in all, I thought I dealt with it well enough for now. True, tomorrow Lockhart would be expecting his package, but that was tomorrow. I could always smash something else in his apartment to distract him.

I arrived outside on the balcony, confident in the knowledge that my emerald jewel had not eluded me by coming back in through the French doors. And she hadn't—but that was only because the balcony was not so much a balcony as an enormous sweeping veranda, wrapping around the building with exits here, there and everywhere. There were plenty of guests smoking, several talking on their phones. But no blonde. Not my blonde.

Disappointed, I turned to head back inside.

I could hear the hooting of an owl as I went. At first it held no message for me, but then, turning it over in my mind, it occurred to me that this was no ordinary hooting. It was the hoot of a golden-blonde goddess calling to my very core.

She stepped out from the shadows and waved me to her side. I hastened there at once.

"Was that you hooting?" I asked.

"Hooting?"

"It sounded like a hoot."

"I was trying to get your attention."

"By hooting?"

"Enough with the hooting!"

I said no more on the topic. Still, it seemed like a weird way to start a conversation. What ever happened to "Hi"?

"I'm glad to see you," I told her.

She made a face. It was a beautiful, heartwarming face, but she was plainly harried. She had no time for sentiment. "You're in danger here!" she whispered.

"I'm sure you're in danger too!" I whispered back.

"No, you are."

"I really think it's you."

"Please don't argue!"

"I just—"

"You don't—"

"Let's just agree that we're both in danger," I offered.

She nodded hastily. "You can't trust anyone."

"I can trust you."

An attractive compliment, I thought, but she had no time for it either. "Meet us at the river at midnight."

"Is there a river?" I wondered. I didn't remember any river, and I had been all over the woods and back. "Us?"

"Trust no one," she repeated.

I didn't know how I was supposed to trust no one if she was also requesting that I meet with her and some*one* at midnight. "This river—"

She said no more. Footsteps on the stone tile behind me brought me around with a start. When I turned back again, she was gone.

There were only about fifty exits she could have used.

Enescu Fleet greeted me in the moonlight. He held up a martini glass, gleaming ever so softly, and if I hadn't had more important things on my mind I might have demanded to know where he had found that. The Fleets definitely had a knack for unearthing alcohol. They would have done well during Prohibition.

"You look all worked up," he said.

I helped myself to his martini glass. Slurping down about half, I handed it back and wiped my mouth. "Where's the Wolf Valley River?" I asked.

The sound of a man speaking nearby belayed my geography lesson. Holding a finger up, I crept carefully around the corner and discovered the speaker leaning against the building, muttering into his phone. Was this the man who had frightened away my blonde?

He certainly frightened me. Dressed all in black, he was as sinister as his clothes—sinister black hair (slicked back), sinister eyes, a large, crooked nose (which I suppose wasn't especially sinister) and one of those ridiculously thin beards (which was). The hair ran along his jaw in a narrow strip about the width of a wafer and looked like a pain to trim. Between him and Director Dean, I didn't know what the world of facial hair was coming to these days.

I must have come in at the tail end of his conversation, for he was saying into the receiver, "I can't give it to you if I don't have it." Then, trying to break in on the flow of speech on the other end, "Dude… dude…dude, calm down. Calm down. Dude—"

Then he noticed me.

I don't know what compelled me to stand there staring at him for so long. Bad manners, I guess. The man in black didn't care for it. Or me. He clicked off the phone and swiveled his glare in my direction.

Before I could offer up any explanation, Fleet joined us. Smiling at the phone, he said, "That was some spat you were having. Lovers' tiff?"

Now, see, that's what's funny about people. There are two types in this world, those who can say whatever they want to whomever they want—and saps like me, who could never get away with a remark like that. See me ask a creepy stranger if he's having a gay quarrel, and I would be sailing over the balcony before I could say, "Just joking, folks!" In fact, I'm not sure I could have managed the comment with an actual gay man. It's all about tone.

Sure enough, his remark caused no hard feelings. The man in black sniffed amusedly. It wasn't an especially effusive sniff, but it appeared to appreciate the unofficial male code regarding good-natured ribbing. I refer to the code that states that any man may make a derisive comment about another man's sexuality, provided that

A) the comment is made in obvious jest, with the further stipulation that such a comment shall in no way constitute a theme or motif with which the first party shall undermine the second party's ability to get on with chicks, and,

B) it's said in the right tone.

The third stipulation is optional and reads, simply, that the first party is brawny. Mr. Black patently respected this code.

Fleet, having invoked it, did not linger, another part of the agreement. (The vanquishing male shall not stand forth, giggling at the wittiness of his remark.) He moseyed back inside, probably to root out the rest of his secret martini stash. It was just me and Dr. Thin Beard now. We both smiled.

I expected his smile to fade before mine, but it actually grew more amused by the second. In a strange, hypnotic way, I found myself growing more amused too. That sense of someone tinkering with my reality became more pronounced than ever.

By the time he spoke again, I was practically chuckling. "Did I hear someone say you're John Hathaway?" he asked, smiling in the moonlight.

"That's me," I said, smiling in my own share of moonlight.

"I know that it's not," he said, and we both laughed. Me not all that amusedly.

16 — The Third Man

I suppose, strictly speaking, he hadn't violated any unofficial male code, real or implied. And yet I resented his comment, resented the ever-loving balls out of it.

Who was this guy to say I wasn't who I said I was, even if I wasn't? He couldn't even grow his beard out properly.

"I don't know what you mean," I remarked, and my smile had vanished, as had my implicit chuckle.

He continued on happily, "Of course you do. I suggest you meet me in Studio D in exactly one half hour. We can discuss terms then."

"What terms?"

"You know."

"I don't, dammit!" I didn't know a damn thing—why wouldn't anyone believe that? "Where's Studio D?"

"Ask Google Maps," said this offense to humanity and departed in an ooze of smugness.

I considered asking, "What's Google Maps?" but remembered it at the last minute anyway, and besides I wouldn't have given him the satisfaction.

"You appear to be brooding," said Fleet, returning with his martini glass replenished.

"I've had a shock," I said, and helped myself to another gulp of his drink.

"You must have heard about the suicide. Just learned about it myself."

"Suicide?" It took me a moment for this to sink in. Suicide? That's what he said, and yet I couldn't understand it. "Who committed suicide?" I asked.

"Then you didn't hear?"

"I never hear anything!"

"It was several months ago. Guest of the casino jumped." He jerked a sober thumb up toward the roof, the area between the battlements. "The police put it down to bad gambling debts, but no one could find any evidence of this. Some called it murder but that never stuck either. It's something of an unsolved mystery in these parts."

If I had been less preoccupied, and a little fuller of proper human emotion, I might have analyzed this poor man's end. As it was, I was more concerned with my own.

"I think I've just been blackmailed."

Fleet registered a sympathetic scowl. His tanks were always full to the sloshing point with proper human emotion. He set his martini down on a passing waiter's tray and asked how much they wanted.

"Nothing yet. Call it a prelude to blackmail."

"Who was it?"

"The creepy guy on the cell phone. He said he knew I wasn't Hathaway and to meet him in Studio D in half an hour."

"Then let's meet him in Studio D."

I blinked. I liked his cool, never-say-die attitude, but I couldn't share it. I shook my head. "I'm thinking of making a break for it. Which way do you think is north?"

Fleet adjusted my finger in the correct direction. "I believe running is a mistake," he said.

"Why? What is there for me here? I mean, everyone has been very kind, but I'm not going anywhere, am I? This is the best way out."

"That's probably what our friend on the roof thought."

"This is totally different. I'm not proposing to jump, only dash. And why shouldn't I? I don't know who I am. Clearly I'm a rotten John Hathaway."

"You're a perfectly adequate John Hathaway, probably better than Hathaway himself."

"This guy seemed to think otherwise."

"And what about the girl?" Fleet asked. "What did she think?"

I paused.

"You've seen her again, haven't you?"

I unpaused. "How'd you know?"

"The look on your face. Not to mention that business with the urn. Nobody would have careened across the party like that simply for one of Jack's hors d'oeuvres. His caterer isn't that good. You and she spoke?"

"She asked me to meet her tonight. Her and somebody else she wouldn't identify."

"What time did she propose meeting?"

"Midnight."

Fleet looked at his watch. "That gives us just over an hour."

"An hour for what?"

"Studio D. Come, I know a shortcut."

His shortcut proved effective enough. Along a couple service corridors, which smelled of old paint, into an elevator, and there we were. Somewhere in the casino.

"Come," said Fleet again, and I continued to follow, dodging drunks and gamblers and other Wolf Valley revelers, until we arrived at the entrance of an auditorium labeled "D."

There was a poster here done up in lights inside a clear plastic frame. A member of the casino staff blocked our view of it. He was diddling with the paper inside. He finished tacking this up, shut the panel and switched on the encircling bulbs. All this to unveil the loathsome guest from the party: pencil beard and all, under a banner that read "Ronald the Remarkable." I assumed the latter was a matter of opinion.

It appeared my blackmailer was a hypnotist and had shows nightly.

Our journey through the maintenance corridors, and down an elevator playing "Light My Fire" on oboe, had nerved me for a brawl. I was ready to do battle with this remarkable rat.

I squared my shoulders and pushed forward.

Fleet held me in place. "Regarding the Grecian urn at Lockhart's apartment," he asked, "I assume it contained no secrets? Before you smashed it, I mean?"

"What? No, nothing. It was only a hunch."

"An excellent one. One must always look for connections. Do you remember Keats's other famous ode?"

I thought about it and replied, " 'Ode to a Nightingale'?"

"Excellent." He pointed.

I looked behind me and saw the entrance to a private room. It had a burgundy-leather door with brass studs and appeared to be closed off except to the very highest of high rollers. Above the door read the phrase, "The Nightingale Room."

"Something to consider," said Fleet, his expression twinkling as it had done on numerous occasions during our young friendship. "Ever since you told me about the young lady's clue, I have been thinking about all things Keats. She made no further mention of it tonight?"

"Um, no. No, she didn't." (Well, she didn't.)

"Odd. And she gave no indication what it could mean at the time?"

"Nope. It was just said out of the blue, no explanation." (It was.)

"Very strange. Ah well, we just need time to think." He twirled me back around toward Studio D. "This way," he shoved me, and I had no reason to doubt him.

The theater was empty, with only a few houselights on. We trudged down the aisle and up onto the stage, where a few more lights could be seen backstage. Fleet took it from there. More trudging, a bit of tramping. Pause to talk with showgirls. Back to the trudging. Finally, we came to a dressing room door. We knocked.

"Who is it?" demanded the occupant. We seemed to be getting that reply a lot lately.

"Me," I said. See him refute that. Jerk-off.

The door whipped open, and a thinly bearded face poked out, his black eyes darting between me and my elderly muscle and back to me again. "I said no cops."

"You didn't say anything of the sort."

"Right." The Remarkable was a fair man. He supposed he hadn't said that.

"And I'm not a cop," replied Enescu Fleet, cheerfully pushing his way through.

"Better come in," said Ronald. Not that he had any choice.

The dressing room was a mess, quite a contrast to the one belonging to Wilson Croker. Croker's room had the look of an exclusive country club. Ronald's looked like someone had hit it with a club, and not a very exclusive one.

"Sit," said the slob, tossing a pile of black laundry out of our path. He shoved a seat my way. Fleet preferred to stand.

"You're that detective," the remarkable one remarked. "I was reading about you in the media guide."

"Retired detective."

"Whatever." His voice was as thin as his beard. He was flustered. He looked back at me. "And I said half an hour, chum. That was like six minutes. Don't you got a watch?"

"No," I said.

Fleet had circumnavigated the room and was now standing behind Ronald, running his hand along his dressing table.

The hypnotist didn't seem to like the positioning. "Hey, look, I don't want any rough stuff here. I made a simple business proposal to your boy. If he took it the wrong way—"

"Nothing of the sort. We are very interested in your information. If it's good, we will gladly pay for it."

"Oh." That held him for a while. "What do you wanna know?"

"What you know."

"Oh yeah? I know this guy isn't John Hathaway."

"And how do you know that?"

"I've met him. The real John Hathaway."

"When was this?"

"Yesterday. He came backstage. He said he had a package for Wilson Croker, and I said did I look like Wilson Croker, and he said no; no, I didn't. The thing is, Croker *had* been here. He sneaked out the back when this guy showed up. I didn't see what business this was of the guy, so I didn't mention it."

"And why *had* Croker sneaked out the back?"

"I don't see what business that is of yours."

Fleet stepped closer, his hand instinctively going to Ronald's shoulder. "That's not very valuable information."

"No?"

"No."

"Oh," said the Remarkable Ronald. He paused. "Yeah, fair enough. Let's forget the whole thing."

Fleet knew a cue when he heard one. "That is exactly my friend's predicament. He *has* forgotten the whole thing. And everything else, it seems."

"What do you mean?"

Fleet was getting pretty good at telling my story. Not that he needed much practice yarning.

"You mean he doesn't remember anything?" asked Ronald.

"Nothing about himself, no. That's why we were hoping you could supply us with some useful information. In fact, you don't know any more than we do."

"Nope," agreed Ron. He looked at me. "What happened, man?"

"We don't know," Fleet answered for me.

"Loco," said Ron. Back to me: "Not even any flashbacks?"

"No flashbacks," I replied.

"I thought you guys with banged-up brains always had flashbacks. They start out all hazy and wobbly, then you make out a face, then a figure standing on a pier, then a car speeding away. Some *chica* screams, 'Don't do it, Ricky…' "

"No flashbacks," I said.

Ronald understood. He considered this loco.

"I assume we can trust you with this information?" asked my heavy.

"Huh?"

"My friend wouldn't want it spread around that he has misplaced his marbles."

"Sure. Who would?"

"And it would be much more convenient for everyone if you didn't mention that he is not John Hathaway."

"Of course. Who cares that he's not? Not me." He twisted around in his seat, and with the twist came the twisted grin. "You gotta understand," he said to Fleet, "when I realized he wasn't who he said he was, I figured I'd caution him, that's all. I mean, there's people around who would try to use that to their advantage, but me—"

"Exactly," said Fleet. He placed a chair across from the hypnotist and looked him in his beady eyes. "You've been very accommodating. Perhaps you wouldn't mind accommodating me on one other point?"

"Sure."

"We've tried everything to jog my poor friend's memory—"

I frowned. We hadn't tried anything at all. I was beginning to feel rather neglected about it, in fact.

"The medicos are baffled—"

I frowned a second time. What medicos? The medicos didn't know anything about it.

"And I was thinking, perhaps, we could try some harmless hypnotism. We're desperate."

I bounded up. I wasn't *that* desperate. And I didn't view it as harmless. I don't know how you'd feel about it, but I wasn't about to turn over my banged-up brain to some creepy thug—especially not a creepy thug who abandoned his blackmail plans this readily. Where was his moral fiber?

Surprisingly enough, Ronald agreed with me. "I don't know. It's pretty hit or miss. Doesn't work on everybody."

"What in this world has a guarantee?" wondered Fleet.

"And I'm not really feeling it right now, gents."

"As a personal favor to me, then?"

"Well—"

Fleet gave me a look. "How about it? Should we give this a shot?"

I don't know what it was about that glance. He didn't exactly wink. Nothing as clumsy as that. But it was a look of shared confidences, a call to trust him.

"Um—"

"Cool beans," said Fleet. "I will just observe."

17 — Poor Player

Thinking back on it now, I don't remember feeling sleepy, much less very, very sleepy.

I don't remember my eyelids feeling heavy, so heavy I couldn't hold them up.

I don't remember much of anything (what else is new?) except a gold pocket watch twirling on its chain—Ronald's watch, chipped and rather cheap. Then there was Ronald's sappy voice, the smell of something I couldn't identify in the room—cabbage?—then the voice becoming less sappy, then not very sappy at all, then positively unsappy.

And then a hand shaking my shoulder and a voice asking me to wake up.

"Kettledrum!" I replied, starting in my chair. The lights were low, and all I could make out was the intelligently bearded face of Enescu Fleet. "What did he do to me?"

"He did nothing."

"Nothing?"

"Nothing. As we suspected, he's an utter fraud."

I stood up. I felt pretty good. Well rested and loose. I was glad our suspicions about him had been justified, although I didn't actually remember having those either.

"Was I out?"

"You betcha."

"Who put me under?"

"I did."

"*You* did?"

"I did," said Enescu Fleet. "Inadvertently. While I was putting him under, you must have tuned in."

"You put *him* under? How—? Why—? How—?" It was a close race, but *How* won out.

"It was rather easy. First of all, it's a myth that you have to dangle an object before your subject's eyes. Ron would do well to remove that from his act—it's cheap."

I might have said, "Just like his watch," but Fleet carried on without pausing for breath.

"The power of the human voice is enough, if you have the talent. I simply waited for the appropriate moment to lend my voice to his, and the rest was merely shifting his momentum the other way around, like a sort of mental jujitsu. If anything, he put himself under—with my assistance."

My brain felt sore just thinking about it. "Then you really put him in a trance while he was trying to put me in one?"

"See for yourself."

He flipped on the light, and there was Ronald, sitting across from us, not looking all that Remarkable. He was staring straight ahead, blinking. He didn't appear to be breathing.

"Sure he's not dead?"

"Quite sure."

I rubbed my head. Was he sure I wasn't?

Fleet motioned me back to my chair. "I was almost certain that Ronald and I had crossed paths before. But I needed to be sure. Now I am."

"And—?"

"I knew him as Rupert Velazquez, alias Ronnie Becker, alias the Remarkable Ronald. He is a gifted con man who now applies his skills to a lounge act. Hypnotism. It's the perfect semilegitimate job for him. Most mentalists are nothing more than hacks, using shills and other disreputable means to scam their audience. Just like most con men. And most audiences are primed to be deceived. They expect a deception, and that plays into the hypnotist's hands. Ironically, I think

Ronald has started to buy into his own balderdash; otherwise I never would have been able to put him under. He wanted to be put under."

"Loco," I said.

"According to him, he used to include mindreading in his act, but a couple days ago he called the wrong shill up from the audience and made a total ass of himself trying to guess her profession. After that, the casino decided they would downplay Ron's other mentalist abilities. That's why the poster outside only touts the hypnotism now, not that those skills are any more valid."

"But he made me laugh."

"I'm sure he can be very charming when he wants to be."

"No, I mean without me meaning to laugh. On the balcony. It was creepy."

"Ah that. That's a pretty simple trick to learn. It's just a forced reflex action you can suggest to people, akin to chain yawning."

I was relieved. The creep had no hold over me. "You know, I was even beginning to ask myself if he was the one who had blocked my memory."

"You can set your mind at ease on that. He assured me that he had only seen you for the first time this evening. In his hypnotic state, I don't think he could outright lie, only dissemble."

"Did he say much while he was under?"

"Not much, no. He admitted who he was, but when it came to other details, he became very secretive. He wouldn't say why Wilson Croker had come to see him. I also couldn't get him to supply anything about the real John Hathaway. It's possible that he doesn't know anything. I did think it was interesting that Hathaway told Ronald that his package was for Croker, and not for Jack. I wonder if it was a ruse on Hathaway's part to get backstage. It's what I would have done."

I agreed it was a poser, alright. "Remind me to tell you something about that package when we have a moment."

Fleet ignored me. "I worked on Ronnie a long time about the phone argument we overhead on the balcony. I couldn't make any headway at all. When I pressed him, he just kept making a twisted face, like an infant who didn't like the brand of strained peas I was serving. All he would say was he couldn't get it, it wasn't him. When

I asked who it was if it wasn't him, he said he couldn't get it. When I asked what it was he couldn't get, he said it wasn't him."

"Determined mind."

"More like guilty. There's something he's been doing that makes him feel so awful that he can't bring himself to discuss it. Now, if we knew the identity of the party on the other end of the line—but that's not likely. Oh well, I guess it's none of our business. My natural curiosity is getting the better of me again. We learned everything we need to know."

"Do you think we should rat him out to the casino?"

Fleet saw no reason for this. "Aside from attempted blackmail, which he quickly backpedaled on, he's not guilty of any crime that we know of. Other than poor showmanship and a rotten fashion sense. We will leave him be for now, I think. And now I guess we should be getting back to the cabin. Pixie will be waiting."

I peered back at the remarkably silent Ronald. "Shouldn't you wake him, or detrance him, or whatever you call it?"

"He has the ability to come out of it himself. And if he doesn't, I told him to rouse himself when the cleaning staff knocks."

I was satisfied. "Wonder why he was at Lockhart's party? Doesn't seem the posh type."

As always, the detective had the answer. "That's easy. All the contestants on the game show were invited."

"*He's* a contestant?"

"Indeed. There's me, Todd Parnell and Ronnie. He's the third man. It was Jack's idea—play up the casino by featuring one of its staff as a contestant. They originally asked one of the showgirls, Holly Letters, a magna cum laude graduate and head of the local Mensa chapter, but she told them it wouldn't befit her dignity. Besides, she's getting her tassels regreased that day."

18 — STRUTS

It wasn't until we had almost reached Fleet's cabin ten minutes later that I remembered that I still had a bone to pick with the Zen master. I waited until we had alighted from the shuttle bus and were walking the last few steps up the drive. Despite the hour, there were still plenty of people about, so I had to be guarded in my speech.

"He's still expecting his package, you know."

"Who is? Jack?"

We had just finished talking about the art of hypnotism—specifically, why he didn't ask my subconscious mind, while I was under, who *it* thought I was. (Turned out he had, and it didn't know.)

"Yes—Jack. He said he would be very glad to have his package."

"And what did you tell him?"

"What do you think I told him? I said cool beans, and promised to give it to him tomorrow."

"Jack Lockhart," said Fleet, leading the way up the path toward the darkened cabin, "would do well to enjoy the things he does have and not go asking people for more all the time. Look at him. He has a lovely home with a view of an unsolved suicide. He has a Penobscot driver, money, women, an artfully fractured urn. What does he need with a mystery package? I bet you he doesn't even know what's in it. For all he knows the congressman could have sent him a bushel of bumper stickers."

"He's pretty secretive about it," I replied. "He lowers his voice whenever he brings it up, like he'd rather be discussing it in a dark alley at midnight. He—oh gosh, midnight." I looked at my watch. I didn't have a watch. "What time is it?"

Fleet answered twelve exactly.

I swept an agitated hand over my forehead. "The blonde! The river! I nearly forgot!"

"This way," said Fleet. "It's only a one-minute walk from here."

Accurate as always, he got me to the rendezvous at approximately 12:01.

Unlike the main path, the appointed meeting place was totally deserted. There were no guests, no roads, and the bungalows were less than a suggestion through the bramble.

With nothing but the moon to light our way, we stepped up to the edge of a short cliff and looked out over the river. There was a small boathouse visible from our view, lots of trees and not much else.

I wasn't happy. "How do we know this is where she meant?"

"It's the only spot on the entire reservation with a clearing at the river. That's probably why you haven't noticed it before now. If she said the river, she meant here."

I nodded. And waited. After about five minutes of silence, punctuated by the steady *splook, splook, splook* of the current below, Fleet drew my attention to the boathouse.

"They left a light on for us."

I had noticed this too. One window, lit. It struck me as sinister, that window. Maybe it was the contrast. There was the rest of the landscape, lying there minding its business, and then *Bing!*, a shining white rectangle. It didn't belong.

"Odd time of year for it," he said. "I'm pretty sure they closed up shop weeks ago."

"Then who's in the boathouse?" I prompted.

"Precisely. You stay here and wait for your date. I'll check it out."

I didn't enjoy my time alone. The clearing definitely felt colder and spookier after Fleet's departure, and I kept hearing strange noises from the woods behind me. Snaps and slithers and the occasional resounding thump. I felt like someone was watching me again.

I considered doing the hoot of an owl to announce my presence, but decided, on second thought, I'd better skip it. If there were some kind of grizzly or werewolf in the fold, an owl snack would probably be just what he was after.

I rubbed my hands for warmth and tried not to let the place creep me out too much.

"Nothing," spoke my friend, and I sprang three feet in the air and nearly took a header into the river. Fleet snagged my jacket and reeled me back in. He suggested I watch my step in future, and I suggested, *in future*, he not sneak up on me like a bloody Comanche. "The shack is empty, except for a single canoe and a raccoon. I don't know who turned the light on."

"Must have been the raccoon," I said.

"There were also tire tracks adjacent to the boathouse."

I was pretty sure raccoons didn't drive, even in Maine. "People towing their boats up?"

"Perhaps, but not in October."

I nodded.

Fleet shined a pocket torch on my face, and I nodded again. "What did she say about the man accompanying her?"

"She didn't. She didn't even say it was a man. Why, who do you think it is?"

He didn't reply. I guess it was a pretty stupid question. "Shall we go?" he asked.

I insisted we wait another ten minutes. He reluctantly agreed. Ten minutes.

Twenty-five minutes later, we headed back to the cabin. Fleet unlocked the door, and we finally got out of the cold. I was pretty distracted so I didn't really notice him hesitate as we came in, nor did I wonder why he was playing with the light switch by the door. Coming out of my haze, I watched him flip it up and down and up again. "Why was this light off?" he asked.

What was it with this guy and lights? The boathouse's was on and should be off; the living room's was off and should be on. What did it matter?

Fleet wasn't so easily satisfied. He called out Pixie's name, and only after she had come scampering out to us did he give it a rest. He scratched her head with all the vigor of before, but you could see his faith in concierges would never be the same. "He just left," he muttered, in time with the frizzing. "Just turned off the lights and left, the bastard. I hope you sweated up his sport jacket good and proper."

I assured him that I would chop some wood in it tomorrow. Meanwhile, the mention of the garment reminded me that I would be glad to get it off and me to bed.

"You've had a long day," Fleet agreed. "You can have the bed upstairs."

"There's an upstairs?" I asked, surprised that I hadn't noticed this. He pointed up, and I observed the second level. It was above the top of the stairs (which, of course, it would be)—the third step of which I was currently sitting on.

"It's more of a loft area," he explained, "just room enough for a bed, a table and a few odds and ends. You can sleep there tonight, and I'll take the sofa. You need the rest more than I."

I didn't argue. He went to take Pixie for her nightly stroll, still muttering, "He just left," while I climbed the stairs up to my bed. As I came up over the ridge, I saw the bed, as to be expected. I also saw the table, a lamp and the concierge—who apparently hadn't left. He was lying on the floor, tied up and muzzled.

I stood there blinking at him, wondering if he was more of an odd or an end.

By now, you'd think finding bodies at my feet would have been old hat to me. Not so. I enjoyed the experience entirely anew.

He was tied up with an old extension cord, and I couldn't understand why. There were so many other things he could have been doing instead—like not being tied up with an old extension cord. As my host had done before me, I looked askance at his behavior, wondering if this was what they taught concierges these days.

He said something. Sounded like "Mmm," but not a happy "Mmm." The kind of "Mmm" that indicates that someone has duct-taped your face.

I stared at him. I was about to head back downstairs—maybe somebody down there would know what to do with a bundled-up concierge—when a fireplace poker came down on my head.

That was the hitter's intention, anyway, a full and robust swing at my poor battered coconut. Through some miracle I managed to weave out of the way. The assailant hit nothing but air, putting him down 0-1, and when he swung a second time the poker connected with the wood railing and sent what I could only hope was an unpleasant whizz-bang through the guy's nerve endings.

Seeing him stumble back in pain, I felt a burst of confidence. Nearly having my head split in two had emboldened me. He came at me again, and I watched in wonderment as my left hand ensnared his poker arm. Then my right hand got in on the fun. I connected to the side of his head, and the punch sent him to the floor. It was astounding. I knew a martial art! Some sort of physical form of Fleet's mental jujitsu, perhaps.

Could it be, I asked myself, that I was more a man of action than I had thought? Was it possible that I was some sort of spy or assassin?

It made sense when you thought about it. Spies and assassins are forever getting their memories erased. If you are a spy and/or assassin and you *haven't* had your memory erased, then you are doing something wrong and probably get snubbed at the company picnic. And who else but a spy would have cryptic messages given to him, not to mention have to fight off midnight marauders? Yes, it was all coming together. I hurled myself forward.

It was too dark to see my combatant's face, but that didn't keep me from swatting the poker from his grip as though it had been some mere plastic plaything. He responded by swatting me aside as though I had been some mere plastic plaything, and it occurred to me then that maybe I wasn't a spy or assassin, after all.

He followed up with a punch to my belly, and I curled to the floor, thinking that perhaps, at best, I was a housepainter or maybe a clerk in a bookstore. (But not one of those bold and adventurous clerks, always climbing the upper shelves for customer orders. Just a nice, quiet employee who kept to himself and never tried to lift with his back.)

Still on the floor, I saw a beige pant leg scuttle past me and on instinct reached out and grabbed it. My opponent toppled forward, grasping desperately for the railing. He latched on somehow, entangling himself in the spokes, and I got up and kicked him. I missed and almost immediately found myself skimming down the stairs, touching every third one, if that. The assassin snagged my elbow as I sailed by, and suddenly we were careening through the railing arm in arm, like a pair of Elks Club members out on the town.

There was about a ten-foot drop, during which my life flashed before my eyes—what there was of it—and then a thud. I landed on the sofa, he, not so lucky, on the floor behind the sofa.

He climbed to his feet and staggered out onto the deck, limping. He was wearing a beige jumpsuit and black ski mask, which wasn't a bad idea. It *was* pretty cold outside. He vanished into the night.

A couple minutes passed, and I heard the door open, followed by the pattering of tiny paws on wood tile. Moments later I became aware of a Maltese face licking mine.

Enescu Fleet also appeared, leaning over my busted torso. "Honestly," he said, "the sofa is fine with me. No need to put yourself out."

19 — And Frets

I didn't sleep well. In fact, sitting in the audience of Studio A early the following morning, I couldn't say for sure that I had slept at all. It was becoming a bit of a habit with me.

I couldn't blame my exhaustion entirely on Miss Fleet's accommodations. Some of it, I was sure, stemmed from the fact that it was currently six in the morning and no human person was meant to be awake at six. They were shooting the game show today, and for some reason they liked to start *early*. (And they called me wonky in the head.) I was dressed in my jeans and one of Fleet's sweaters, my Oxford broadcloth having been torn asunder during my postprandial brawl last night.

The authorities had more or less settled the matter of our midnight marauder. They (in the person of the reservation sheriff—a mellow, round-bellied man called Greene) said they had no idea what was going on and felt it unlikely they would ever know what was going on. It was just one of those strange occurrences. We were told, however, to let them know if it occurred again, because that would make it not only strange, but also out of the ordinary.

I couldn't get much better out of the Fleet man. He seemed to know more than he was saying. It seemed like everyone was concealing something on this trip. The only person who wasn't concealing anything was the concierge, who poured forth his testimony the instant the duct tape came off. According to what we could piece together, the marauder had gotten in through the deck window and, once inside, had struck the concierge from behind with the fireplace poker. He had gone to great effort not to kill him, Fleet had concluded, hitting him in the precise location to induce unconsciousness and not a cracked skull. Of course, the man hadn't acted all that pleasantly disposed toward *my* skull, but when I pointed this out, I was told not to raise petty objections and that these were mere details, details.

I had the feeling that the concierge would have gladly spoken more about his ordeal, but other than the bonk, he hadn't much to report. He had been hit while climbing the stairs to the loft—no doubt to lie down and take a nap in my bed, the slacker—and the masked man simply had to yank him up the last few steps before applying the binds.

I would have liked to have known what Pixie, the Wolf Valley's most fierce watchdog, was doing during all this, but any criticism of the wombat princess passed unheard. It was her owner's considered view that the girl had cleverly spirited herself away to some strategic position, lying low, waiting to pounce.

The intruder, he felt, had been there looking for something. What, he did not know. My suggestion, that the man could have also been there to take me out, Fleet dismissed entirely. As far as the resident detective was concerned, the pouncing and the poker proved nothing. They were details, he said, mere details, and I didn't speak again until morning.

If you could call it morning. I had nodded off for the ninety-sixth time when the special guest contestant woke me. He clasped me on the noggin and said, "No good sleeping now, the show's about to start."

I was amazed to see him wearing one of those tissue makeup dickeys. I would have thought the world's most fascinating man would have exuded some special elixir from his pores, masking all blemishes and imperfections.

"Wake me when you name the killer," I said, drifting off. "You do name a killer in this game, don't you? Right. Wake me then." I felt my head tilting forward again, but Fleet held it in place like a palmed melon.

"You're not still sore from last night, are you?"

"I think I landed on my ass funny. Other than that, I'm great."

"I meant the attitude I adopted with the sheriff. I might have come off as a shade disdainful when you spoke."

"Ass," I said again. It was a word with many useful functions.

He took the seat beside me. I had been told that this seat would be occupied by Jack Lockhart, but the beverage giant hadn't arrived yet.

"Perhaps it hasn't occurred to you," Fleet whispered, "but I was trying to protect you."

I muttered, "Protect me"—laughably—and he said, "Yes. Protect you."

"If you had continued to stick your oar in, the sheriff would have asked you your name and address. A central witness in an assault? A key figure in the brawl? Your info would have been his first priority. And when you couldn't supply it, don't you think he would have grown suspicious? Your only option would have been to own up, and even if he believed you, where would you be? Under the care of some nice men in white smocks, that's where."

My eyelids shot open. "I hadn't thought of that."

"No."

"I'm amazed he didn't ask for my info anyway."

"He did. I talked him out of it."

"You didn't hypnotize him, did you?"

I hadn't seen Ronald the Remarkable this morning, and the last thing we needed was another casino employee wandering about with swirling eyeballs.

"It wasn't necessary. Once I was able to point out that you were nothing but a cipher, he agreed to allow you to remain anonymous, as a personal favor to me. The clincher came when I explained that you were Ate's married lover and didn't want your name bandied about."

"I bet she liked that."

"She did express herself very vividly on the topic when she arrived home last night. But the key was she waited until after the police had left before speaking her mind. She's a good girl."

Which was more than you could say about me, I realized. The good part, not the girl. Well, that too. "Sorry I doubted you."

"Mistakes all around," he said. The smile faded from his face. "Here comes my daughter now."

I couldn't help admiring Ate's work ethic. Up at five, half an hour of some deranged stepping exercise, which woke me from my half sleep, a modest breakfast, a quick shower, and here she was twenty minutes later, toiling away to make sure every detail was correct for her game show. She truly was a network goddess. I didn't know what it was I did to earn my monthly envelope back home, but if it was anything as stressful and thankless as this, I was happy to forget.

She didn't look all that excited to see us. I wasn't certain if this had more to do with the broken railing in her loft (another byproduct of the brawl), or the notion, among certain members of the Wolf Valley Police Force, that I was her married lover.

I was inclined to think it was more the latter.

"They want you in the contestants' row in five minutes," she told her dad, hardly moving her miniature red lips as she spoke.

She was definitely brooding over the fake-lover thing and not the railing. Home repairs can be pretty annoying, I'm sure, but this went beyond oak and varnish. No amount of wood putty can refit the banister of a girl's virtue. Byron said that. Or if he didn't, he should have.

"I guess I should be going, then," Fleet replied.

"Go," she said.

I felt bad about their rift. I would have tried reuniting them, reminding them of some cherished bond, but I didn't know of any.

It was probably just as well that I said nothing. She didn't look all that pleasantly disposed toward me either. She didn't say anything, but she seemed to be thinking that if she had taken a clandestine lover, she could have done a lot better than some tousled nitwit whose sweater didn't even fit him.

"So," I said, hoping to break the strained silence. "How's this game show work again?"

Father and child turned and blinked at me. The less temperamental male fielded the question.

"It's easy to grasp once you understand the structure," he answered, removing the dickey and handing it to a passing intern. "Let me explain—"

Ate cut him off. "I can explain it better," she said, and her father nodded graciously. He let her have the floor. "Every puzzle has a dead guy," she began. "Along with the stiff, there will be a clue, a couple of actors to find the body and explain the backstory, and three suspects. After the corpse is revealed, the contestants will attempt to name the killer based on the clue left behind by the victim. This will be in the form of an allusion. It might be literary, historical, etc. That's where the trivia comes in. While the contestants think about the allusion and try to solve the murder, Croker starts doling out hints. Eventually someone gets the reference and buzzes in with their solution."

"How does the victim leave behind a clue that both fingers his killer and contains some kind of cultural allusion?"

"It's easy. Consider this example from the book. Let's say the victim is a sports enthusiast, and after getting gunned down with an Uzi or whatever, he staggers across the room and selects a Babe Ruth baseball card from his collection. That would be his clue."

"Seems to me," I said, "that after getting shot up with an Uzi the last thing I would do is grapple around for clues."

"It's a puzzle," said Ate, and I smiled weakly and asked her to continue. "Of the three suspects," she went on, "we learn one is named George Herman."

"Why?"

"It's his name. The other two suspects are called something else, but it doesn't matter because Herman is your killer."

"How?"

"Babe Ruth's real name was George Herman Ruth."

"No kidding," I remarked. "Brilliant. And that's all there is to it?"

That was all there was to it. "Points are totaled based on correctness, speed and an explanation of how the contestant arrived at the solution."

"Sounds like *Hollywood Squares*."

She nodded and said it was nothing like *Hollywood Squares*.

"Sounds complicated," I offered.

She nodded again, but in agreement.

I glanced back at the stage with my newfound knowledge. The three detective armchairs were arranged to the side. The Remarkable Ronald had plopped into his, looking like he had slept in his clothes last night. On the other side of Fleet's throne sat the man Todd Parnell—the egghead Hell's Angel from Jack Lockhart's party. I still didn't get that guy. And then there was the empty podium on the opposite end of the stage. We were still awaiting the arrival of Wilson Croker for that.

The delay gave me a chance to take a better look around the set. It's amazing how much better you see things when you're awake. You focus and absorb. The first thing I focused on (and absorbed) brought me bounding out of my chair. This didn't make Miss Fleet any happier. The sudden spring in my step got tangled up with the lack of spring in hers, and we ended up twirling about like a pair of mambo instructors.

But it was worth it, even if it meant absorbing her dagger glare, as well as a steady look of disapproval from her father.

I had no time for lengthy explanations.

"The back row," I said, pointing.

And what of it? you are no doubt asking yourselves. How does the layout of the auditorium justify jumping up and fondling a girl like a ripened butternut squash? Hasn't the woman been through enough?

That was almost certainly what father and daughter were thinking, and I could only hope that my parting words, uttered before I disappeared up the steps, would clarify my behavior—

"It's her!"

20 — His Hour upon the Stage

By the time I reached the back of the auditorium, my mystery blonde had left her seat. I charged out after her through the closest exit.

She was nowhere to be seen. The back door opened onto a miniature lobby, and like everywhere else in this freakin' casino, it had about eighty different exits and entranceways. I picked the one on my immediate left, a tiny sliver of a door with a digital keypad on it. I caught up to it before it could swing shut again.

I was in the more industrial area of the casino now, the back rooms, and I could see almost at once that I had chosen badly. There were no blondes here. Not even any brunettes in blonde wigs. Only a lot of fluorescent lights and Director Dean standing down the hall, waiting for the elevator.

He had his shaggy head down in anticipation of the *bing*, and when this sounded a few moments later, he shuffled forward onto the car with the same distracted expression. It was then that I noticed he was limping.

Those of you with an excellent attention for detail will recall that the last thing I saw before passing out on the sofa last night was the marauder's prominent limp. Landing in a heap on his knee, or perhaps it was his ankle, he was forced to flee on half power. And here we had Director Dean limping up a storm the next day. Significant? I think so.

Thanks to a set of stairs at the other end of the corridor, I had no difficulty in catching up with him on the bottom level. "Hey," I said, as he tried to step out from the elevator car.

He stumbled back with a yelp. I think my *Hey* must have startled him. He peered out at me with a scowl and then appeared to place me. "Oh, it's you, Hathaway." He was a coy one, this guy.

"Where'd you get that limp?" I demanded.

Hercule Poirot probably would have slipped into the topic more smoothly, but he also would have waited until the last chapter with everyone assembled in the drawing room, and who has time for that?

"What are you talking about?" he asked, knocking into the sliding elevator doors as he tried to exit.

"You're limping."

"So what?"

"You weren't limping yesterday. I find that significant."

"Find it any way you like," he snapped, making it out of the elevator at last. He stepped across the hall, arriving at a door labeled "Video Booth."

I cut him off at the pass. He couldn't get away from me that easily. I was loose and limber, ready to play. Also, he did have that limp.

"What's wrong with your leg?" I said, holding the booth door shut with my left hand.

"If you must know, I have a bad knee. It tweaks me in cold weather. Maybe you noticed we had a flurry of snow this morning."

I had noticed. "And you expect me to believe that?"

"What the hell is the matter with you? Would you let go of that door, please!"

"No."

"I'm calling security."

"Do it," I said, not giving an inch. "Maybe when they arrive you can explain about your so-called bad knee."

"Why would I do that?"

"If they want to know."

"Why would they?"

I was beginning to sense that we were getting off topic here. "Did you, or did you not, try to kill me with a fireplace poker last night?" I asked.

"What!"

"Why do you have a bad knee?" I rephrased. Vary my pitches—that was my strategy.

Director Dean was plainly feeling out of his depth. Figuring, no doubt, that the easiest way to get rid of me was to explain everything, he said, "It's an old hockey injury."

"You're too skinny to play hockey."

"I didn't play, and shut up. I got the injury senior year in high school, trying to film the ice-hockey captain's girlfriend coming out of the arena."

"And he busted your knee?"

"She did."

It seemed plausible, and yet I wasn't sure. "Then you weren't concealed in my hostess's loft last night, waiting to spring out on me when we got home?"

Hearing myself ask this, I realized I wasn't at my best that morning.

Dean seemed to think so too. Wrenching my hand off the door, he suggested that the next time I drop off one of my parcels, I better check and make sure I didn't leave my brain inside it.

The mention of parcels reminded me of Jack Lockhart, my soon-to-be neighbor in the audience. What with all the excitement last night, Fleet and I hadn't settled on anything there.

Dean was gone now. I missed him.

I'm not sure why I didn't head back to my seat. Jack Lockhart perhaps, or maybe just good, old-fashioned laziness. Whatever it was, I remained rooted to the linoleum, and it was fortunate that I did.

At the other end of the hall, there was a curve, and beyond that, I knew from our explorations yesterday, another stage door. I mention this because as I stood there alone with my thoughts, I heard that door click softly shut.

It was the softness that attracted my attention more than anything else. Anyone without an ulterior motive would have banged the door proper. That was what I had done with mine. All the doors in the studio were heavy and unwieldy. The lightest touch caused them to make a noise like a metal dumpster falling on another metal dumpster filled with several more dumpsters. It was for that reason that each door had a sign posted on it that read, "Quiet Please, Filming in Progress."

As anyone familiar with human nature knows, the one way to ensure a noisy exit is to post a sign that reads, "Quiet Please."

But this person had heeded the request. He or she was moving about cautiously, and I wanted to know why.

I walked toward the source of the silence. I could hear breathing. It wasn't mine, because I had long since suspended that practice until further notice.

Behind me was another door. I figured it probably led to a utility closet or something. I turned the handle and slipped inside.

If it was a utility closet, it was the largest utility closet I had ever been in, not that I could remember ever being inside a utility closet. Even in the dark, it felt large and airy, the size of several utility closets combined. I was beginning to think that it wasn't a utility closet.

I backed away from the door. The tough part was waiting quietly, and not kicking anything while I did.

I kicked something about ten seconds later. It twanged and skidded across the floor, and that's when all sorts of interesting things started happening to me.

First, the door opened, and I found myself face-to-face with my fellow trespasser. I giggled—I actually giggled at seeing her.

It was my bold and enigmatic blonde. She looked as dazzling as ever, lit in the light of the corridor, soft and moist and every ounce a tender embodiment of all that is pure and good in the world. (Not that I go overboard every time I see her or anything.)

She gasped when she saw me, but it wasn't an unpleasant gasp. There was a good deal of joy mingled with surprise. I really liked that gasp.

I had so many things to say to her. I started with "Uh."

She said, "Heh."

"You didn't show up last night," I told her.

"And you didn't come alone," she told me.

I bridled at her criticism. She never asked me to come alone. I reminded her of this, and she admitted freely that she guessed she hadn't, no.

I sighed. If people would give better instructions on how they wanted to meet me, there wouldn't be all these mixups.

"How'd you get down here?" I wondered.

"I doubled back and came in through the stage doors on the set while the page was distracted. I wanted to talk to you somewhere private."

I nodded. Talk was good. Private was okay too. Just then, the lights came on around us. She gasped again, not nearly as pleasing as the first time.

I was about to ask her why she thought I was in danger, when a voice drifted in from behind me. It said, "—years on a desert island," and in a flash I realized that Enescu Fleet had just been introduced by the game show announcer. In another flash, I saw that I was on the stage on the other side of the curtain.

It was still decorated in the hunting-lodge motif. I saw the chessboard in the center of the room, the three bottles of wine on the sideboard and the obligatory corpse laid out between them.

I stepped closer.

I would have commended him on his method, the way he hadn't stirred an inch the whole time we were there, had it not struck me, in a third flash, that his method was a little too good.

This was no simple actor playing a corpse. If anything, it was a corpse doing his finest imitation of an actor. He hadn't taken a breath for a solid minute, and there was a pallor of death about him no makeup artist could have achieved—not even if supplied with fifty tissue dickeys. I wondered who he was, or rather had been, and what was going on.

I didn't intend to wait and find out. I turned back to the blonde, only to find that she was no longer present. Sensible of her. I still had time to flee before the curtain rose, and I fled now.

About halfway home, I spotted a crossbow lying on the floor between me and the exit. It had been the crossbow I had kicked in the dark, and it was the crossbow I now hurdled over with an effortless spring.

I didn't have the slightest impulse to pause and examine it. Why characters in stories always lunge for the nearest murder weapon and grip it to their chests, just in time for the authorities to arrive and finger them with it, I will never understand. Just asking for trouble.

I reached the door and was grappling for the handle when a buzzer seemed to go off in my subconscious, like a tiny trivia contestant ringing in with his answer.

The corpse. There was something about the corpse.

I spun back around and stared. The announcer was introducing Wolf Valley's own, the Remarkable Ronald, but I wasn't listening. All I could hear was the steady shuffling of my feet across the wood planks and the ceaseless ticking of the grandfather clock. I approached the body, and my blood turned to ice water as I beheld his mustached face and black-framed glasses.

It was Wilson Croker. He had fooled me twice before but not today. The crossbow bolt, the rigid limbs. The man was dead, deader than few pompous-windbag game show hosts had ever been. At my cabin, no one could have mistaken the thespian touch. (Okay, I had, but I had other things on my mind at the time.) There, he had been acting, clear and simple. His performance today had expired long before I arrived, and with it, the performer. No one was that good an actor, Shakespearean trained or not.

If I hastened to exit before, I hastened even more now. I more or less staggered from the scene. In my hurry, I became entangled in the crossbow again. It latched around my leg, panting for attention, and I jumped and kicked and spat strange oaths against the bowstring industry.

Then the curtain went up.

Then the audience ceased applauding, and the cameraman ceased listening to his head mic, and the other two actors in the sketch said, "What the hell."

And then everybody saw the body (not the body they expected to see), and everybody saw the crossbow, and everybody saw me gripping the crossbow to my chest like a baby koala bear.

Perfect.

21 — Hathaway Doesn't Have a Way

I slept very well. In fact, lying there on my cot as a special guest of the Wolf Valley Police, I couldn't think of a person sleeping any better. It was funny. I should have found the whole experience a lot more traumatic. I had been detained for questioning in connection with the violent death of Wilson Croker. I had been seen, by about eight dozen witnesses, standing over the body, holding the murder weapon. When asked for my name I had no choice but to take the fifth. And when it was explained to me by the sheriff that the fifth didn't apply, I had no choice but to respond that, for me, it was going to have to apply.

It didn't look good.

And yet I felt relaxed. Soothed. Almost a little bored. I guess I had faith in my star.

The digs didn't hurt. The Wolf Valley knew how to treat their suspects. The place reminded me more of a tribal-reservation Mayberry than any cell I could have envisaged. The cot was nice, the food was nice, and Sheriff Greene's sister, who came by after I awoke to see if anybody needed anything, was nice. She looked like a linebacker with bangs, smiled a lot and told me all about the sheriff as a boy and the two of them growing up in Canada. She also served me a delightful Penobscot treat, a rustic dough wrapped around crumbled lamb and veggies. I later learned that her husband hailed from the Isle of

Rhodes and the delightful Penobscot treat had, in fact, been a gyro. Tasted damn good wherever it came from.

After Greene's sister left, I took a glance out the outer window, to break up the monotony, and whom should I see but my previous benefactor Emilia—faithful Aunt Sarah, as always, lingering in the background. (Little Sam was not present, being otherwise engaged kicking something, no doubt.)

My cell was an early twentieth-century design, with an open window (this a foot above street level—very quaint). It was the perfect height for the little one. Observing me, she poked her apple-cheeked face through the bars and asked me if I had bitten somebody. (It struck me as an odd question, even for her, until I learned that Aunt Sarah had been telling her all about card sharks at the casino.) I replied that it hadn't gotten as bad as biting, no, and Emilia inquired whether I had started my tunnel yet. I told her that I hadn't, and she said that I should get going on it soon because the Cricket Men needed me. She also mentioned something about the Pine Tree Emperor, which I didn't quite follow. Just before leaving, she remembered my puzzle and asked how I was proceeding with it. I replied that it still had me stumped, but I had the assistance of a real-life private investigator to help me now. She appeared to revel in this tidbit most of all, and after adopting a fedora made from her lunch bag (not a very well-boxed fedora) she scurried along in search of Clues.

No sooner had she gone than my old buddy Roy from the bus came inside to drop off some paperwork for a new fishing license. Talk about old-home week.

He peered in at me as he entered, and I heard him ask the sheriff in a low voice if they had run me in on the Keats murder. The officer hadn't heard of anyone called Keats getting killed, and Roy nodded and said that if they did find a murdered poet, I was the man they should question.

I drifted off to sleep again here. As my eyes drooped shut and I succumbed to the soothing sounds of the tribal flute playing on the sheriff's portable stereo, I remember thinking that I hoped the county would stick Roy with a stiff fee on that license renewal.

"Up and Adam," said the sheriff, jolting me awake. It was early afternoon now, and he was standing at the door, his apple cheeks not quite fitting between the bars. He turned the key in the lock, and I watched in amazement as the gate swung open. "Come on out," he remarked. My God, he was mellow.

I was still the only guest in residence, so I had to assume he meant me. I stood, stretched and exited. I didn't dawdle (if nothing else, I was beginning to get a chill from that early twentieth-century window).

Normally the prisoner would have had his personal effects returned to him at this juncture. Since I didn't have any, the sheriff issued his discharge with a cursory nod. For him, that was pretty animated.

Fleet was waiting for me in an inner office. The sheriff resumed his seat at the desk, while I remained in the doorway, wondering.

"Don't worry," said my own real-life private investigator. "I've explained everything. He knows the truth now."

I still hesitated. When it came to Enescu Fleet and his explanations, there were always many truths from which to choose. I waited to learn which one we were dealing with today.

"I've explained all about the memory glitch and the missing blonde."

This was better.

"So I guess you're not Miss Fleet's married lover," muttered the sheriff with a good deal of irony.

I said no. No, I wasn't. Miss Fleet and I were just friends, I told him, and the sheriff opened his mouth to speak, and then seemed to think better of it.

"You might as well sit down," he said.

I stepped more fully in the room. My resemblance to some cautious animal accepting a morsel of food was still pretty pronounced.

"I saw the blonde today," I informed them, taking a seat like some cautious animal accepting a chair. "In the hall outside the stage."

"In the vicinity of the body," grunted the sheriff, and I should have known he'd put the wrong construction on it. These mellow lawmen are still lawmen at their core.

"No!" I replied, and would have brought my fist down on his desk for emphasis had it not been so amply covered in papers and lunch plates and what looked like a partial jigsaw depicting a kitten. "She had nothing to do with that!"

Fleet tugged me back into the chair. "Calm yourself. The sheriff and I know that neither of you could have killed Wilson Croker."

I liked this better. "Why not?" I asked, wishing I had phrased that a little differently.

"The coroner got back to us with a time of death," Fleet replied, "or rather, a time of death it couldn't be."

"Huh?"

"Croker had been dead for at least twenty hours when you found him. Maybe more. The authorities haven't been able to pinpoint it yet, due to the condition of the body."

"What's wrong with it?" I wondered. "I mean, beyond the obvious?"

"It was kept on ice," said the sheriff, and I was happy to see him making a contribution. I couldn't help noticing his eyes straying to the kitten jigsaw every now and then, as if one more chunk of whiskers couldn't hurt anybody.

"Ice?"

"Most likely kept outside," explained Fleet. "Possibly at the boathouse by the river."

I shot him a look.

"The temperature coming off the river is frigid, and last night it probably would have dropped well below freezing. I mentioned to the sheriff that we saw a light on in the shack on our way home."

As long as that was all he mentioned. We could leave the blonde and her suggestion of a riverside rendezvous out of it.

"Any way you slice it, he wasn't shot today. And you didn't shoot him."

"Well, I could have told you that," I said, realizing how easily these things could get worked out once you sat down and discussed them openly. "Where do we go from here?" I asked.

"We wouldn't mind knowing what became of your memory," said the sheriff.

"You and me both," I agreed, but I was thinking more about leads. "Wait. We know Croker was alive yesterday at noon."

"Do we?" asked Fleet.

"We met with him, remember?"

"I remember. The man we met wasn't Wilson Croker."

Yesterday this would have had me reeling in my chair, at a loss to comprehend. Today I was still at a loss to comprehend, but I didn't reel. I merely scratched my nose, adjusted myself on the creaky plastic and said, "He wasn't what now?"

"The man we met wasn't Wilson Croker. I am certain of that now. I suspected something at the time but didn't know what to make of it. Now I do. The man we met was merely playing the part of Croker."

My baffled stare became more baffled. Fleet continued:

"Don't get me wrong—he did a serviceable job. The haughtiness, the pomposity, all well portrayed. Too well portrayed. The disguise was also flawless, but you stick most men behind an enormous mustache and glasses, and they will carry off that deception pretty well—especially around those who don't know them. But he slipped up.

"I first suspected something was amiss when he told us that an actor's job is to *lay* there. It should have been *lie* there. It's a common enough mistake, but not one I would have expected from a man of his background. That's when I decided to test him. He had already corrected me on the *Macbeth* quote—no doubt because he was an actor himself—so I checked to see how he would do with the Victorians. I led with a little false Tennyson, and he bought it hook, line and recitation. The real Croker took a degree in English literature from Oxford. He never would have let my gaffe pass unnoticed."

"What gaffe?"

Fleet stroked his beard. I thought for a moment he was going to give us the recitation anew, but he decided to go with the abridged version. "When Tennyson said in his poem 'In Memoriam' that it is better to have loved and lost, he wasn't referring to a woman. He was referring to the memory of a man."

"One of those, eh?" said the sheriff.

"It's not what you think," Fleet told him, launching into a thirty-second discourse on the social mores of the time and how men in the Victorian era were always writing each other poems and doing each other's hair and how it didn't mean anything.

I remembered most of this from my schooling, wherever that was. Fleet's refresher was all very informative, but I wasn't sure how it related to the question of the false Croker.

"You see, I had left myself open for another Wilson Croker zinger. But none ever came. He wasn't Wilson Croker. You add that to the supposed time of death, and you have an impostor setting up a perfect alibi."

I understood now. "An alibi for whom?"

"That is the question."

I let the words breathe a moment before replying.

There were quite a few ins and outs with this puzzle, not to mention several literary references and a few more Wilson Crokers than I would have cared to have had in a single sitting. I gave the details a few more flips in my mind before continuing:

"So this guy plays Croker, disguising the fact that the real Croker is already dead?"

"Yes. In fact, I will do you one better. I suspect, Sheriff, that another body will shortly be discovered in the area."

Greene responded by leaning forward. Gliding over the kitten pieces, he selected a fax from his stack of papers. "We have. Came in this morning. John Doe found stabbed to death down by Sheriff Soaring Dove's jurisdiction. I thought it might be Keats."

"It's not Keats, Sheriff. If you look into it, you will discover your John Doe is an actor from the show. Are there any missing per chance?"

"One of the new guys is. A Nick something. I have it here somewhere. We were debating putting out an all points on him."

"There is no need. Sheriff Dove's Doe is our Nick."

It was beginning to make sense to me. "So the murderer gets one of the actors to play Croker to set up his alibi, and then double-crosses his cohort?"

"I'm inclined to think that the dead man knew nothing of the Croker murder. He was nothing but a pawn in a very deadly game of chess."

This reminded me of the chessboard on the set. With the show postponed due to a real murder, I had been dying to know how the board related to the three bottles of wine (and whether the answer had anything to do with Babe Ruth). Probably not the time to ask.

Fleet was musing. "The question is, who does the Croker deception benefit the most?"

"Lockhart," whispered the sheriff, looking mellow and thoughtful.

He seemed to realize his customary reticence wasn't going to cut it here, and after a pause of perhaps ten seconds, carried on:

"He's the man for my money. With Croker gone, he becomes the head mongoose at the top of the Wolf Valley Casino. I don't think Wilson Croker had any heirs. On top of that, I heard the two men had been quarreling lately about the running of the place. And then there's the Tribal Council."

"What about it?" asked Fleet.

"The council will be opening up a seat to an outsider. Their aim is to connect with the growing business community on the reservation. There will only be one seat available, and both Croker and Lockhart have been vying for it. Whoever gets it will sit in on every important decision affecting the reservation and its businesses, from accounting practices to zoning."

"Interesting."

"I thought so. What's more, I have been gathering info on folks, their whereabouts and activities from around twenty hours ago—you know, when Croker was most likely shot—and Lockhart is the only suspect without an alibi. He says he was called to a powwow with the tribal elders at the time, but there was no such meeting. I checked."

Fleet sat back, tapping the tips of his fingers together methodically. "Things certainly do seem to be pointing in Jack Lockhart's direction. But do you think he has it in himself to commit murder?"

"Maybe not, but that overgrown delinquent he has working for him certainly does. His so-called driver Neptune. Look at his rap sheet. Drunk and disorderly. Aggravated assault. And his weapon of choice would be a bow too. He hunts deer with one every year. One of these automatic contraptions would be a child's toy in his hands."

Fleet agreed that Lockhart made a lot of sense as our suspect. "It's something to think about."

The sheriff looked almost apologetic. "I know this Lockhart is a friend of yours, F."

"Not that good a friend," said the detective, who had plenty to spare. "If he's our man, you won't see me running any interference."

We probably would have wrapped it up here, for I was free to go and we weren't making any tremendous headway. But then I had to go and stick my oar in, as Fleet had previously described it.

You know how it is when you get gabbing, three men of the world kicking around ideas about the latest crossbow murder. You become overly laid-back. You speak injudiciously. As the faux Croker had done, you slip up.

I was thinking about finding Croker in my cabin that first morning and what a funny coincidence it had been, when it dawned on me that I had the entirely wrong angle on it.

More to myself than anyone else, I said, "Then that stunt at the cabin wasn't a stunt at all. Croker really had been shot with a crossbow!"

The minute I said it, I wished some efficient casino stickman had been there to scoop the words back as a nonroll, or whatever you call it in craps when the dice go shooting out of your hand in a haphazard fashion and land in somebody's mai tai. I needed a do-over.

There were no do-overs with the Penobscot police. Greene said, "What's that now?" (In England, it would have been "What's all this, then?" I knew this because I had a British accent.)

I said, "Uh."

"What stunt at the cabin?"

Fleet cast a long, hard stare at me, which is to say it lasted about eight-tenths of a second. He was very economical with his stares. "I think you misheard, Sheriff. He said the stunt at the *clappin'*."

"Stunt at the clappin. What's a *clappin*?" asked the officer.

"I believe it's a mighty Norwegian sea monster," said Fleet. The witticism didn't go down very well. Greene said he was pretty sure that was a *kraken*, to which Fleet replied that one man's *clappin* is another man's *kraken*. "Seriously, though," he remarked, "I think when he said clappin', he meant when the curtain went up on stage this morning. Everyone was clappin' because the show was about to start. And then, of course, everyone realized that Croker was really dead, and they stopped clappin'. And that brings us up to the present moment."

The sheriff stared at him. "But what was that about Croker being shot with a crossbow? Are you just realizing that now?" he asked me.

"I'm slow," I said, and Fleet supported this.

"I think we should be going now," he added, prompting me to rise with him. "Any objection to us poking around Croker's dressing room?"

The sheriff blinked a moment and then replied, "It's not standard for PIs to be given the run of the place, much less retired PIs."

Fleet's smile seemed to indicate that there are retired PIs, and then there are *retired PIs.* "We'll be good, I promise. A little favor, from one Canadian to another?"

The sheriff tossed him the keys.

Evidently, today, the retired PI was Canadian.

22 — Where the Answers Lie

In what I thought showed great restraint, Fleet didn't grill me the instant we left the police station. Without a word, he accepted the dog leash from the deputy outside, slipped a little something extra in that man's shirt pocket, and that was that for the moment.

We strolled along for about a minute and a half, at which point he paused and handed me a leather jacket he had draped over his forearm. "You look cold."

I slid it on and was surprised to find it fit me perfectly. "Where'd you get this?"

"At your cabin—or clappin' as it is sometimes called. I went back to check out a few things this afternoon and found it behind the sofa. Don't bother rifling the pockets, looking for any identification. I already looked, and they were empty."

I ceased rifling. I wondered what he had been doing, going back to my cabin, and what business he had going through my pockets.

"You have something to tell me, I think?" he asked.

I don't know how well I told my story this time, but I held nothing back. I just let it flow.

At the conclusion, Fleet smoothed his beard and said it was all very interesting. "Then this is what you have been keeping from me all this time?"

"Yes."

"Now I know everything you do?"

"Pretty much. Sorry for the secrecy, but I didn't know what to think about Croker. I thought it had to be a prank."

"It does have a disturbingly playful facade, this murder. I'm not sure what to make of it."

We wound our way up the path toward the casino. "What were you looking for at my cabin?" I wondered, feeling it was my turn to ask the questions.

"Your canoe."

"My canoe? I have a canoe?"

"The canoe from your cabin. I was pretty sure the canoe I saw at the boathouse last night was yours. If it was yours, then yours would still be missing from your cabin. It was."

I shook my head. "Someone swiped my canoe?"

"I think the murderer hid the body in your canoe the morning you and I met. He then used it to transport the body to the boathouse."

I mentally traced the path the corpse had taken the last couple days. Bedroom to canoe, canoe to boathouse, boathouse to casino. It had gone on some adventure, that cadaver. Something still bugged me, though.

"You don't mean to say that you saw a body in the boathouse last night?"

"My dear boy, if I had seen a frozen game show host last night would I have concealed it from one and all for this long?"

I gave him a look, and he conceded that he might have, but in this instance he hadn't. The boathouse was clean.

"And the killer really used the canoe to transport the body?" I asked.

"Like a sled, yes. The path was cold and hard enough to facilitate the trip. What I would like to know is how he got the body into the studio this morning. That took some craftiness."

More than I had, that was for sure. "The whole thing makes my head spin."

Fleet nodded his. "I don't know how Croker wound up in your cabin, or who shot him and where, but I think it's pretty clear from your description that after you and the dying man spoke, the killer arrived on the scene and dragged the body out through the window. The canoe was lying there, making the ideal hiding place. From what I can see now, the murderer was hiding in the gazebo while we were outside fetching Pixie. He probably wanted to gauge our reactions, not realizing that you had a poker face to end all poker faces. When we didn't seem interested in the canoe, and in fact didn't appear to have the slightest concern about anything amiss at all, he must have figured that neither of us had seen the body in the bedroom."

"He was watching us from the gazebo?"

"Out of Pixie's sniffing range, yes. Watching, armed with the crossbow. I think it's pretty safe to assume that your reticence saved our lives."

The rest of the walk didn't take very long. It would have taken a lot less long if not for Pixie. Fascinated by all the wondrous odors I had picked up at the station, she tripped me up every few steps, sniffing vigorously at my pant legs. In due course, we arrived at Studio A and the dressing rooms. Proceeding past the police tape, we entered the one where, a day earlier, we had met with the fake Croker.

The room had changed significantly. Gone was the tidy organization and in-your-face order and method. From the bookshelves to the desk to the pictures on the wall, everything had the look of having been ridden hard and put away wet. "The sheriff's men sure are messy," I said.

Fleet did not immediately reply. Pixie was busily shooting to and fro, alive with the discovery that there was more to life than pant legs. "I would be willing to bet that this is how the authorities found the office," he remarked.

"But it looked peachy when we left it yesterday."

"Which means that between then and now someone has rifled it. Any thoughts where the safe is?"

We found it quickly enough behind one of the theatrical posters—which is to say Fleet found it, while I stood by, cracking my knuckles.

It was the only picture on the wall not hanging at an angle, and I wondered if that was what had drawn him to it. He slipped it off the hook, revealing a metal face and keypad.

"Any ideas?"

I shook my head. He turned to the safe and entered a rapid four-digit code. It opened. (I was beginning to resent playing his investigational straight man.)

"How—?"

"Lucky guess." He pointed to the top of the bookshelf, romantic literature. "The *K's*," he said.

These were almost all Keats. I selected one of the collected works and paged through it. I found the answer in due time on the dust jacket, under a biography of the poet.

"1821," I sighed.

"Well done. I considered 1795 but went with the 1821 first."

"John Keats, 1795-1821. Then that's what Croker meant by *The answer lies with Keats*."

"Perhaps. If so, then it's all in here. Let's see what the big secret was, shall we?"

He reached inside and pulled out a packet of papers. "The solutions to today's puzzles," he commented, setting this portion aside. He thumbed through the next stack. "Newspaper clippings." We looked at these together.

They all centered around the suicide Fleet had told me about. They detailed the victim's jump (how he had busted the lock to get to the roof and then flung himself over the side), the discovery of the body by one of the hotel staff (a hysterical woman called Nadine) and the subsequent police investigation (which never went anywhere).

Something about the reports felt off to me. It wasn't until we had flipped to the last page that I realized what this was. Despite the fact that he had been staying at the casino when he was killed, no one seemed to know the dead man's name. Another of those chills ran down my back.

Fleet had noticed this too and told me not to worry. If he saw me wandering off toward the roof with a pair of bolt cutters, he'd put me in a half nelson straightaway.

"But how could no one know who he was?" I asked. "Where did he sleep? He must have registered."

Fleet slid the papers back into the safe, including the puzzle answers. I guess it wasn't in the cards for me to know the solution to the chessboard and the three bottles of wine. I saw he had held one packet back. "What's that?"

"Apparently the real Croker had more than a passing interest in my attending the show." He held up a clipping. "It details the Hopkins case, my last before I retired. I think Croker was investigating the suicide and wanted my help."

Underneath the clipping was a folded blueprint. Croker, it seemed, had been present for the construction of the casino. "Now what do you make of this?" asked Fleet. He placed his finger on the Nightingale Room, where someone had scrawled the name *Sophia* in pencil. "Who's Sophia?"

"Croker's girlfriend?" I wondered. Didn't feel right.

Fleet didn't appear all that pleased with this explanation himself. He closed the safe and replaced the poster.

This done, he tilted the left side a little to the right and then the right a little to the left. Not quite satisfied with this either, he stepped back and gazed at it.

"What's wrong now?" I asked. It looked fine to me, though I supposed it could have stood to go up a touch on the right.

"Someone else has been in that safe."

"I'm sure someone was. Newspaper clippings don't sprout up by themselves."

"I don't mean Croker. Whoever it was replaced the poster perfectly on the wall. Subconsciously he or she didn't want to draw attention to it by leaving it askew. Of course, with everything else in the room cockeyed, that's exactly what he or she did do."

I could have told him that. I had noticed this out-of-place tidiness too, remember? Of course, I had no chance to point this out. Fleet had scooped up Pixie and was in the process of getting her to relinquish a piece of police evidence in the form of one of Wilson Croker's emery boards. The subject of posters, however straight, sort of fizzled out from there.

"Now we need to figure out what is missing."

"Is something missing?" I asked.

"Bound to be. The same as at your cabin."

"Are you talking about the canoe again?"

"No. I am referring to what was missing inside."

"What was missing inside?"

"The white elephant."

I had to assume he meant this literally: the porcelain statuette from the mantelpiece with the chip in the trunk. I couldn't understand anyone coming back for that thing. It was ghastly.

There was a lull here. Fleet peered around for Pixie, while I went to the shelf and slid the collected poems back in. Or I tried. Something seemed to be impeding its path. I reached behind it and hoicked out a brochure of high-end vacation spots.

"The fake Croker was reading that when we arrived yesterday afternoon," said Fleet. "Whoever put him up to the impersonation promised him enough cash to take a long vacation."

"You sure they weren't in on it together? He could have been scoping out places to go on the lam."

"People don't go on the lam to Palm Springs. My guess is the ruse was suggested in the form of a bet. I think we're dealing with a gambler here."

We were certainly in the right place for it. I flipped over the brochure. "Hey, did you see this?" I showed him a list of names carefully printed on the back. For the most part, it was people who worked at the casino. John Hathaway's name was scrawled at the bottom.

Fleet accepted the page. "No doubt they worked out a list of people the fake Croker could not meet while in costume. People who knew the real Croker and would pierce the disguise at once. I'm sure that was part of the bet: *Can you fool someone who has never met Wilson Croker in person?* You will notice that I am not on the list."

"That's why he let you in. And that's also why he got all irksome when he realized who I was—or thought I was. When we knocked, you identified yourself but didn't mention me as Hathaway until we came in. He needn't have worried."

"I wonder why Hathaway's name was the last on the list."

"Maybe the real Croker met him most recently?"

"Possibly. Yes, you may be right." He didn't seem to think I was right. He brooded over the catalog a moment longer and then returned it to the shelf, nodding toward the door. We were going. I placed the poems of Keats back on the desk.

Before we left, I glanced at the poet's biography again. His famous epitaph brought a sardonic smile to my lips.

Here lies one whose name was writ in water.

How appropriate.

23 — And So Do the Suspects

Fleet wanted to check out the backstage area next, so we checked out the backstage area.

We banged around a storage room for perhaps ten minutes—kicking up dust and cobwebs and at one point some scurrying rodent (which Pixie got a big kick out of).

Then we struck gold. Shoved to the back, where no one would pay it any attention, was an ancient grandfather clock. Fleet slid a gloved finger down the side. No dust. "This hasn't been here very long."

"Must be the broken one," I said, remembering our prop discussion the previous day.

I thought back to the set where I had discovered Croker. I could still hear the *tick, tick, ticking*. There had been a working clock there this morning.

"Somebody must have replaced it before the show."

Fleet beamed at me. "Well done. We'll make a detective out of you yet."

"Do you think it's important?"

"I don't know. It may be. It may be nothing."

I sighed. I was beginning to think we had disrupted that tiny ferret from its home for no reason.

I paused. "Can you hear that?" I asked.

Fleet listened.

"Sounds like voices," he said, "coming from the main studio."

"The scene of the crime," I remarked.

I had been waiting all afternoon to say that.

"I'm telling you, you don't have it in you."

"Why do you say that?"

"Instinct supported on a bedrock of outwardly unimportant facts."

"What the hell does that mean?"

"It means you suck. Look, some people have the killer instinct; some people don't. It's nothing personal."

We had tracked the voices, one female, one male, from the storage room, down the hall and into Studio A. (I'll leave it up to you to figure out which sex was giving the other hell.)

Clanging in through one of the heavy metal doors, we found a veritable party in progress.

Ate Fleet was in the center of the room, holding a coffee mug, her face as flushed as ever. Across from her stood Director Dean, his face also pink with exasperation.

At the buffet table—these people catered everything!—one observed the showman Ronald. Beside him stood Todd Parnell, ex-champ of the game show circuit, fondling the goods on the pastry tray. In a distant seat in the empty auditorium sat Jack Lockhart, leaning back like a Broadway producer running through a few rewrites for his latest blockbuster. In a seat more distant than that sat the silently menacing Neptune, looking silent and menacing.

And before them all lay the stage. Here a good deal of police tape met the eye, cordoning off the murder scene. It didn't look all that strange, considering the format of the show.

Dean spotted us first and his bug-eyed stare went immediately to me.

"What the hell is *he* doing here?" he gasped, pirouetting out of crossbow range. He was still limping but he didn't let this slow him down.

A quick footnote on the limping situation. I had mentioned my suspicions to Fleet at the tail end of our walk up to the casino. He commended me on my powers of observation, but suggested that I might employ these more consistently. It seemed that Dean had been walking with a limp all weekend, long before the tussle in the loft. I might have noticed this (I was told) had I not been so intent on stuffing my face at the buffet.

"The police have dropped all charges," explained Fleet to the room, and the lack of cheers all around touched me deeply. "Whoever shot Wilson Croker did it the day before. If it wasn't Hathaway, then the question becomes who among us had the best motive and the weakest alibi? The police have asked me, unofficially, to look into the matter."

It occurred to me that while the real Hathaway might not have done it, the real me still had the weakest alibi and the most intriguing motive—in that I didn't know that I didn't have one. I refrained from announcing this to the gathering, however. I had learned my lesson at the sheriff's office. It also occurred to me that the police had never asked Fleet to do a damn thing.

Police approved or not, the man knew how to command an audience. Everyone gave him their attention.

"Shot the day before?" asked Todd Parnell. He had a voice that managed to be both reedy and resonate in one breath.

"You're investigating?" asked Dean.

"Anyone want half of this bear claw?" wondered the Remarkable Ronald.

Fleet ignored them all. He had his methods. Beginning with Dean and Ate, he asked, "We interrupting some kind of argument?"

His daughter rolled her eyes. "It's nothing. I was explaining to everyone here how we need a new host. Dean seems to have this ridiculous idea that he can fill Wilson Croker's shoes."

"It's not a ridiculous idea! If not me, then who?"

"Oh, I don't know. Any driveling drunk off the craps table, a cardboard cutout. This guy," she said, tipping her head toward me.

I frowned. I didn't mind coming in behind a driveling drunk, but surely I could rank higher than a cardboard cutout.

"The fact is," said Dean, "I have the most experience and have logged the most hours behind the camera."

"Yes, behind the camera. Don't forget the *behind*, Hitchcock."

"It's better than anyone else here, and don't call me Hitchcock. If anything, my style more closely resembles a Scorsese or Coppola. The fact is—"

"The fact is," interrupted Ronald, "the network needs fresh blood. No pun intended. We should do a show about me. The Remarkable Ronald straight into your living room." If he hadn't twiddled the tips of his fingers as he said this, he might have found support for the idea. As it was, the room gave him a collective snort.

"Oh, now we're really in the land of the ludicrous," said Ate. "Just what the network needs, a mind reader who dazzles one and all by surmising that the woman in the meter-maid outfit is a preschool teacher."

"You know perfectly well that was a slip-up."

"Allowing you onstage is a slip-up. Any stage."

"Don't be that way. We Latin bloods have to stick together."

"I'm Penobscot," muttered Ate, inching away from her fellow Latin blood.

"So you think Ronald-TV is a bad idea, *chica*? Why? Tell me your thoughts." He put his hand to his temple. "Your beauty prevents me from locking in."

"And let's keep it that way," said his "chica." "The idea is insane, Ron. What would the network want with a washed-up mind reader?"

"You call me washed up?"

"What would you call it? The casino has already canceled half your shows and cut back the rest of your performances by half an hour. Your act was always drivel; now it's reduced-fat drivel."

"Croker didn't seem to think so. He often attended my performances."

"In order to torture himself. Croker was this close to canning your sorry ass, and you know it."

The discussion had now teetered into the personal. As always, I looked to Fleet to impart his calming influence, bringing everyone around to their better selves. It didn't appear necessary. On this occasion, Dean was the man with the diplomatic flair.

"Would somebody like Alex Trebek do?" he asked Ate.

"What?"

"Would Alex Trebek satisfy your perverse need for a personality? Your need for a 'name.' "

"Let me get this straight. *The* Alex Trebek? The very-famous-game-show-host Trebek?"

"The very one."

"You could get him?"

"I think so. I went to film school with a neighbor of his. I don't think the big man would mind serving as our show's honorary host. As a favor to me."

Ate stood digesting this tidbit. "Let's talk," she said, and their hostilities ceased. They adjourned to the buffet table. I can't be sure, but I think they split that bear claw.

I welcomed the calm after the storm. The food, the conversation, a crime scene a couple feet away—everything was back to normal now. Even Pixie was enjoying herself, clawing the stuffing out of one of the armchairs.

Fleet pressed his advantage. "You don't mind if I ask you all some questions, do you? You could wait and talk with the police, but I think you will find my questions—"

"Oh, just ask them," snapped his daughter.

Fleet thanked her. He pivoted toward the auditorium. "You have no objections, do you, Jack?" The tycoon shook his head, and Fleet gave him a stately bow. "You've been awfully quiet through all this."

Lockhart smirked. Or so it appeared from that distance.

Neptune, meanwhile, could have been tossing kisses to the stage for all I could make out from the buffet. Even still, I wouldn't have bet against him covering that expanse in a few ready bounds. You never knew when his employer might require his "driving services."

Lockhart could take care of himself for now. "You have such a lovely speaking voice, F, I didn't like to interrupt. I was quite put in mind of Wilson in his *Hamlet* days. It's a pity you never took up acting. You would have made a grand Prospero."

Fleet made no comment on this, except for another bow. His daughter, wishing to move things along, said, "The questions, Dad."

He thanked her again. He faced the stage. "I have only two. First, who authorized the show to start this morning? Come now, it had to be one of you. It wasn't Croker."

Dean shuffled nervously. "I guess—"

"Yes, Dean?"

"—I did."

"And why was that?"

"I thought, um, the cameraman said we were ready to go."

"You thought the cameraman said you were ready?"

"That's what I thought."

"But the cameraman had said nothing."

"No. No, I realize that now. I got confused."

Fleet absorbed this testimony with a solemn nod. "You know what I think. I think you started your show Croker-less on purpose. You did this for one of two reasons. Reason one—you already knew Croker was dead and were getting impatient waiting for his body to be found. I have seen many a murderer crack for want of discovery of his crime."

"I—"

"Reason two, you didn't know Croker was dead and wanted to embarrass him. It is pretty well known that you despised Croker, that he treated you like a toady and a hack, and that you would have liked nothing better than to be rid of him. Or, if nothing else, take him down a peg. This was an excellent opportunity for that. Croker was late, ridiculously so. No one could find him. He was holding everyone up doing God knows what. By starting the show without him, you would literally shine a light on his own ineptitude. So then, my shaggy friend, which of these two reasons is it?"

His shaggy friend paused in thought. "Reason two was the non-murder reason, right?"

"It was."

"That's the one. If you want to know the truth, I didn't think it through. Croker's absence was pissing me off, so I started the show. He always pissed me off, even in death."

Fleet seemed satisfied with Dean's evidence for now. "Who was to play the crossbowed corpse in today's sketch?"

His daughter fielded that one. One of the regular actors, she said—we had met him at rehearsal. He was to be the corpse in sketches one, two and six today.

"And why didn't he play his role in sketch one?"

"He said he had a note in his dressing room instructing him not to go on this morning."

"Indeed. And where is this paper now?"

"The police took it with them. I think they want to dust it for fingerprints."

"Of course they do," said Fleet. He moved on to the detail of the clock. "A handsome piece you have there. But it's not the clock you had on stage the day before. Someone broke that one. Who was that?"

Dean did another shuffle step. He looked like he couldn't catch a break.

"That was my fault too. We were blowing off some steam, me and one of the actors. We were tossing a football around the set, and I went long and barged into the stupid clock. I didn't think I hit it that hard, but then Nick noticed the pendulum had snapped off. At first, I didn't care, but then I remembered we had a puzzle with the clock later in the week. Croker would have insisted on a working prop; he was like that. So we sent for a replacement. I didn't realize it had come in that quick. One of the guys must have unloaded it."

"Yes, one of the guys," answered Fleet. "This actor friend of yours—Nick. You realize he is dead—murdered?"

"Yes. The sheriff called."

"You don't seem all that broken up about it."

"What do you want me to say?! That he was my best friend ever and I don't know what I will do without him?"

"Tennyson would have."

"Huh?"

"Not important. Please, continue your hysterics."

Dean took a deep breath. "Look, I didn't know the guy very well. I—he—things are unraveling here."

A kindly hand went to his shoulder. "I think that's enough, Dad," said Ate, coming to the director's defense. "Dean's had a full serving of Fleets today."

Her father seemed to agree with her. "That was all for Dean anyway. I may have more questions as we go. I would ask that everyone—"

"Not leave town?" sneered the Remarkable Ronald. He was sitting in one of the armchairs (Fleet's, I believe) and had his shoes up on the contestant podium.

The detective smiled at him. "Indeed. Not leave the reservation, in fact. And how fitting that you should be the one to echo the policeman's dictum, Ron. It's almost as though you've had experience with the authorities before."

This shut up Ronald. He stood up and dusted off his shoeprints with the sleeve of his black pullover.

"And I must apologize," continued the acting inspector, "but I do have another question for Dean. Where would this new clock have come in? Let's say, if it were delivered after hours?"

Dean almost laughed. This one was easy: "Around the back, in the loading area. They're doing some new construction there for the casino. Hardly anyone goes back that way but workers and delivery-men."

"How convenient. Thank you, Dean."

Dean nodded, happily dismissed.

Fleet had one last point to cover. With a pensive look on his face, he stepped to the contestants' row and pressed each of the three buzzers in turn. When he came to Parnell's, nothing happened. No buzz, just a dull click.

"Todd, your buzzer isn't working."

It was Parnell's turn to react. "What are you talking about?"

"Your buzzer. No work-y. The line must be loose."

Parnell spun around in rage, directing most of his hostility toward Lockhart. "So, you call me out of retirement, invite me to do your show, then make sure I can't buzz in?"

"Calm yourself," said Fleet, two words that were rapidly becoming his catchphrase. "Once the show began they would have realized the mistake and repaired it. No need for all this huffing and puffing."

"Still," said Parnell, standing down. "It pisses me off. I think someone did it on purpose."

"Oh, I'm sure someone did. For what purpose, we will learn in time."

So saying, he exited the stage, having given his all. He didn't exactly break his staff, as Prospero would have done, but he was finished. For now.

"Jack, if you have a moment, I would love a word." He took a seat beside Lockhart. The performer had become the spectator.

24 — Motivational Motive

With Ate and Dean talking shop over the pastry tray, Fleet and Pixie having their word with Jack Lockhart, and Ronald sporting that thin little beard of his, that really only left Todd Parnell, trivia geek, for me.

I found him presiding over the coffee pot. He had hardly moved an inch since we got there.

I gotta say, there's something about people who are good at games that makes them not quite right in my estimation. They constantly appear detached from reality, lost in a world of stats and strategy. The ex-champion definitely had this quality. No doubt Todd Parnell felt he had better things to do than schmooze with me—such as mentally cataloging the historical kings of Sweden in order of shoe size. As a result, he seemed to view my presence as a distraction, an insect caught in the perspiration of his mental calisthenics.

My opening remark didn't help. "So you're the trivia phenom, huh?"

He peered across the coffee pot at me. His frizzy receding hairline glimmered in the stage lights as he tried to decide whether or not to commit to a greeting. Looked like not.

I plodded on. "They say you were once the Tiger Woods of question games. No one could touch you when you were going good. Pretty cool."

Parnell accepted the tribute with a creepy, buck-toothed smile. I felt his goggle-eyed stare burrowing into me.

"Tiger Woods is this real good golfer, you see."

"Nonpareil," said the phenom.

"Pardon?"

"A better description than 'pretty cool,' " he grinned, "would be nonpareil. No one has ever matched my feat, and no one ever will."

It was no skin off my nose. I helped myself to a cup of coffee, since he wasn't exactly offering, and said, "So what do you think that chessboard and the three bottles of wine were meant to signify in the first puzzle?"

He must not have been in the mood for guessing games, which was ironic, so I changed the subject back to his self-imposed retirement.

"So what question did you miss on? It was probably something ridiculously simple. You brainy guys always seem to go down on the easy stuff."

I had meant it as a compliment, but I could see how rehashing his failure might disguise these intentions.

"Did I hear something about half a bear claw?" I wondered, changing the subject yet again.

Parnell appeared in no better mood for discussing bear claws than he did for playing guessing games. "Who *are* you?" he asked.

"That's hard to say."

"You're always around Enescu. Is he your keeper?"

"I wouldn't call him that, no."

"Well, you can tell him from me that it's lucky someone did kill Croker. If not for that, I would have wiped the floor with the old man. When it comes to brain games, these old guys can't keep up with youth."

"I'll let him know," I said, and quietly edged away from the refreshment table. I joined Pixie and Fleet in the tycoon section.

"I can't fathom it," Lockhart was saying. "An impostor, right in our midst."

These words gave my spine a chill until I realized they weren't talking about me.

Fleet smiled grimly. "Yes, and now Wilson Croker is dead, and the man who played Croker is dead. Fascinating, isn't it?"

"I can't fathom it," said Lockhart.

"Neither can the police, to be honest. They have their suspects, of course."

"Who?"

"You, for starters."

During this discourse, Lockhart had taken out a pair of nail clippers and was idly pruning his cuticles. (The kindest construction I could put on this was he had jumpy nerves and needed something to do with his hands.) At these words, he snipped wide of the mark and cursed vividly. "Me? Why on earth would anyone suspect me?" He caught Pixie's eye as he asked this and peered away with a shiver.

"You have a rotten alibi for one."

"What are you talking about? I was nowhere near the body!"

"Come, Jack, you can do better than that. Croker was killed a day ago."

"Yes, yes. Yes, of course. Yesterday morning, the sheriff said. I was in town. Meeting with the Tribal Council."

"You weren't, Jack."

"Dammit!" The sports-drink colossus returned the clippers to his suit jacket and pulled out a nail file. An emery board. "You got to help me, Enescu. Someone is framing me."

"Grr," said Pixie, to make it clear that it wasn't her.

"How so?" wondered Fleet.

"I did get a call from the tribe, or so I thought. It was very early, around eight. I went into town, but no one was there. The call was a fake."

"Like Wilson Croker," muttered Fleet to himself. "Who took the message?"

"Neptune."

Fleet peered up at the driver/receptionist. He gave the hulking Penobscot a friendly nod. "You trust him?"

"Implicitly. He saved my life about a year ago. Why would he try to destroy it now?"

"People have unusual motives. And loyalties change."

"Not Neptune's."

Fleet moved on. "You have to admit, you had motive. Getting Wilson Croker out of the way to run the casino on your own. Who knows, maybe you even inherit his share."

"I inherit nothing."

"How do you know? Is there a will?"

"No." Lockhart paused. "There isn't a will." He seemed very sure. "We talked about it, Wilson and I, but he never made one. I don't think he even had any next of kin, aside from some useless nephew or cousin or something. I told him he was making a mistake, but he wouldn't listen. He never listened."

Fleet tickled Pixie behind the ear. "This is all fascinating, Jack, but the fact is, with him dead, you can do things your way, both here and on the Tribal Council."

"I could before! Dammit, this is ridiculous!"

"Woof!"

"People don't spear their partners with crossbow bolts so they can run their businesses with a little less irritation."

"Woof!"

"Everything was fine—"

"Woof!"

"I—"

"Woof!"

"Wilson and I—"

"Grr."

"Would you shut that mutt up, please!"

Fleet gave his friend a cold, hard look. "That's up to you, Jack. You're the one making all the racket. Pixie doesn't like racket. She doesn't like liars either."

Lockhart returned the cold look with interest. He spoke softer but no less forcefully. "Look, Wilson and I might have had our differences, but that was all. I barely knew the man outside our mutual investment. We were business partners. With him out of the way, I have more trouble now than I had with him here, and that's the truth. Now then, if you don't mind, Fleet—"

"You missed the pinky, Jack," said the unflappable PI, pointing to the emery board.

"Woof," added the unflappable Maltese, who probably thought someone had said *Pixie*.

"Your pinkie finger. You forgot to file it."

"Frig my pinkie finger."

"You might well say that, since it helps convict you."

"What?"

"A funny thing happened while we were examining Croker's office," said Fleet. "Pixie went straight for an emery board she found on the floor. I didn't see why; her fingernails looked fine to me, but now I understand what she was trying to tell me. It was your emery board, Jack. You see, very few people had access to Croker's office, and fewer still habitually use a nail file. I happen to know that my daughter rarely uses one, and Wilson Croker didn't seem the type. Not many men bother with their nails. You're very vain, Jack."

"Sod off."

"The emery, in itself, doesn't mean much, even if we can prove it belongs to you. You could always claim that it was left there earlier—although this is also doubtful, considering Croker's devotion to tidiness. The important detail, though, is what the emery reminded me of. When we left the impostor yesterday, he said you and he had been in conference. Something about advertising revenue. You see the significance of this? No one who truly knew Croker would have been fooled by the actor's disguise. Not for an instant. It only worked on us because we had never met him. If you had seen the impostor that day, and never mentioned it, then you also must be the one who hired him. And killed the real Croker."

"It's a lie! I never saw Wilson or anyone resembling Wilson that day."

"The actor and the emery board say different."

"Hearsay."

"Whose? The actor's or the emery board's?"

"Sod off!"

"You already said that. Ah well, if there's anything to it, I'm sure we'll find a witness who saw you coming or going."

"There isn't anything to it," spouted Lockhart.

"Glad to hear it, Jack, glad to hear it." Fleet stood. Pixie, after another suspicious look at the beverage magnate, jumped down and gave the rest of the aisle a good snuffle.

Lockhart drew himself up in his seat. I suddenly realized he was glaring at me. I had been listening so intently and without speaking for so long that I had almost forgotten that I was there.

"And you," he snarled.

"Uh?" I replied. When men like Jack Lockhart snarl at you, all you can say is *Uh.* (Unless you're Enescu Fleet, but how many of us are?)

"I still want that package from you. Understand?"

"Uh," I said.

"Not gonna happen, Jack," Fleet remarked.

"What?"

"He doesn't have your package."

"What!"

"You see, he isn't really John Hathaway. A minor deception, hope you don't mind. Very Wodehousian. Toodle-oo."

25 — An Affair to Remember

I don't think I've ever been happier to be outside in the cool breezes again, breathing the crisp New England air. Not only had things become strained with Jack Lockhart, but Todd Parnell and Ronald had also spent the past twenty minutes glaring at me. What with that, my lack of Hathaway-ness, and Dean pressing to have a "Dean Driskill Presents" tacked on to the show—apparently Dean's last name was Driskill—you can see why I was happy to go. An October chill was a welcome change to this cauldron of warped feelings.

Fleet seemed pretty ready to vacate as well. What I had initially mistaken for retreat, however, was in actuality a bold advancement into the enemy camp. Specifically, we wound up in the courtyard of Sprightly Sports Drinks.

We had come there by way of the construction area Dean had mentioned. Fleet glanced around a little—he seemed particularly interested in the security cameras—then we made our way to a ridge behind the offices.

"Hopefully Jack's consternation will keep him out of our hair for a while," he said, pausing behind some dumpsters with an excellent view of the studio exit.

"Wait for it," he told me.

I waited for it, and presently the studio doors opened and Neptune burst through, followed by Lockhart. They got in a sedan and sped off. (So Neptune did drive, after all.)

"He's probably going to see his lawyers. Good. I'd prefer not to be interrupted inside."

"Where inside?"

"Sprightly Sports Drinks," he remarked, handing me Pixie's leash.

I can't speak for the fur ball, but I found our tour of the up-and-coming beverage juggernaut pretty informative. I got to see the test kitchen where they create all their wacky flavors, had a peek at the art department—the color of the week, *mauve*—and even got to meet the complete writing staff, the brains behind all the pithy riddles adorning the labels. His name was Tim, and if his story was to be believed, he hadn't been allowed to roam outside the writers' lounge since sometime last November. Still, the Kiwi-Strawberry made me chuckle.

I didn't see much of Fleet during this time. Almost immediately after receiving our tour badges, he had bumped into an old lady friend, a chemist.

She had short gray hair, a firm profile and no shortage of eye makeup. She looked more like an aging brothel madam than a scientist, and her words of welcome echoed this. If I remember correctly these were, "*F*— me! It's Effy,"— then she completed their reunion by pouncing into Effy's arms. From there, things just got weird. She asked him what he was doing in these parts, prompting Fleet to reply, *Oh, you know*. He then asked her if she had a few minutes, to which she remarked for him, she had several.

The last I saw of them, they were strolling off to the lab—Fleet pulling out a test tube from his pocket and speaking to her about it in hushed undertones.

From my location, attempting to get Pixie's leash disentangled from one of the test-kitchen stools, the tube looked to be filled with a dark liquid, such as coffee. When I heard his chemist friend mutter something about French roast, her undertones not being all that hushed, I figured I had scoped it out correctly. Fleet must have slipped some from the urn during our recent visit to Studio A. But why? It didn't taste all that great to me. Why study it?

When we met up again outside, I didn't bother to ask for an explanation. I knew better than that. Nor did I seek to confirm his quintessential twinkle. The mustache and beard concealed much of the smile, but it was unquestionably there, twinkling away.

I pretended not to notice.

"Where now?" I asked.

"The roof," he said, waving over a doorman to handle Pixie.

I have to say, his technique picking the lock to the roof was nothing short of astounding. I didn't even realize he had picked it at all until he was proceeding through the doorway, slipping his tools back into his pocket. Most people fumble with their house key longer than he did with that lock.

I won't glamorize the roof for you. It was cold. Really, really cold. I no longer felt all that pleasantly disposed toward the crisp October breezes.

Fleet had stepped over to the edge and was peering out at the lush emerald landscape. It had a nice view; I'll give it that.

"This is where he jumped," he said.

"Who?"

"The unnamed casino guest. He threw himself off here."

I could see why. You probably warmed up on impact. I zipped up my jacket and asked what we were doing up here.

Fleet didn't answer. "Come," he said, heading in.

"What did that accomplish?" I demanded.

"I'll tell you presently."

Hah! I thought, and in we went.

Our next item of business was Nadine, the woman who had discovered the suicide. After all the excitement of the roof and coffee test tubes and the color mauve, the visit struck me as anticlimactic. I couldn't figure how she had any bearing on our current investigation at all, and already my feet were getting tired.

We found her working the reception desk at the Ivory Buffalo Hotel. I could see at a glance that she wasn't going to be an easy witness.

She was perfectly attractive—in a middle-aged, woman-next-door kind of way. She had dark auburn hair, hardly any makeup, and features that tended toward the earthy variety. She had a nice smile, though. Not that she used it all that much.

Hearing what we had to say, she wiped the Welcome-to-Wolf-Valley expression from her face and said in heavy Maine-ese, "No one seemed to *keah* much what I had to say then. Don't see why anybody should *keah* now."

Fleet assured her that we would be hanging on her every word. "You found the body on your break?"

"Yeah."

"In the alleyway between the casino and the Ivory Buffalo?"

"Yeah."

"You knew the dead man pretty well, then?"

Nadine looked startled. "How'd you know that?"

Fleet replied that he hadn't known for sure, dusting off that old until-you-just-confirmed-it-now comeback detectives seem to enjoy so much.

"I had my suspicions," he said. "I grant you, there wasn't much about you in the papers. But what little there was agreed on one point, that the discovery of the body had affected you profoundly. You were practically beside yourself and had to be sedated. The police attributed this to a natural sensitivity, but it seemed to me, reading between the journalistic blather, that there was more to it than met the newsprint. Then, of course, there was the location of the body. Seemed an unusual place for a nice lady like yourself to spend her lunch, in the alleyway between the two buildings. It occurred to me that you must have gone there looking for something. And you had found it."

"You seem to know it all," said Nadine. "He and I used to have our rendezvous'es up on the roof. Don't look at me that way. It was nothing like that. Trevy used to bring lunch, and we'd have a picnic. That was his name. Trevy. Trevor."

Once again I found myself musing that, sometimes, not knowing your name can be preferable to knowing it. (I refer to those times when your name is Trevy.) I shivered visibly, and when Nadine asked me if I had a problem, I blamed it on the October breezes.

"When he *neva* showed, I went looking, like you said. I don't know what made me think he might have—"

Fleet gave her hand a light squeeze. "We can pass over all that. You didn't consider him suicidal?"

"*Neva*. He was mysterious, not giving me his whole name, not explaining why he was really *heah*. But kill himself? It didn't make sense."

"He never told you his job?"

"No. I sort of *figu'ed* he was some kind of *coureah* or something."

"A courier?"

"Yeah. I saw him with packages a few times, but he wouldn't say what was in them."

Fleet gave me a look. "They say Trevor had gambling debts?"

"He didn't gamble." She was certain on that point.

"How did he seem that day? The day he jumped?"

"Weah'd," said Nadine. It took me a couple minutes to realize that this was *Weird*. "I saw him in the morning, and he acted like he didn't know who I was. Then he busted the lock on the roof and, and—it didn't make any sense. He didn't need to do that!"

Fleet gave her hand another soothing tap. "I don't want to appear harsh, but why didn't you say any of this to the police?"

I expected Nadine to come over all shy and embarrassed. She didn't. She merely shook her head and replied that nobody had asked her. "Besides, I'd given him one of the rooms in the renovation area for free. Trevy wouldn't have wanted me to get in trouble for that."

"Pardon me!" I interjected, and if I sounded like a haughty English aristocrat, I didn't care. I felt like a haughty English aristocrat. "Do you mean to say that you clammed up on the whole affair, saying nothing? You cared about this guy; you should have told people about him. Nobody knows a thing about the man. The papers, the press, nobody. He's a total blank."

Nadine looked pretty blank herself. "Sorry, with your accent, I can't always follow you *theah*."

We left shortly after that. About halfway across the lobby, Fleet held up and went back over to Nadine. He returned a few seconds later.

"Good news. In exchange for the sheriff going easy on her, she agreed to talk to a friend in security. We need to have a look-see at something."

"What kind of look-see?"

"The footage of the construction area last night between ten and midnight."

I still didn't get it. Five minutes later, we were crammed into a tiny security booth, a man called Hank sloshing soda on me on my right—and on my left, a man known as Butch telling Fleet that it was an honor to meet him and was he actually the guy they had based all those beer commercials on?

Fleet made polite conversation with the guards while Hank (or it might have been Butch) fiddled with the computer.

The main casino, explained Hank and Butch, had a more elaborate security center than theirs. Fleet waved away this self-effacement. He had everything he needed right here, he said.

It didn't take us long to find what we were looking for. The footage at 22:59:06 showed an overhead perspective of a man in a jumpsuit and stocking cap rolling a crate across the construction area. You couldn't see his face from our angle, and he soon disappeared out of view of the camera. Before he moved out of the frame, I could make out the words "Tip Tock Clocks" burned into the side of the crate.

"The grandfather clock?" I asked.

Fleet nodded. "This is the footage of the delivery guy last night." He paused. "It is also the footage of the murderer."

26 — An Acquaintance to Forget

Fleet spelled it out for me after we had left the booth. The killer had arranged to pick up the new clock from the shop in town. On the way back, he had stopped at the boathouse, packed the body up inside the crate with the clock, and that was that. Easy.

Fleet was sure a forensics test on the clock would confirm all this. Not that these details seemed to matter to him.

"This doesn't get us anywhere," he said. "We're no closer to identifying the murderer than before."

I wasn't so sure about this. If the killer had picked up the clock, then someone from the store would be able to identify him.

A call to Tip Tock quickly deflated this theory. No one had seen him. The alley behind the shop was just broad enough for the extrawide van he had used. Once the crate was loaded in the back, a gloved hand had reached out from the driver's side window, slid the clipboard inside and signed for it. All without revealing his face.

The man had thought of everything, down to the most minute measurement.

I figured that this must let Dean off the hook, since he had ordered the clock and wasn't likely to have gone to all this trouble to conceal picking it up.

Fleet did not agree. According to him, Dean was the ideal candidate to have picked it up. Who better than he—the man who had broken the clock in the first place? He was still a viable suspect, in other words, which was funny since I had suspected him from the beginning, only for the wrong reasons. Fleet did not appear amused.

"What about Lockhart?" I asked.

"What about him?"

"Is he still a suspect?"

"Everyone is a suspect until I say they aren't," said Fleet. We continued our walk through the casino in silence.

He didn't truly perk up again until we passed the Nightingale Room, and there it was only to greet his daughter, Ate, who was on her way somewhere.

She seemed jumpier than usual.

"Dean just got off the phone with Trebek's people," she told us, hardly bothering to slow down. "Everything's all set."

Fleet looked impressed. "Our mild-mannered director has hidden depths."

"I guess so. Anyway, I gotta run. Lots to do to set up."

"One last thing, honey. It's about John Hathaway."

She came to rest by a tribal statue. Her face was as hard as the marble behind her. "What about him?"

"Are you sure he checked out of the hotel?"

"I don't know. He said he had."

"But you've already told me that his word is not to be trusted."

"You got that right."

"Then he might have fibbed? In other words, he could still be in the hotel, lying low?"

"I guess. What does it matter?"

"I'd like to talk to him."

"Why?" She scowled at him and then repeated, "I mean—why?"

"I think he is involved in all this somehow. I know he is. His input might be helpful. Speaking of which, how much do you know about this suicide from a few months back?"

She reflected. "The suicide? Very little. It was before my time. I know the police thought it was suspicious but couldn't prove anything. Why?" The word of the day was *Why*. "Do you think Hathaway was involved?" She sounded hopeful.

"Not at all. It was also before his time. But Nadine told me something very interesting about it."

"Who?"

"Nadine, from reception. We questioned her about the suicide. After we had finished, I went back to ask her a favor, and that's when she mentioned that I wasn't the only one looking into the suicide. Before going to earth, John Hathaway had posed her some guarded questions of his own."

This surprised me. The playboy Hathaway concerning himself in such noble matters? There must have been a buxom babe involved in this somewhere.

Ate was also amazed. "Are you sure it was Hathaway?"

"According to Nadine, yes. He may have simply been paying his respects to a fellow courier, but somehow I don't think so."

"Wait a minute. Was the suicidal guy a courier too?"

"I don't think he was, no."

"You're making my head hurt, Dad."

Fleet apologized. "I think people assumed the man was a courier, but he wasn't. I would like to know what he really was. Apparently, Hathaway would too."

"Well, I wouldn't know anything about it," said Ate.

"No, but you might have some pull getting us a room number. Hathaway's room number. If he is lying low, then what better place than his room? Tell me, how well do you know this Nadine?"

Ate smiled. "Sorry, Dad. The staff won't give out room numbers. People are always trying to trick them, and they're very savvy. Give it a miss."

I knew the Fleets pretty well by now and could say with some certainty that this discussion had not run its course. Telling Enescu Fleet that something wouldn't work would only spur him on to make it work.

It never came to that. For the last couple minutes, her father had been gazing in the direction of the Nightingale Room. He drew Ate in closer and asked, "Do you know this guy?" He tipped his head toward one of the casino guests.

"I thought you did," she said.

I had noticed him myself—not that anyone bothered to ask me. He had been standing on the edge of the high-rollers' room for the better part of our talk, an overnight bag slung across his ample shoulder. Every time Fleet shot him a glance, he shot one right back.

"Here he comes," I said, resisting the urge to say *cheez it!*

The man addressed himself to us as a whole. He looked like a newborn panda bear someone had dressed in a golf shirt and trousers.

"Did I hear one of you say John Hathaway?" he asked, and we agreed that he had. "I went to school with a John Hathaway. I'm Claude, Wilson Croker's nephew."

27 — Unexpected Recognition

Thankfully Ate bought me some time to think, drawing me aside before the conversation could get rolling. She did this, I knew, to establish her own escape route. Whatever the reason, I appreciated it.

"I meant to tell Dad something," she remarked. "I got the strangest call this afternoon. It was from the Tribal Council Orphan Fund in town, thanking Wilson Croker for his donation."

This *was* weird. I wouldn't have pegged Croker as the charitable type. Everyone was surprising me today.

"I'm amazed," I said.

"Me too, but that wasn't the weird part. A pile of stock certificates for Sprightly Sports Drinks, totaling ten thousand shares and accompanied by a stock power signed by the dead man, was discovered in their offices today. It had to have been slid through the slot late last night or early this morning, before they opened. All of which would have been fine, except that Mr. Croker had been dead since yesterday morning."

"Early yesterday morning."

"Exactly, which means the donation must have been made after Mr. Croker's death."

"The ghost of Croker making amends?"

"I don't know. But it seems weird. See what the PI man has to say about it, would you?" And with a nod to her father, and a lesser one to Croker's nephew, she skipped off.

I hate to make snap judgments about people, but I disliked Claude Croker from the moment I saw him. I disliked him even more watching him converse with the PI man. It wasn't only that he appeared to be a grease ball of the worst description. I'm sure there are grease balls out there who possess an inner charm. This one did not. He had a jaded, supercilious demeanor, no doubt inherited from his uncle. Even from across a crowded casino he annoyed me.

The only consolation was I wouldn't have to be John Hathaway in his presence. If Claude knew the real Hathaway, Fleet would have to leave that deception alone for once.

"Oh, Johnny," said Fleet, not leaving it alone for once. "Come and say hi to your old school chum."

Unable to speak, I drifted over to where they stood. As much as I wished to bolt, part of me was curious to see how Fleet was going to reshape my face into one Claude would recognize as his old school chum's.

"I was telling Claude that you have probably changed a good deal since the fifth grade."

I loosened up. "No doubt," I agreed.

I didn't envy Hathaway growing up with this thug. Along with the winning personality, he had the breadth and width of a fullback. Two fullbacks. He was almost completely spherical, in fact, with a giant shaved skull to match. He must have been a joy at ten years old.

"You look different," he said, squinting at me.

"The years," I said, "they age."

"And your hair's a different color."

"The lighting."

"And I don't remember you having that fruity accent."

I glanced at my cohort, who replied for me, "The acoustics."

Claude no longer seemed all that interested in his old chum's transformation. I took it that he and Johnny hadn't been all that close. "I guess you heard someone killed my uncle, Hathaway?"

I replied that I had heard something about it, yes.

"It's a tragedy. I was headed for Amsterdam when I heard. Came here instead. Arrived about ten minutes ago. I'm Uncle Wilson's only heir and figured it was my duty to be on hand." He gazed between the two of us, his pudgy features working something through. "So what do you think my uncle was worth anyway?"

Fleet remarked that these details would likely come out after the inquest, to which Claude nodded and took out a pack of cigarettes. Along with his other charming traits, he stank like a damp chimney. Seeming to recall that you weren't allowed to smoke inside the casino, he scowled and jammed the pack back in his pocket.

"Haven't I seen you around somewhere?" he asked Fleet.

I thought a good rejoinder here would have been "Not if I saw you first," but Fleet, courteous to the last, merely replied that it was entirely possible.

"That's it, I saw you in the hotel magazine. You're that geezer from all the game shows."

I thought a good rejoinder here would have been "Who you callin' a geezer?" but Fleet merely inclined his head in the affirmative. He appeared amused by the guy.

Claude continued to be contemptuous. "These game shows are ridiculously easy. I always know the answer before they ring in. Every time." He turned to me. "Remember that trivia club they had at school, Hathaway?"

I said it wasn't a very vivid memory, no.

"You remember. All the geeks who couldn't make the cut for chess club were there. Man, I used to enjoy whaling on those guys." He chuckled lightly, reflecting on happier times.

"Was Hathaway one of your whalees?" asked Fleet.

"Hathaway? Nah. I never whaled on Hathaway. He was always too fast a runner." Here he let out another guffaw and pushed me into a cocktail waitress.

I collected myself, apologized to "Bertha" and rejoined the conversation.

Claude had taken out his cigs again. Realizing that he had already tried this, he cursed. "Man, you can't do anything in this Podunk casino. No smoking, no decent chicks"—he turned and glared at the advertisement for the Remarkable Ronald—"the shows all suck. Idiot couldn't mind-read his way out of a paper bag. Preschool teacher, my ass. Even the tables stink. The stakes they cut you off at are crap."

"You would like something a little higher?" asked Fleet.

"You got it. I asked them to put me in the high-rollers' room, but the stakes start at ten grand, and they seem to have this issue with extending credit. My funds are mostly tied up in investments overseas, you see."

Fleet agreed that this was often the way. "We too have longed to breach the inner sanctum known only to these high rollers."

"The inner what?"

"Sanctum. The Nightingale Room beckons to us, calling for us to sip a beaker full of its blushful Hippocrene."

"Huh?"

"We're lookin' for some action."

"Me too, man. Me too." Back to me: "Remember the blackjack we used to play at school, Hathaway?"

"Not especially."

"You remember. We played behind the schoolyard once, me, you and the Collins boys. I told you I was going to beat you up at recess for some reason—you were always pissing me off about something—and you challenged me to a blackjack match instead. You made such a big deal about it in front of the older kids that I had to agree. Poker was more my game, but I played your blackjack, and you took ten bucks off me. I always figured you must have stacked the deck."

"That would have been a lot of years ago," I argued.

The decades meant nothing to Claude. For him, it would always be fifth-grade recess. "Man, was I going to kick the crap out of you. But then we had all those snow days, and by the time we got back, you had been transferred to some sissy boarding school."

"Sad," I said. Tragic, you might even call it. "Well, anyway—" I started to say.

I'm pretty sure things would have wrapped up here. Claude and I had very little left to say to one another, especially with him brooding on that ten dollars and me not exactly offering to make amends. It wasn't as though I could. Even if I felt like paying off Hathaway's debts, I had no money. I didn't even have a wallet.

I was about to inch away, when Fleet went and stuck his oar in again.

"I have a thought," he said, and I didn't care for the sound of this. "It sounds like you two old chums have much to settle."

"Huh?" said we old chums.

"Did you know, Claude, that Johnny here has developed into quite a poker player since you saw him last? Perhaps you could settle your differences that way?"

"Huh?"

"The matter of the ten dollars. I'm sure that has been gnawing at you all these years."

"Well—"

"Of course it has. Ten dollars? Why, it is a fortune in your youth. And what if you compound it over twenty years? It must be worth thousands now. The only manly thing to do is settle it over a deck of cards."

"Go mano a mano?" asked Claude.

"Exactly the mano breakdown I was thinking."

"For how much?"

"Ten thousand dollars is a nice figure. I could stake Hathaway if he doesn't have it."

Claude tried to whistle. He looked like he was blowing invisible bubbles. "Ten *G's*, huh? Where are we going to play?"

"Not behind the schoolyard, that's for sure. How about the Nightingale Room? It's an appropriate arena."

Claude seemed to agree. "But wait, I still don't have any money. I mean, on me. Usually ten grand isn't a problem, but the Swiss banks are on holiday and—"

Fleet had a ready solution. "I'm sure the casino wouldn't mind extending you credit if you explained it to them properly. After all, you are Wilson Croker's only heir, and therefore stand to inherit a bundle."

"That's true."

"I will have a word with them for you, if you like."

"Thanks."

"Excellent. And we will meet back here, when? Midnight? Perfect. We—I—excuse me a moment, would you?"

During these arrangements I had made several attempts to horn in. Seeing these methods fizzle, I said, "Hey!" and that got me recognized.

"What are you doing?" I whispered, once Fleet and I had stepped aside.

"Don't you see? It's the perfect way into the Nightingale Room."

I gave him another of my befuddled looks.

"There is something in that room," he explained. "The answer lies within, I'm sure of it. We must discover the significance of Croker's last words."

"We have. The safe, remember?"

"Hah," said Fleet, and now I knew where his daughter got it. "The safe was nothing. Don't talk to me about the safe."

"But the safe had it all," I pointed out. "It was secret, it held papers about stuff, and the combination was all Keats, all the time. It was perfect."

Fleet shook his head. "If Croker wanted you to look in his safe, he would have given you the combination. Why play games? No, there's something more to this business."

"And you think you'll find it in the Nightingale Room?"

"I won't know until I try."

This time I shook my head. "You can get into the Nightingale anytime you want. You're Enescu Fleet."

"Thank you for that, but in this instance it's not enough. I have been inside once, and the pit boss watched my every move. They don't care for people loitering around their clientele. They're a skittish bunch, these high rollers."

"But what good is playing Claude going to do?"

"Since I don't know what we're looking for, I need more time. This will give me the perfect opportunity. I can search the room on the pretense of watching you. Meanwhile, you can grill Claude about this flimsy alibi of his."

"What do you mean?"

"He didn't arrive ten minutes ago. He couldn't have. Claude Croker has been here all weekend, while his uncle was still alive. I think that is significant."

"How do you know this? Did you see him?"

"No, it was something he said. But this isn't getting us anywhere. You can draw your own conclusions when you question him."

"While playing poker for ten grand?"

"Exactly. And don't worry, this fits in with our story perfectly. I remember reading that Hathaway is an excellent cardplayer."

"But I'm not John Hathaway!"

Fleet slowly nodded. He kept forgetting that, he said, and I told him to remember it now.

"And while you're at it, remember that Jack Lockhart, owner of the high-rollers' room, knows I'm not John Hathaway."

"Jack Lockhart has his own problems. He's not likely to balk about your continued imposture when he knows that one word from me will have the police on his back. No, Jack isn't our problem. It's the poker. How's your game?"

"How should I know?"

"Can you play?"

"Poker? I don't know, let me think. A full house beats a straight, right?"

"I believe it does."

"I guess I know how to play."

"How about strategy? How are you on that?"

I told him that I knew a full house beat a straight.

Fleet nodded again. "Perfect."

28 — The Mysterious Mr. Hathaway

I told Fleet about the ghostly charitable contribution on our way back to the cabin. He was interested, but not overly so.

The lack of dialogue on the charity topic gave me a chance to ask about this poker death match tonight. I wondered, once again, why we couldn't ask our local sheriff for his support, and Fleet insisted, once again, that we had to go about this casually. There was no sense in tipping off the murderer.

I didn't see how we could. If I had no clue what we were doing, I couldn't figure how the murderer would. I was still sorting out exactly what we were supposed to be looking for in this wondrous Nightingale Room, when I paused. It seemed a sprocket had come loose in our GPS.

"This isn't the way to the cabin."

"Who said anything about the cabin?"

"You said the room."

"Exactly. John Hathaway's room."

I sighted the reception desk for the Ivory Buffalo on the horizon and immediately stumbled backward into a crapshooter. The roll came up boxcars, and a cheer burst out around the table.

"Since my daughter has declined to sit in, one of us needs to get the room number. I would go now if I were you. It appears Nadine just went on break. I would tackle the fellow with the bald spot. He looks helpful."

I told myself that I could do this.

It wasn't a crime to ferret out a person's room number. The most the clerk could do was give me a squiggly eyed look and refuse to unbend.

"Um," I said, stepping up to the desk.

The balding clerk, labeled "Aubrey" on his shirt pin, smiled broadly. "Good evening, Mr. Hathaway, what can I do for you?"

I said um.

I hadn't expected this. All I could think was Aubrey must have overheard Fleet introduce me as Hathaway at some point. Helpful—but I still had a lot of arduous spadework to do.

"Um, about my room," I said.

"Misplace your key again?" he asked.

The old man had got it right. Hathaway hadn't checked out. Not that this did me or anyone a whole lot of good.

"Um," I said.

"Let me get you another key," the clerk smiled.

I had to admit, this was proving a lot less arduous than I had originally envisioned. Aubrey stepped to the card reader behind the desk, and presently he was handing me a key, one of those generic credit card–shaped thingies, without a number.

That, of course, was still the rub. The room number.

Aubrey to the rescue again. Reading the bewilderment in my eyes, he smiled and said, "Room 1214, sir."

Well, there it was. I said thanks, or maybe it was just um, and turned to head back across the marble lobby.

I froze. For the first time since Aubrey had come into my life, spewing key cards and room numbers like a slot jackpot, I found myself drawn to him.

I had an idea. In fact, I couldn't think why I hadn't thought of it earlier.

"Say, Aubrey."

"Yes, Mr. Hathaway?"

"Can you tell me the name of the man in Bungalow 6?"

It was so simple. Bungalow 6 was my cabin. I must have checked in, ergo the efficient Aubrey must have my name in his computer. My real name.

"I think I might know the guy," I remarked casually.

Aubrey frowned, becoming suddenly dour. "I am sorry, sir. I am not at liberty to give out guests' names," and with these words, Aubrey and I ended what could have been a beautiful friendship.

I returned to Enescu Fleet, but not before brooding on life a moment. Seemed funny, life, but maybe that was just me.

We rode the elevator up in a pensive silence—me, Fleet and the dog, Pixie. Fleet had collected her from the guard on the way: a sound move. It was good to have her along should we need anyone to piddle.

The doors slid open onto the twelfth floor, and out we stepped. Down a long, elegant corridor to the right, carpeted in burgundy and peach, and there we had it. Room 1214.

I knocked.

We stood by in silence for perhaps two minutes, and then Fleet shook his head. "Nobody at home. I guess we might as well go in."

I stared.

I suppose I should have expected this, but somehow it never occurred to me that we would be breaking and entering.

"You said you just wanted to talk!" I exclaimed.

"We can't talk if nobody's home. We'll go in and wait for him."

"We can't!"

"We can. I saw the clerk give you the key. Nice work, by the way."

I had meant it from an ethical standpoint.

"We need to see what's in that room," said Fleet. "It's vital."

This obsession he had with searching rooms was beginning to concern me. I quickly knocked again, adding a desperate backward gaze to the process.

Silence and more silence. Reluctantly (on my part) we proceeded inside. Or, I should say, we proceeded inside after about twenty tries with the key card. Twenty one was the charm, giving us the green light. I could have done without the silent criticism of the retired detective's eyebrows, not to mention the derisive growls of his tiny

Maltese pup. Those key cards are not as easy to use as they look, especially when your hand is shaking.

Young Hathaway did pretty well for himself. His accommodations were none too shabby. He didn't have an enormous room, but it was a decent size and had a nice view of the pine trees.

It seemed like more room than any one man could need, though one had to budget for the stream of floozies he had pouring through the place on a regular basis. Your average floozy demanded more.

Whatever his attractions to the opposite sex, he certainly shunned the cleaning staff. Dishes were piled up from meals long past. The bed looked like a small melee had broken out on it, and the sofa didn't look much jauntier. I made an effort not to go near either one of these. "Where do you think he is?" I asked, as Pixie wound herself into a frenzy, attempting to scurry in six directions at once.

"He could be miles away by now," replied Fleet, unwinding her.

"I thought you said he hadn't checked out?"

"That was before the murder. Whatever he got himself into this weekend has only gotten stickier, and men like John Hathaway do not stick around when the going gets sticky. They scoot. Frequently without bothering to pack," he said, indicating a wardrobe of shirts and slacks, all good quality.

It all sounded plausible to me, but the place still gave me the heebie-jeebies. I kept expecting its occupant to come stumbling back in at any moment—drunk and disorderly and what-the-hell-ing. Rogues might scoot, but that didn't mean they wouldn't come scooting back again for their shirts and slacks. From what I had seen, a couple of these were Pima cotton, and those don't come cheap.

"He should have let housekeeping in more often," I said.

"And risk tipping off the men after him?"

"Are there men after him?"

I didn't get it. What could he have had that anyone could want? His parcel? What was this parcel, anyway?

I didn't say it, but it seemed pretty likely to me that John Hathaway was currently lying face down in some tribal stream somewhere:

the fourth corpse behind Trevor, Wilson Croker and that actor, whose name I had already forgotten. Nick—that was it.

Stepping to the other wardrobe, I found another boodle of clothes. As these were largely female, pullovers and capri pants and things, I gathered that one of Hathaway's girlfriends had skedaddled with him. Either that or he liked to indulge in some very special fancy time, all by himself.

"Take a look at this," said Fleet. I came over to the bureau, where the detective was holding something up in the sunlight. "A ticket stub to the game show this morning. It appears that I may have underestimated our Mr. Hathaway."

"He was there?"

"From the looks of it, yes. Or someone was, on his behalf."

"What about the famous parcel?"

"No trace of it."

I frowned and peered up at my reflection. We had hardly seen one another since the morning I had awoken in my cabin. I had almost forgotten that feeling of a stranger staring back at me.

I needed another shave.

My analysis of the only face I would ever have was interrupted by the piercing barks of Pixie. For reasons known only to her Maltese mind, she had taken a sudden interest in the adjoining door. Her vulgar shouts, coming at a moment when I was trying to decide if my hairline was receding, caused me to whip around, scattering an open bottle of hair dye. (Apparently somebody had been altering their appearance this weekend.)

I got quite a bit of it on me in the process, and when I consulted the label, was not encouraged. The folks at "Hair Da Belle" advised against getting their product in contact with carpets, wood surfaces and fabric. Although they didn't explicitly state it, keeping it away from living things probably wasn't a bad idea either.

"It says here," I said, over the sound of Pixie's barks, "in the event of prolonged contact with skin, remove. I guess they mean the hair dye."

Fleet wasn't listening to me. He had stepped to the connecting door. In the hopes of silencing the raging pup, he now opened this.

This would have been fine, had the door to the next room been shut. It wasn't. The internal door was wide open, the entranceway currently occupied by a maid dusting the doorframe. At the sight of Pixie rearing up at her, she let out a squeak and sprang back. Pixie, in turn, sprang forward. She shot past the panting maid, past the panting maid's cleaning cart and through the open door into the hall. She disappeared into the peach distance, a fluffy white blur.

Enescu Fleet, with a nod to the help, went after her. That just left me, my splattered sweater and the huffing maid. Once the maid had slammed shut the door, that just left me and the sweater.

I retired to the bathroom to see what I could do with a dab of hot water and soap.

Not a whole lot. I dabbed and rubbed for a couple minutes and then shut off the tap.

I could hear something.

It sounded like it was coming from behind the shower curtain, a sort of huff or puff. I listened a little closer and determined that it was actually coming from the hallway outside. Realizing I still had the key card, I went to let Fleet back in.

I don't know what prompted me to peep in the peephole first. I suppose it was only reflex, or perhaps I thought I would simply find the maid without and didn't feel like startling her into any more hysterics. In any event, I gave the peephole a gander, and what I saw had me springing back into the room—startled and hysterical.

The person at the door, currently fiddling with that pesky key slot, was Jack Lockhart's enormous driver, Neptune.

I thought about dashing through the adjoining door, in the manner of darting Maltese, but the maid had locked and bolted that exit. I turned and shot back inside the bathroom.

As this seemed to hold limited powers of concealment, I turned and shot inside the bathtub behind the shower curtain.

This seemed better. In fact, when I discovered a lovely young blonde standing to my left, I knew I had made the right decision. It was clearly the people's choice.

29 — Reunited

If I remember correctly, I said, "Hi." Not much on it, but it was honest.

It was pretty remarkable, I thought, how we kept running into each other like this. The cabin, Jack Lockhart's party, backstage at the game show, and now the bath. If I could have thought of a clever quip about it all, it probably would have broken the ice, but since I couldn't think of a clever quip, I stuck with the *Hi.*

She said hi back, and before you get carried away with any elaborate fantasies, she was fully clothed. (You can't have everything.) Nonetheless, whether clad in a gray cable-knit sweater and contrasting black capri pants or not clad in them, she was a welcome sight to my weary eyes. I was delighted to share an uninterrupted moment with her for once.

I was also a little surprised.

I considered the evidence. There she was, dressed, hiding in the bath, trying not to make a sound except for those muffled huffs. It seemed to me, my PI-ing instincts honed to perfection from prolonged association with Enescu Fleet, that she was hiding from someone. Since Neptune had only now arrived, it couldn't be him, so it must have been from me and/or the F-man.

"Were you hiding from us?" I whispered.

She nodded and asked me, still in a whisper, who I was hiding from.

"Neptune."

Her eyes widened. She said shhh! No sooner had the puff left her lips than I heard the hotel door click shut in the foyer. Neptune was coming into orbit.

There was very little to do in this hiding place of ours, but I wasn't complaining. She stood there, I stood here, and from the other room there came the sounds of rifling.

"You smell nice," I whispered.

She repeated her shhh!, and I receded into the soap dish, abashed.

The girl looked apologetic.

Seeming to feel her reply was a tad abrupt for such a handsome tribute, she smiled and pointed to the shower gel. I nodded. Then I remembered where we were, and I frowned.

I thought about it. *Her* bath gel in Hathaway's shower. *Her* capri pants hanging in the spare wardrobe in Hathaway's room. *Her*self in Hathaway's shower in Hathaway's room. I was beginning to get an idea of how she had spent the last two days, and my frown deepened.

A sound like Neptune placing the chaise lounge in a half nelson drifted in to our ears, prompting my companion to lift her reserve briefly. She must have figured it was safe to speak.

"You smell nice too," she whispered, and I said shh. I smelled like hair dye and damp Maltese, and she knew it.

We heard a door slam. "Did he go?" she whispered. I peeked out from the curtain.

Nothing there—not that I expected to see the man standing at the sink, plucking his eyebrows. I had to explore further.

I stepped out and listened. Silence.

For an instant I caught a glimpse of the two of us in the mirror, me and the blonde, and thought we made a rather attractive—

It didn't matter.

"Wait here," I whispered.

"K," she whispered.

The room was at rest. I glanced to the left, and then to the right. No Neptune. I was about to head back and release the blonde from her porcelain captivity when I had an inkling. The balcony. The room had a very nice one, half obscured by the drawn curtain. It was entirely possible that Neptune had stepped out onto it. Why, I couldn't say, but I couldn't say why he had been ransacking the room either. It was worth a look-see.

I moved across the carpet, keeping an eye carefully cocked on the sliding door. It was so carefully cocked, in fact, that after about four steps I took a header over a large, unseen object on the carpet. This large, unseen object was Neptune.

It appeared he hadn't stepped out on the balcony, nor had he given up and left the room. He had been searching under the bed. (Until I stepped on him, that is.)

The spot I had squished must have been of a soft and highly personal nature, for when he grabbed on to my jacket a moment later, it was not at all playfully. With a jerk, he tossed me against the bureau. In response to this, I knocked off several pictures from the wall and got more hair dye on myself. The room was determined to turn me into a blond yet.

After a momentary pause, I climbed to my feet and shook the wisps of carpet lint from my person.

I decided it was about time that I started taking matters into my own hands. Ever since awaking the previous morning without a thought in my head, I had been putting up with one dismissive gesture after another: cryptic old codgers who wouldn't let me in on their secret detective techniques, sexy blondes who wouldn't stay put for two seconds (and then when they did stay put, they went and hooked up with playboys in designer shirts), and now hulking henchmen who thought they could fling me about with impunity.

I'd had enough.

I'm pretty certain that Neptune, given the chance, would have let the matter rest. He had searched, he had flung—there was nothing else keeping him here.

I couldn't see eye to eye with him on that.

I can't honestly say if I acted judiciously or not, running up and tackling him from behind. It seemed like a good idea at the time, but maybe that was just the hair dye talking. Anyway, that's what I did.

If nothing else, it surprised Neptune. He was definitely startled. After we had bounced off the wall, the dresser and a numbered lithograph depicting a bowl of pastel-colored fruit, I saw the look in his eyes, and it was the look of a man astonished. He saw that I had pluck, and I think it impressed him.

Unfortunately, good impressions don't last very long.

Mine with Neptune lasted about five seconds. After that, he climbed to his feet, grabbed me by the scruff of the neck in one hand—the scruff of some highly personal area in the other—and hurled me over the bed. This could have been very painful on my highly personal area, had the area in question not cleverly receded to some unspecified location, disassociating itself from the entire affair.

I stood up and dusted more lint from my head. The place really needed a cleaning.

It's funny. On gray November mornings, when there is nowhere to go and nothing to do, I often sit back and ponder how I might have proceeded from here. Sometimes I feel I would have given up. Other times, I think I might have damned the consequences and charged into the Valley of Death. In any event, the point never arose. I was still making up my mind when I saw Neptune flinch. Looking closer, I realized he had something on his back. Looking closer still, I saw that this something was a lovely young blonde in black capri pants.

I was impressed. Not only by the size differential, which was mesmerizing—picture a hummingbird pecking at the back of an oversized raven, and you will have it—but by her spunk and enterprise. She might stay in Hathaway's room, she might use Hathaway's shower gel, but when it came to me and a giant Penobscot beating the stuffing out of me, she was willing to risk life and cable-knit sweater to lend assistance. That was my idea of Woman.

I couldn't let her handle him all on her own. Neptune had staggered out into the middle of the room, and like any senseless brute with a blonde inexplicably entwined around his torso, he was endeavoring to back up and squish her into the wall.

I got there in the nick of time.

I grabbed hold of his jacket and dug in the best I could to slow his backward descent.

I pulled and jerked so effectively that he finally switched it out of reverse and pitched forward onto me.

Hitting the carpet first, I barely had time to roll out of the way before the smackdown. Down went the brute, zoom went the blonde cowgirl, and ouch went I, receiving the cowgirl special delivery in the solar plexus. I was still catching my breath when Neptune, rising up out of the heap, twisted around in anguish.

For a couple of seconds, I couldn't figure what he was going on about. Then I saw it. From out of nowhere, a hand had grasped his paw and was wrenching it behind his back in a compelling judo grip. The hand doing the twisting wasn't mine, and it wasn't the blonde's, so I had to assume, unless Neptune was secretly a contortionist, it belonged to somebody else.

It did. A man had appeared on the scene. He was youngish—about my age. Tall (a few inches taller than me). I suppose he was handsome (about two-fifths handsomer, I guess). And as I have already mentioned, he was twisting Neptune's arm off at the stem.

Could this be Hathaway?

"Not so fast there, big boy," he said—and with the exception of Enescu Fleet, I couldn't think of another person getting away with calling Neptune "big boy" to his face, judo grip or not. "He's a feisty one, isn't he?" he asked us.

I might have told him that it was no good baiting the man. He had hidden depths. And sure enough, with one arm literally tied behind his back, he slowly lifted himself off the rug. Our brave preserver tried to turn the screws on his lock hold, but Neptune was too much for him. It was like trying to keep a judo hold on a grizzly bear.

A couple seconds later they had risen fully off the floor together. A few seconds after that, Neptune had backed up and smashed Hathaway into the one remaining wall portrait our brawl had not disarranged. (Better a congressman's nephew than a luscious blonde—that's what I always say.)

That did it for the judo hold. Hathaway crumpled to the floor, and Neptune became whole again.

He wanted no more of us. Rubbing his bent limb with a growl, he turned and bolted for the exit.

Half a second later, he was sprawled out on the carpet again, put down by the most elegant blow to the jaw you have ever seen. Enescu Fleet had delivered the punch. (George Foreman had nothing on him.) Appearing in the doorway at precisely the right moment, he had shot from the hip—a sort of upward, open-palm motion. It floored Neptune once and for all, and that, at long last, was that.

I stood up.

I helped up the female brawler in the room first, and then the other male, the infamous Hathaway.

"Thanks," he said. "And thank you, sir," he remarked, nodding toward Fleet. He faced me again, and I saw he was scanning my face, as though prompted with something rare and beautiful. Were there no limits to this man's flirting? "You really don't remember me, do you?" he asked, shaking his head.

"Should I?"

He shook his head again. He was a big head shaker, this one. "I might as well 'introduce' myself, I guess. Though I have to tell you, this seems kind of weird." He stuck out his hand. "Enescu Fleet."

I gaped. Enescu Fleet (my Enescu Fleet) also gaped. Even the dog gaped, in her way.

I found words before any of them. "You're—what?"

"Enescu," said the man. "It's Romanian."

"I know—I—" I shook my head. Now he had me doing it. "If you're Enescu Fleet, then who is he?" I pointed a shaky finger at the old man with the tweed jacket and powerful right uppercut. "And," I added, not content to stick with one question at a time, "who's John Hathaway?"

Enescu Fleet (the Younger) laughed. "Why, that's easy," he said. "You are."

30 — Who, What, When

I won't even attempt to set down the tangle of voices that followed these remarks. Of all the confused jumbles, this set a new standard. For a while, I don't know who held the lead, me or the older Fleet. We both spoke freely and rapidly, demanding qualifications in the free-for-all.

I think I won out in the end. For every question I asked, four more occurred to me. I asked these too, until all that could be heard was me asking and young Fleet attempting to reply. Add Pixie's yips into the mix, and it was no wonder that the first Fleet felt compelled to silence us all by applying a heavy fist to the metal adjoining door. It had been through a lot today, that door.

"If I could have everybody's attention, please," he said, and we all gave it to him. The large pumpkin-shaped dent he had put in the panel spoke for itself. "Thank you. Ladies and gentlemen, there is much to discuss here."

He paused, as Neptune pulled himself into a chair. "I have nothing to say," said the Penobscot, and Fleet nodded amiably. This was not a problem, the old man replied, for the driver had nothing he could tell us.

"You see, I know everything, my humongous henchman. I know why Jack sent you up here, and I know what you were looking for."

"You know nothing."

"We'll have to agree to disagree, then. You say I know nothing; I say I know everything. Perhaps the answer lies somewhere in between. On one point we will remain in absolute accord, I think. You're not going anywhere."

In order to nip in the bud any objections Neptune might have, Fleet removed a Glock from his belt and fingered this meaningfully.

The gun surprised me. I thought these gentleman detectives always quelled the opposition with nothing but a haughty stare and the undeniable facts of the investigation. I asked him about it later on, and he said simply, why shouldn't he carry a gun? Guns come in handy.

"Now then," he remarked, nodding toward the second Fleet, "we will hear from you."

"Delighted. What would you like to know?"

"What in God's name made you say you're Enescu Fleet?"

"Oh that." He touched a hand to his hair. This was a little on the long side, but well styled, despite the commotion of the last few minutes. "You mean you don't remember me either?"

"Of course I don't."

"You do know who *you* are?"

"Of course I do. I'm Enescu Fleet." There was a ring of defiance in his tone.

"No one said you weren't."

"We can't both be Enescu Fleet."

"Who says we can't?" asked Fleet #2. Up until now, he had been speaking in a generic American accent. He now switched over to a more mellifluous British inflection. "You don't mind if I shed the facade, do you? I've been trying to sound vaguely Midwestern—Ohio or someplace like that. Ohio's in the Midwest, isn't it? Anyway, I'm not sure how well it came off."

Fleet #1 didn't care how #2 spoke. As long as he got on with it, he muttered.

The youth took a deep breath. "You haven't talked to your cousins in a while, have you?"

"Of course I haven't. Who talks to their cousins?"

"Well, if you throw your mind back, you might remember one in particular. This cousin moved overseas thirty years ago, and with your financial assistance, opened a bookshop. That bookshop became a chain of bookshops, and that cousin became a bookshop tycoon. He later married a charming Scottish lass, and some years after that, having found themselves sadly unable to conceive a child of their own, they adopted an heir. Me."

The light of recognition was slowly illuminating the older man's bearded face. "You're Arthur's boy?"

"Yup."

"He wrote to me about you."

"He could do no better thing. I am a fascinating subject."

"It was decades ago. They had gotten in contact with some agency. They really named you Enescu?"

"In your honor, yes. It was Dad's way of paying you back for the bookshop loan."

"He could have just repaid me," grumbled Fleet. "So there really are two Enescu Fleets in the world?"

"The standard quota. If it helps any, up until recently, I had always detested the name. I prefer to go by E. F."

"F?"

"No—E. F., the initials. *E F.* Why would I go by 'F'?"

"That's the nickname people used to call me. If you say the *e* and *ef* together, it sounds like an *F*."

"Ah," said E. F., pausing. "Does it?"

Fleet declined to reply. His phone had just chirped with a text message. Looking up from this, he said, "Now that we know who you are, I think you might explain *why* you are. You can start with why we are only learning of your presence now."

"That's complicated."

"Simplify it."

"I had suspicions, you see."

"Suspicions of whom? Me?"

"Well, yes. As it happens, yes. I saw you hobnobbing with my suspects—"

"*Your* suspects?"

"And I didn't know if I could trust you. That's why we hid when you barged in here. This break-in, by the way—not very sporting. Not the British thing to do."

"I'm not British," retorted Fleet. "You are!"

"Right. Of course. Tough keeping track of who is from where this weekend. It wasn't the Romanian thing to do, then. And bringing the dog—I'm surprised the little hound didn't sniff me out. Something wrong with her sniffer, do you think?"

"Never mind Pixie's sniffer."

" 'Pixie'?"

"Never mind," said Fleet. "Why didn't you trust me? We're semi-family."

"I told you—it got complicated. We had never met, and I didn't know how corruptible you were. I knew you had been advising Hathaway and didn't know what to think."

"I was helping him."

"I see that now. You have to understand, I have been under no small amount of stress this weekend. I couldn't even leave the room. I had to send Lesley here out on my behalf."

We were making progress. The mystery blonde was named Lesley.

"And what brought you here to begin with?" asked Fleet.

"Ah that. Now we get to the nitty-gritty."

"Excellent. I want complete details," remarked his second cousin twice removed, or whatever he would be. "But not before Mr. Hathaway leaves us."

I was shocked. That is, I was once I realized he was talking about me. Shocked and annoyed. I knew these gentleman detectives liked to keep their Watsons in the dark, but this just seemed malicious.

"Why?"

"It's nothing personal. It's just that my daughter is all worked up. Something has gone awry with her game show again, and she's been sending up SOSs to me by the bucket load. I won't be able to pull myself away for some time, but you could go in my stead."

"But this man knows who I am!"

"And now so does everyone. You're John Hathaway. As I suspected from the beginning."

"But—?"

"As a favor to me, Johnny, please go. There is nobody else. Nobody else she trusts."

"She doesn't trust me. She hates me!"

"She's like that with everyone. Go. And don't forget, you need to get ready for your poker match in a couple hours."

I could see nothing more would be gained by arguing. Fleet had his methods, and I would have to lump them. It hardly seemed right, though. He got to learn about his name, but I would have to wait to learn about mine.

I paused at the door and looked back at the room, four sets of eyes urging me onward. (Five, if you counted Pixie's.)

"I need a new shirt," I told them. "This one is covered in hair dye." It was some slight comfort to me that the ruined garment had been borrowed from the man ejecting me.

Young Fleet came to my assistance. "You have a whole wardrobe full of them," he said. He opened the wooden doors and showed me. "Take your pick. I recommend one of these subtle checks. They didn't fit me very well, but they're sure to fit you. They're yours, after all. Oh, and here's your wallet. I was holding on to it for safekeeping."

I grabbed one of the subtle checks from him and slid it on.

He was right. It fit me perfectly.

31 — Roles Reverse

Ten minutes later, I connected up with the distressed daughter in Studio E. She cast one look at me and rolled her piercing black eyes up toward the stage lights.

"You?" she said, and I said, *Yes, me.* I was in no mood for her half-Spaniard haughtiness.

"What's going on?"

"Never mind what's going on. Where's Dad?"

"He's coming. He had to attend to something and said he'd be right down. He sent me in the meantime."

"Hah!"

"Enough with the *Hahs*. I ask you again, what's going on?"

"My career is coming apart at the seams, that's what."

She gestured around her. I noticed the studio was packed with the familiar band of rugged stagehands, poking switches and screwing in lights and so forth.

"I talked to my bosses at the network about our new host, and we're a go for the show. *Deadly Allusions.* These people are setting up for tomorrow."

"That's good."

"And we're all expecting the arrival of Alex Trebek in the morning."

"Fantastic."

"Is it? *Is it?*"

I didn't know. Wasn't it?

"It's not. Why? Because Alex Trebek isn't coming."

"You just said he was. Did he cancel?"

"He was never coming."

I shook my head and told her that I couldn't follow any of this.

"I can't follow any of this," I said. "The Trebek motif is especially baffling. Perhaps you'd better start at the beginning."

"I will. It's—you explain," she snarled, and I noticed Dean Driskill standing nearby. He looked like he had recently been mauled by a baby wolverine.

"Well…" he said.

Ate Fleet waved aside this unmanly dithering. "Tell him what you told me. About Trebek."

"Alex Trebek is to be our honorary host," said Director Dean, in a thin, weak voice.

I looked at Ate and then back to Dean. "So what happened to him?"

Dean sighed. "Not you too!"

"Not me too what?"

"You misunderstood too?"

"Misunderstood *what*?"

"What honorary means."

I thought about it. "I don't think so. What did I misunderstand about it?"

"That Alex Trebek isn't really coming. That's why he's honorary!"

I looked at Dean, then looked back at Ate.

"Oh yes," she said, "he's completely serious."

"Let me get this straight," I replied. "You think honorary means, what, fictional?"

"No, not fictional exactly."

"Honorific?" asked a passing stagehand.

"Maybe," said Dean. "What's honorific mean?" We told him, and he shook his head. "I'm thinking of a different word."

"Virtual?" I wondered.

"Closer."

"Figurative?"

"No."

"Nominal?"

Dean's face brightened. "Yes, that's it. This Trebek business is all nominal, like an honorary degree. When some celebrity gets an honorary degree from a college or university, he doesn't have to go to any classes, does he? It's all nominal. It's the same with an honorary host. Otherwise, you'd just call him a regular host, wouldn't you?"

I didn't know what to think now. Maybe I didn't know what honorary meant, after all.

"So, what you arranged with Trebek's people is what exactly?" asked Ate.

"I arranged for him to lend his name to the proceedings. In an honorary capacity."

"Don't say honorary! Never say honorary again! What good does his name do us?"

"It's like an associate producer credit. Associate producers don't do anything; they just lend their names."

"I'm an associate producer," said Ate coldly.

"Well, there you are. The Trebek name gives the show a certain, um—"

"Panache?" I inquired.

"Yeah, panache. What's panache mean?"

I tried to explain, but he said it didn't matter.

"The point is, people hear the name and say oh, Alex Trebek, he's cool; I guess I can give this show a chance. Then they watch, and they forget all about Trebek, because they're hooked. All you need is the 'Alex Trebek Presents' in the opening credits, and you're set. The name is all that matters. Once you have that, it's totally, uh—"

"Eponymous," said the stagehand, passing again, and Dean nodded and said yeah, eponymous. Then he paused and looked like he was going to ask what eponymous meant.

Ate Fleet was in no mood for any more definitions. "And this audience we're supposed to hook, we do this without a host?"

"No, we have a host. Me."

Ate looked at the stagehand, then at me, and then back to Dean. "You?"

"Of course. I know you have some reservations about me as host—"

"Not reservations. Abject horror. You don't know anything and have no personality."

"But I can do it. This is what I've always longed to do," said Dean. "Host."

His associate producer probably would have had more to say on the topic. I might have too—and I'm not sure the stagehand would have remained silent much longer. But on the cue "host," a pudgy hand prodded me in the back.

I turned to behold the repulsive form of Claude Croker. I really wished he would quit manhandling me.

"Hey, sister," he asked, "where's mama bear?"

"What?"

"Where's Fleet, Hathaway?" Claude said, and I realized that I *was* Hathaway.

"He's coming."

"Well, tell him to cinch up his support hose and get down here. The casino has finally advanced me credit. Oh hey, there he is."

Enescu Fleet had, indeed, arrived. Also the lovely Lesley, Sheriff Greene, several of the sheriff's deputies and Enescu Fleet (the second). The Fleets were in.

The sheriff was speaking in that understated, resonate tone of his. "And that's why we really need you to stay out of it until after the inquest, F. I've been hearing it from the council, as well as the governor, and it's probably best if you left this to the pros."

"I understand completely," said Fleet. "Would you have any objection to my performing one last act as an unofficial investigator?"

"What's that?"

"Solving the murder of Wilson Croker."

The sheriff perked up at the offer. His face didn't show it, but I could tell that on the inside he was totally perky. "You can do that?"

"With your indulgence."

The sheriff considered the proposition for perhaps one-tenth of a second. Then he replied, slowly and purposefully, "Okay."

"Cool beans. And would you mind helping me out with another request? Get everyone assembled in the Nightingale Room as soon as you can."

"Okay," agreed Sheriff Greene again, and went over to sample the ever-present buffet table.

Ate appeared at our side. "Dad."

He paid her no heed. Instead, he peered over at Claude Croker. "Claude, it appears that the match between you and Johnny will have to be postponed. I need the Nightingale Room for more official purposes."

"Dad—"

"You were all keyed up for it, Claude, I can see that—"

"DAD!"

Fleet gave his offspring her due attention. "You spoke, honey?"

"Did they tell you?"

"Did they tell me what?"

"My show airs in ten hours, and I have no host and a director who's about to have his head smashed in by a falling stage light, assuming I can figure out how to loosen the bolts. Everything's a mess."

Her father was nothing if not sympathetic. "Now what has become of that bold and independent young lady I know, the spitfire who told me she didn't need her old man gumming up the works at her place of business?"

"That independent young spitfire is dead."

"Not the tumbling stage light, I hope."

"Dad—"

Fleet placed a loving hand on her shoulder. "Even the strongest among us needs help every once in a while. I'm pleased to see that you can still admit that. How would it be if I readapted your show to serve both of our purposes?"

"How?"

"The Nightingale Room has admirable facilities for filming, yes? Excellent. Oh, Claude." Back to Claude Croker, who was still absorbing the snub of forty seconds ago: "Another change. We will hold our match, only I will be sitting in for Johnny."

"You play poker?"

"I do. Quite well, in fact. But it is not poker that I had in mind. We shall string along with your other suggestion and make it a trivia death match."

"I suggested that?" wondered Claude.

"Indeed you did. When you were describing what a cinch these trivia game shows are. This will be along those lines, except heads up. Mano a mano. Why? You don't wish to back out, do you?"

Claude Croker was struggling with emotion. He was a gambler, and gamblers never enjoy backing out. "No. No, it's fine. But why should Hathaway get a ringer and not me?"

"But of course. Who did you have in mind?"

"Um—" said Claude. He paused, gazing around at the crowd of faces. "Well—"

"I'll do it," said a reedy voice. We all turned to see Todd Parnell sitting in Dean's director's chair. I hadn't even seen him arrive.

"Mr. Parnell," Fleet smiled. "Ensconced among the crowd as usual. How fitting. You wish to compete against me?"

"Sure. Why not?" said Todd, grinning that insipid grin of his.

Fleet turned to his daughter. "Your thoughts?"

Ate Fleet was thinking. "I guess this could work. We could film tonight, and that would still give me time to show it to the network and see what they think."

"Whatever makes you happy."

"Okay, let's do it. Anything is better than Dean Driskill trying to be Wilson Croker."

"Will you have to check with him? Director Dean, I mean?"

"Oh, he will do what I say," she said, and buzzed off to make the arrangements.

I pulled Fleet aside. "Is this really the time for games?" I asked.

"It's always the time for games. Especially when they finger a murderer."

"As long as you know what you're doing. Speaking of which, where's Neptune?"

I was not amused when Fleet answered orbiting in eighth place around the sun.

"Don't worry. I left him upstairs."

"Without anyone guarding him?"

"He'll be fine. Pixie's there."

I stood speechless at the obvious pride in which he had imparted this statement and was still speechless when he said, "You understand you will have to do the searching while I stall. Much of this riddle has revealed itself, but not all. There is still one piece of the puzzle left to be found in the Nightingale Room."

I knew the heavy lifting would land on me. "I still don't know what I'm searching for."

"Something that's not supposed to be there. You'll know it when you find it," said Fleet, and with these words of wisdom, he made way for Dean Driskill, coming through.

Dean didn't seem to have any problem with the new format of the show. "I like it," he said. "It's Hollywood and Vegas and trivia grudge match all rolled into one. How would the questions go?"

"I was thinking that we would pose these to each other," said Fleet. "Riddles based on the first episode of *Deadly Allusions*. I assume you still have the questions?"

"Sure, but I don't know how long it will take to ask them. Probably not all that long. We could ask Tim for some more, I suppose."

"And who is Tim?"

"The riddle writer from Sprightly Sports Drinks. He consults on the show."

"Then by all means, bring us Tim."

"Okeydokey."

"Divide up the riddles, and Todd Parnell and I will each take half."

"Wouldn't it be easier if I read the questions?" Dean asked.

Fleet shook his head and explained that it would work better this way. More Hollywood, he said. More Vegas.

Dean nodded. He liked it. "Okay, we should be set up in a couple hours. By the way, do either of you know how to spell Trebek?"

"With a *k*," I said.

"That's what I thought. Thanks."

And on this note, he departed.

32 — The Riddle

I didn't see how any of this was going to catch us a murderer. Nor did I know when I would be privileged to learn how John Hathaway (if that was my real name) came to be mixed up in it all.

Despite this, I still found myself drawn in by the seductive lure of Parnell v. Fleet. There was a peculiar energy in the air as the two combatants took a seat at the main poker table in the infamous Nightingale Room. The inner sanctum, as Fleet liked to call it, had a kind of winter ski-lodge feel, not unlike the TV set where Wilson Croker's body had turned up. It had atmosphere. It also had heavy mahogany paneling, two hand-carved fireplaces and an actual crystal chandelier hanging down in the center of the room. Pretty nice.

It was a slow night for high rollers, so no one had to be shifted around very much. Those who did didn't really complain, and by the time the match had started, most of the poker players had stepped away from their games to watch.

Several of them appeared to be taking side bets, with Claude Croker joining in on the fun. I heard later on that he had actually made a bet *against* Parnell (who was favored to win four to one) in order to hedge his original bet with Fleet (on my behalf, at even money). It all went a bit beyond me, but the upshot was he couldn't lose, no matter who won. If Fleet proved victorious, then Claude, ironically, would clean up. He wasn't as stupid as he looked.

The Nightingale had a decent-sized gallery of seats, used for various televised poker matches, and it wasn't hard to squish in somewhere. Most people sat, but I tried to stay mobile, poking behind vases and picture frames. "Searching" the place. I also did my best to question Claude Croker about that flimsy alibi of his. He had chosen to remain on his feet as well, giving himself a ringside view of his investment(s).

"So you arrived here this afternoon?" I asked, lifting up a tray of hors d'oeuvres and peering under it.

"What of it?"

"I was just thinking."

"Well, knock it off."

"I was just thinking that if you had arrived earlier, much earlier—"

"Shut up, Hathaway."

I probably should have been more intimidated by Claude. A few short hours ago, his childhood bullying had been entirely theoretical for me. I was the honorary stand-in. Now that it turned out that I was that poor, oppressed youth, after all, I might have been expected to shy away from my tormentor. I really didn't. I don't know whether it was having no memory of him or the fact that he had since grown into a giant dough ball, but he had no effect on me.

I continued, undaunted:

"We both know you're lying, Croker. You didn't arrive this afternoon. In fact," I smiled, and I guess one might call it an epiphany, "that was all done for our benefit, wasn't it? That's why you were so intent on seeking me out. You needed someone who knew you, someone to say they saw you arriving. When you heard my name, you chose me."

Claude jerked his giant bullet head around. "I told you to shut up!"

"I remember."

"Well, are you gonna?"

"No."

Claude struggled to speak. Then, with an easy smile, which looked horrid, he took a seat. He was exhibiting way more restraint than I would have given him credit for.

He wasn't the only one to show hidden depths that night. Director Dean did *not* make an ass of himself, as Ate Fleet and I would have wagered he would (say, at twelve to one), and, honestly, he did a respectable job filling in for Wilson Croker. He attempted a rather foul British accent at the start, which I personally found over the top, but other than that, not too bad. He didn't embarrass himself.

It wasn't until he had made the introductions—"Alex Trebek Presents Trivia Death Match, a Dean Driskill Production"—that I realized that every person who could have any connection with Wilson Croker's death was present, including the Remarkable Ronald.

Jack Lockhart, no doubt wondering what had become of his henchman, came in late, at first refusing to remain and then reluctantly taking his seat beside the sheriff and his deputies.

We began.

The first twenty minutes are hard to describe. It really was like a murder-filled crossword puzzle come to life. Fleet and Parnell, as you would expect, had each memorized their portions of the *Deadly Allusions* episode, keeping the felt clean.

Back and forth they went, asking each other riddles:

A man with a dagger in his back walks into a bar. The suspects include three associates, each of whom share their name with a historical battle…

Three students dressed as villains from Shakespeare stand over the body of their professor, his head bashed in with an antique typewriter…

Four supermodels, named for famous lakes, discover a strangled corpse…

Host Dean sat between them in the dealer's chair, a plastic smile on his stubbly face. Occasionally, he would slip in some tidbit regarding the question they had answered, a little background on Shakespeare or geography or what have you. When he didn't have a tidbit, he tended to fall back on his painted grin and fake accent, which at times sounded almost Swedish.

Even with these miscues, it was all very informative. For about a quarter of an hour, we learned all about literature, art, music, baseball, food and obscure word origins. I finally got the scoop on the one about the three bottles of wine and the chessboard. It turned out to be very clever, although I noticed Fleet changed the crossbow to a rifle.

At first, I chalked this up to respect for our dear departed host, but the real reason soon became apparent. Fleet and Parnell had been freestyling up until then, tossing out tidbits and facts and basically jamming on the trivia like an intellectual jazz duo.

Then it came to Fleet to recite a new riddle—only this one, I knew, hadn't come off any episode sheet.

"A man with a crossbow bolt in his chest," he said, pausing for significance, "staggers into a cabin. With his last ounce of strength, he mutters, 'The answer lies with Keats,' and expires, never to speak again."

With the same cheesy grin, Dean Driskill rotated to his left, encouraging the riddle along with a wordless gesture. He must have suspected something was amiss with this particular clue, however, for his eyes betrayed a childlike confusion. "What do you think of that one, Todd? It's a doozy, isn't it?"

"It's impossible!"

After a long pause, too long really, Dean rotated back. "He says it's impossible, Enescu."

Todd Parnell struck the table with a tattooed fist. "It can't be solved! There are no suspects, no context, no details at all! It's impossible!"

"It does seem kind of impossible, Enescu," agreed Dean, rotating to Fleet, then Parnell, and then back to Fleet.

"That's only because it is," said the detective, sending a whisper through the audience. "Or so it has probably seemed to Wilson Croker's murderer at any rate," he added.

Dean blinked at him. He didn't know which way to rotate.

The world's most fascinating man stood up.

"Perhaps I'd better explain," he said.

33 — Why

"Please indulge me while I give you a few details," he began, speaking to the audience. "The murder of Wilson Croker is a complicated puzzle and, as such, its solution cannot be blurted out. It requires a little setup first. Let us begin with the suspects."

He peered into the seats, sighting the Remarkable Ronald sitting several rows back.

"First of all, there is Ronnie Becker. He might easily have killed Wilson Croker. He would have done almost anything to protect his position at the casino, a position that was growing more and more tiresome in the eyes of the powers that be. Was Croker in danger of learning Ronnie's secret, that the latter was nothing more than a con man and a fraud? Or had Croker known about Ronnie's background all along, and was using this as a wedge against him?"

These all seemed like pretty rhetorical questions, so none of us answered.

"Perhaps it was ambition that drove the murderer to kill," Fleet went on, sweeping back around and facing his host.

Dean hastily reassembled his cheesy smile. "Who, me?" He was probably still asking himself what this had to do with *Deadly Allusions* and the four supermodels named for Great Lakes.

"Of course you. Dean, the once-oppressed toady. Dean, the also-ran who now runs the show. Dean, the man who would be host."

I've always wondered why private detectives do this: list their suspects out one by one, drawing out their secrets and emotionally pantsing them before their peers. Seems to me, if you know who did it, just say it.

"Let's not forget the nephew, Claude Croker," Fleet continued, and here was a suspect I could get my head around. "Wilson Croker's sole heir. Men with far more scruples than you, Claude, have committed murder for far less."

Claude was sitting directly in front of me, and I saw him bridle. It took him a second or two to work out Fleet's insult. "Hey!"

"You, more than anyone else here, benefited from your uncle's death."

Claude worked out this implication even faster. "But I wasn't even in town at the time!"

"Weren't you?"

"I arrived today, hours after the body was discovered. You two saw me!"

"Did we? Or did we see what you wanted us to see? Had you actually been here for days? I ask because you let slip a curious detail when we met. You mentioned Ron's act and implied that you had witnessed a mistake during his mind-reading session. But how could this be? The casino had pulled that portion of his act two days ago. You couldn't have seen it yourself, only arriving this afternoon."

"Somebody told me about it. Said it was a big rip-off."

"Did they? You have a remarkable empathy, then. The outrage you exhibited seemed very personal. You must feel things very deeply for your fellow man and the price they pay for entertainment."

Claude puzzled over this one longer than before. "Um, yeah."

"It's no matter," said Fleet. "If you did come here to see your uncle before his death, then you would have been caught on camera. They're everywhere, you know."

Claude bounded up. He burbled something about not having to sit here and listen to this, only to find himself jammed back in his seat by the grip of justice. This grip of justice was mine.

"Sit down and shut up," I said.

"Okay, okay. Dammit, Hathaway, not so rough. Okay, maybe I was here earlier. I came here a week ago to ask my uncle for money. I'm staying at a cheap motel in town. It's all I could afford. Look, I didn't kill him—you gotta believe me. Yeah, I need money. And yeah, he laughed in my face when I asked, but I didn't kill him. I was working on him, trying to soften him up." He rubbed his backside. "Jeez, Hathaway. I think you made me bruise my coccyx."

I missed the next few seconds, trying to blot from my mind the mental image of Claude Croker's coccyx. When I came to again, Fleet was standing over Jack Lockhart, beaming down at him with that twinkling stare I knew so well.

"And then there is the business partner, my old friend Jack."

His old friend sat with his arms folded, glaring up at him from beneath a rich man's brow. "And what motive am I supposed to have?"

"Nothing too grand on the surface. You have plenty of money of your own. Then again, there is the matter of your alibi. It doesn't hold up. And there's the will."

"There is no will."

"Oh, but there is. I have it right here," said the suddenly very unpopular detective, producing the item from beneath the buttery folds of his tweed jacket. "Your man Neptune was kind enough to provide it for me. You really should have hung on to it yourself. I'm surprised you didn't shred it."

The sheriff snatched it from his grasp. Together with his deputies, he pored over the packet.

"Looks genuine," announced Greene.

"It is. It was drawn up years ago in England, which is why nobody knew of its existence. Nobody but you, Jack. You're the primary beneficiary."

There was a short hubbub here, during which Lockhart muttered something about holding on to the document, should Wilson's murder ever get resolved. He was practical to a fault, that Lockhart.

"I understand Croker had no real family," said Fleet. "Sure, there was the nephew Claude. But his uncle had no intention of leaving him anything. Wilson Croker was a man of business, and the finest mind in business he knew, next to himself, was you, Jack. You and you alone could do something worthwhile with his legacy. That's why he left you his money."

"I didn't want his money!"

"No, which is why you sought to disassociate yourself from it the best you could. But it didn't work. He was probably always getting you into trouble that way when you were young. You grew up in England together, didn't you? Somewhere near the town of Bingham?"

"How'd you know that?"

"You both have a porcelain souvenir from that remote hamlet. Yours is a yak. Croker's was a white elephant. More on that elephant later. Speaking of hamlets, that was another of your missteps. As much as you tried to put up a smoke screen after the murder—distance yourself from Croker and any motive you might have had to kill him—you slipped up again. You mentioned his Hamlet."

"So?"

"Wilson Croker hadn't performed Hamlet since his early youth—in England."

"Okay, so we grew up together. So what? That doesn't mean I killed him."

"No, but that's how the killer wanted it to appear. And you knew it. Already you felt you were being framed. I wonder what made you think that? It couldn't only be the phony phone call you received, luring you away from the casino. It must have been something else. Perhaps you received another phone call, leading you to the body?"

"You can't—"

"Prove it? No. No, I can't. But you weren't in the audience. Where were you? Don't answer that. The point is, you were being set up to take the fall. You had to act. You began by suppressing the will. That wasn't difficult. You knew Croker had it; he had probably even given you the combination to his safe. It was an easy matter to send Neptune in to find it among his effects. Once you had the will, *poof!* went your main motive for killing him. But there were problems. Trifles. One was a minor provision in the will, a charitable contribution of some Sprightly stock. You had come to terms with turning over Wilson's wealth to the loathsome Claude, but you couldn't abide the orphanage losing its money. That's your real problem, Jack; you're an old softy. You knew Claude would never give anything to charity, and even if he would entertain the suggestion, you had no way of communicating his uncle's exact desires without bringing suspicion on yourself. So you forged Wilson Croker's signature to some Sprightly stock certificates and had Neptune deliver these to the orphanage before their offices opened. You probably thought people would assume Croker had made a contribution the evening before his murder. Who'd question a bunch of orphans? And this may well have been the assumption too, had Croker's actual time of death not been the previous day. It was a nice thought, but one that nearly undid you."

"Then you believe I'm innocent?"

"Of course you're innocent. I also think you were hornswoggled. I highly doubt Croker ever intended to leave that stock to the kids. It was almost certainly a ploy to gain favor with the Tribal Council. He would have revoked the provision the minute they gave him his council seat."

"You know, I bet you're right. I'll be a son of a—"

"Yes, and don't interrupt. I said *trifles*, plural, and the second one was the courier Hathaway. It's ironic, isn't it, how parcels kept giving you so much trouble. First a parcel of stock, and now a mystery package from George Hathaway. No doubt you kept asking yourself, who is this man John? He claimed to have a parcel for you, but where was it? He was acting awfully suspicious. Then you heard that John Hathaway—a fake John Hathaway, but you were not to know that—had a package for Croker as well, or so he told Ronald. What was this? Had he had a second will made? Was Hathaway bringing him a copy? Were you still named in it? You had to know, and that's why you sent Neptune to Hathaway's room, to find out once and for all what the courier had brought. The answer is simple. Nothing."

I must have been gaping, because I had to close my mouth and moisten my lips before I could speak. "What did he...I mean, what am I...why am I here?" I asked.

"A very fine question," Fleet replied. "We all assumed that a courier must be couriering something, but this is not so. You are here for another outstandingly simple reason, John. You are on vacation."

"I am?"

"It probably doesn't seem like it, but you are. When Croker collared you and spoke his cryptic last words, you had already been drawn into an affair that you had nothing to do with. You were just in the wrong place at the right time."

He paused and took a lap around the poker table.

"Let us consider those words. *The answer lies with Keats*. These were spoken to you, Johnny, in a cabin two days ago. What do they mean?"

He asked the audience, "Did Hathaway kill him? God knows. Hathaway certainly doesn't. He can't remember."

I didn't like the way this was going. Everyone was staring at me now.

"With Hathaway's memory loss, we come to the true motive for the crimes committed this weekend." He reached into his pocket again and withdrew the test tube I had seen him with earlier.

"I won't bore you with the scientific name of the drug present in this coffee. Instead, I will refer to it by the code name Wilson Croker gave it. *Sophia*. You are looking at the most sophisticated memory-assistance drug ever devised."

"More potent than ginseng?" asked Claude Croker.

"More potent than ginseng," Fleet agreed. "Its exact ingredients are difficult to know without the precise formula, but thanks to the analytical efforts of my friend Judith"—he nodded up the aisle to his lady friend from the Sprightly science lab—"we know that *Sophia* affects a person's memory in one of two distinct ways, depending on how it is administered. It can enhance that individual's mind and memory immeasurably, or it can wipe it clean of all personal experience."

"How can it do both?" I asked, fully cognizant that I fell into Group B.

"Perhaps you would care to explain, Judy?"

The brothel madam took the floor. "Glad to assist, F. It's very simple, folks. From what I can tell, analyzing it in the lab, this *Sophia* unlocks a larger portion of our brainpower by inhibiting the preconceived notions the mind has about its own potential. In other words, it allows the mind to forget its own limitations. Once this potential is unlocked, it pushes everything else to the side—past memories, concerns, foibles—all forgotten. The user can then absorb enormous amounts of knowledge and information without any obstacles. Under the influence of *Sophia*, a person could theoretically learn twenty times more, twenty times faster than someone not on *Sophia*. They wouldn't only learn it; they would process it better. It's the ultimate mind steroid."

"You got all that from analyzing it?" asked Claude. It was a pretty good question.

"Not entirely," admitted Dr. Judy. "About two years ago, I came in on Croker screwing around in the Sprightly lab after hours. He told me about a theoretical drug 'a friend' of his had given him to study. Though he didn't say it then, it had to be *Sophia*. He was so thrilled with the results that he told me a little about it, without specifying details. Then he seemed to realize that he had said too much and clammed up."

"Sounds like a wonder drug," Claude remarked.

"The flip side is the memory loss. Properly administered, the user does not really forget his earlier knowledge. The drug simply suppresses the memories that get in the way. I'm no psychologist, but in a funny way it also suppresses ego. Our egos tell us what we are, what we can accomplish, and so on. *Sophia* has its own ego. If it's done right, it takes charge and everything is jake. If it's done wrong, then the memories aren't refiled properly. Knowledge stays put, but personal experience goes by the wayside. That's how *Sophia* can wipe out memory."

"Like an overdose?" I asked.

"Nothing like an overdose," said Judy. "The drug acts completely differently, depending on whether it's being used to enhance or block memory. No matter how it is administered, general knowledge remains unaffected because it's pure, not tied up with emotion or ego. *Sophia* leaves that stuff alone. It's the person's individuality that gets jerked around. The dosage determines how that individuality is filed away."

"And if it is misfiled, then that person is screwed?" I said. "They can't get themselves back again?"

"Nah, they're fine. We never really forget anything. As long as the brain isn't damaged, you can always get everything back."

"Does the *Sophia* wear off on its own?

"Hard to say. Much better to take the antidote."

"Which is?"

"More *Sophia*. Lots more, from what I can tell."

My head hurt. Fleet thanked Judith for her assistance and continued his narrative.

"As you will have gathered, the potential for such a drug is enormous. That was what made it so valuable to Wilson Croker. And so dangerous."

"Uncle Wilson got himself killed over it?" asked Claude.

"In a way, yes. And he wasn't the only one. Originally, there were four. Four men hoping to make a fortune on *Sophia*. There was Wilson

Croker. He had capital and access to the Sprightly Sports lab. Next there was Ronnie Becker."

The audience gasped—yes, gasped—as the hapless Ron's complicity was revealed. He stammered some objection, but Fleet rolled over him.

"Ron brought his shady connections to the party. He may have brought in the third man, Trevor. I don't know. Trevor, some of you may remember, jumped to his death a few months ago. Up until then, he had supplied certain ingredients the Sprightly labs did not have on hand. He also called himself a courier, but he was in essence nothing more than a drug mule."

"Is that why he jumped?" asked Ate. "Was he whacked-out on his own product?"

"The *Sophia* drove him to his death, yes. But he did not kill himself. He was murdered."

Another gasp. Dean Driskill couldn't have asked for a better venue for his first television production. I just hoped they wouldn't have to cut it up too much for commercials.

"The day Trevor allegedly jumped, a very special lady in his life, the lady who would discover his body, swore that he was not himself. While those contemplating suicide often act as such, this struck me as significant. It occurred to me that Trevor may have been doped up on his own *Sophia*. And if he was doped, then someone must have doped him. That person was the murderer."

Here, the sheriff inserted his two cents. As the investigating officer at the time, he didn't take kindly to Fleet's interpretation. "We didn't discover any narcotics in the man's system."

"*Sophia* isn't so easy to identify. Unless you're already looking for it."

"Why couldn't he simply have been depressed?"

"There's a very simple explanation why not, Sheriff. The busted lock."

"I don't follow."

"The lock to the roof was broken. Trevor busted it to get access. You agree?"

"Yeah. So?"

"So? He had no need to bust it. He had a key. It was given to him by his lady friend."

Pause for gasp.

"Nadine told me this right off. Probably you too, Sheriff. 'He didn't need to do that,' she had said, referring to busting the lock. He didn't need to do it because he had the key! Once I realized what she meant, I went back and confirmed it with her. Trevor had the key alright."

"I didn't know that!"

"Nor did Trevor. But he should have known it. I suspect if you check through his personal effects, you will discover it right there on his key chain. He didn't know it was there because he had no memory of it, or anything else."

The sheriff shook his head. "There *was* a key on him we couldn't identify. It never occurred to us that it could go to the broken lock. But why didn't Nadine tell us this at the time?!"

"I can't speak for the lady, of course, but I would guess that her answer would be that nobody asked her."

Sheriff Greene muttered something under his breath.

"Don't be too hard on her, Sheriff. She didn't intend to deceive."

Greene grumbled something in reply. A man of great sympathy, he was not. "I suppose you know the killer's identity?"

"I do. So did Wilson Croker. It was Trevor's murder that originally prompted him to call in a private detective. He wanted the whole business thoroughly and discreetly investigated."

"Who'd he bring in? You?"

"That was his intention, yes. But a funny thing happened on the way to the private detective consultation."

Sheriff Greene had no patience for crosstalk. He had a wonderfully one track mind. "Just tell us who killed the boy! The fourth man in the *Sophia* conspiracy? You still haven't identified him."

"No, the murderer wasn't the fourth man. Not this murder, anyway. Trevor's killer was someone else. He might not have meant to murder Trevor. He probably only intended to wipe his memory, maybe scare him by luring him up on the roof. But things got out of hand, and Trevor fell."

"Who!" said the sheriff. "Who killed Trevor?"

"I would have thought it obvious by now," answered Fleet. "Wilson Croker himself."

34 — How

Once the voices had died down, Fleet continued:

"Keep in mind that some of what I am about to tell you is speculation. But it is also first-rate speculation, supported by the deductive powers of not one, but two first-rate private detectives. I think you will agree, once I have finished, that it is perfectly accurate."

I had no idea who the second first-rate private detective was. I only knew that it couldn't be me. I felt this for two reasons. (A) What little experience I had acting as Fleet's unofficial assistant hardly qualified me for that description. And (B) I hadn't deduced a thing. I sat back, agog to learn more.

"If it had not been for the march of certain events," said Fleet, "we never would have suspected murder in Trevor's death, and certainly we never would have dreamt of Croker himself as the killer. But a tangled knot has a way of straightening itself out if you let it lie. The same holds true for guilty parties. Croker's own actions tied that knot around his neck, in more ways than one.

"Let's pick up the story after Trevor's apparent suicide. Wilson Croker has committed murder. He's covered it up, but how well has he covered it? That's what he needs to know. By chance, he learns that his producer, Ate, has a celebrated father, a celebrated father who is not only a famous detective, but also a detective who has distinguished himself on game shows. Discreetly he makes inquiries about bringing me to Wolf Valley. Ostensibly this is to feature me on *Deadly*

Allusions, but in truth he wishes to consult with me on the death of Trevor. I'll explain why in a moment. *Allusions* is the perfect way to get me here, and he begins to form his plans for me once I arrive. There is only one problem. Ate.

"My daughter, you understand, loves her family, but in small doses—and never at the workplace. She wants nothing to do with me on the show and tells Croker so. She's heard that he's been trying to get in communication with me, and she asks him to get someone else. Wilson Croker is not to be dissuaded, however. He continues to put out feelers on his own. He's fixated on me and will accept no imitations. Ironically, that's just what he did get."

Here Enescu Fleet the Older paused to introduce Fleet the Younger. E. F. took a couple bows, two more than he needed in my opinion, and sat back down again. "My cousin's son," said the elder Fleet. "Clever fellow that he is, he saw a way to capitalize on the name Enescu Fleet after I retired. He became a detective and has already made a real name for himself in England. Made a name with my name, I should say. Wilson Croker wasn't aware of any of this. Like most people, he thought the world had called it a day after one Enescu Fleet. When he put out his feelers, he had no idea that he would be getting this young man.

"Ultimately Croker decides to engage young Fleet in my stead. The Enescu Fleet concept is similar to the family gerbil in that way. One is very much like another. Not being a trivia savant like myself, Fleet #2 needs a cover. Croker insists on this. Under no circumstances can the real reason he is here be known—that should have been the first indication that everything was not on the up and up. Unheeding, my cousin's son falls in with his employer's suggestion. He goes undercover. And so enters John Hathaway.

"John Hathaway, I should explain, is an old school friend of young Fleet's. The two had met up recently at a class reunion, where Hathaway let slip that his Uncle George, the congressman, knew Jack Lockhart. Johnny, in fact, has a standing invitation to visit the casino as Jack's guest any time he wishes.

"Remembering this conversation, the ingenious young Fleet has found his alias. He will become John Hathaway. Jack didn't know George's nephew by sight, and Ate Fleet had never met her cousin. In fact, much like her father, I suspect she didn't even know he existed. Everything seems perfect. And once again, it isn't.

"The real John Hathaway suddenly arrives at the casino, joined by his lovely girlfriend, Lesley. No doubt Johnny's conversation with his old school friend the month before has given him an itch to gamble. Whatever the reason, he is here, and things are about to get sticky.

"E. F., meanwhile, under his borrowed Hathaway alias, has been investigating the death of Trevor. He is making headway. As a matter of fact, he has begun to suspect that his employer is not as virtuous in the affair as one might have thought. He learns about the *Sophia* and the secret foursome behind it, and eventually confronts his employer with the certain knowledge that he, Wilson Croker, killed Trevor himself.

"Much to his surprise, Croker agrees with him. The confrontation takes place in the early a.m. at young Fleet's cabin on the casino grounds, and Croker is only too happy to admit his guilt. Trevor had shown himself to be difficult, he explains, and had to be eliminated. Croker had already double-crossed all three of his partners in the *Sophia* drug deal—Croker's personal drug was greed—but it was only Trevor who threatened to go to the police and expose the conspiracy.

"Hearing this, Fleet doesn't know whether to be happy or confused. Typically, suspects don't delight in their own defeat. Croker's sanguinity is soon justified. From within a small satchel he withdraws a crossbow—a prop from the show, but quite functional. Young Fleet backs away, and Wilson Croker laughs. He's not going to kill him, unless forced to do so. He simply requests that his detective drink a portion of coffee, coffee that Croker now takes the liberty of lacing generously with *Sophia*. He has brought this with him inside a small ceramic elephant—one of his many hiding places for his stash.

"This was Croker's plan all along, the ultimate do-over. Thanks to Fleet's thorough investigation, he has gained knowledge. He now knows what he must do to cover up Trevor's murder, and with the detective's mind erased, there will be nobody left to fill in the blanks.

"This is where my namesake singularly distinguishes himself, proving himself worthy of his adopted label. Grabbing the porcelain elephant, he chucks this at Wilson Croker's head and bounds from the room. The elephant does not break, and it is while Croker is retrieving it that I think another man must have joined him. None other than his other partner. The fourth man. He has been eavesdropping, having followed Croker to the rendezvous.

"It is not Wilson Croker's day. He lunges for the crossbow, but his nemesis gets the better of him. This time it is Wilson Croker at the disadvantage. The fourth man makes his demands. He wants the formula to *Sophia*. With it, he can make his fortune alone, just as Croker had proposed to do. Croker knows he must comply. But then, suddenly, he sees a way out. If only temporarily. He reaches for the coffee. With a sneer he utters the puzzling phrase, *'The answer lies with Keats,'* as a clue to his later self, and he drinks.

"It doesn't take his partner long to figure out what has happened. He knows the effects of *Sophia* as well as anybody. Croker has outsmarted him. The only man who knows where the formula is hidden now knows nothing. The fourth man slaps him, bullies him, but to no avail. He even repeats the clue to him, but this also hangs in the air, unanswered. As Croker had hoped before taking the fateful sip, his partner cannot harm him as long as the formula remains hidden. They are at a stalemate.

"Now, for what transpired next. I personally do not think the fourth man meant to kill Croker. He was too valuable to him alive. And I am quite certain he did not figure out the Keats. I think, in the most appropriate service of justice, Wilson Croker brought about his own demise. Remember, *he* doesn't know that his life is safe with his assailant. All he knows is someone is menacing him with a crossbow, and he doesn't know why.

"The fourth man must have ordered him out into the woods, the only logical place for the shooting to have taken place, judging from the lack of blood in the cabin. They go, and suddenly Croker panics. He tries to escape, the two men tussle, and the crossbow goes off. Croker is hit. He probably got away from his killer momentarily, staggering back to the one place he knew. The cabin.

"Re-enter John Hathaway, the real Hathaway—his girlfriend Lesley faithfully at his side. You will recall that, when last seen, Hathaway was arriving at the casino. At some point during his visit, he has also learned about the false Hathaway.

"Johnny is astounded. Whether he suspects his old friend E. F. or not is difficult to say. He only knows that someone is up to something. He finds out where the counterfeit Hathaway is staying. This probably wasn't too hard. After all, he really *is* John Hathaway. He arrives at the impostor's cabin. He knocks, and when no one answers, he enters. He looks around. There's a fresh pot of coffee on the counter. He reaches for it. He drinks. Lesley, meanwhile, is tired—annoyed. She takes her coffee outside, to the gazebo. She's from England, and she likes the cold.

"And so, there we have it. Hathaway now knows nothing. His memory is erased. The drug makes him drowsy, and he lies down on the sofa and kicks off his shoes. He sleeps. Lesley, out in the gazebo, also knows nothing. Having passed out momentarily from the effects of the *Sophia*, she awakens to see a cabin. She knocks. *Can you help me, kind sir?* she asks. *Eh?* says Hathaway, scratching himself. *Who am I?* she asks. *I don't know, who am I?* retorts Hathaway.

"Lesley goes. Hathaway chases after her. Croker staggers in while Hathaway is outside, and when Hathaway comes back, they meet. Croker tells him the last thing he knew on earth—that *the answer lies with Keats*. Croker croaks, and Hathaway goes back out into the living room, giving the murderer ample time to climb in through the bedroom window, collect the body and stow it in the canoe under the window for safekeeping. Out on the sofa, Hathaway sits, he thinks, and then the most wonderful thing happens. He meets me. Ate, changeable just like her mother, has invited me to the show after all, bringing the total up to two Enescu Fleets and two John Hathaways."

Have you ever seen an audience staring straight ahead, mouths hanging open and eyes swirling ever so slightly in their sockets? Well, that's how we all looked then.

I figured I was best equipped for the reply. I coughed and said, "Then who killed Wilson Croker?"

"You mean, who is the Fourth Man?" asked Fleet. He smiled. "I have arranged a little experiment on that." He ambled across the multicolored carpet and borrowed a walkie-talkie from one of the security guards in attendance. "Yes, hello, video booth—who's this?"

"Sss. Gaburf," responded the walkie-talkie.

"Marvin. Pleased to speak with you, Marvin. Do you have the footage I asked for?"

"Sss. Gaboogle."

"Excellent. Put it up on the big TV."

"Sss. Dingle," agreed the walkie-talkie.

Fleet stood beneath a plasma monitor. Some footage came up.

"I took the liberty of arranging a short montage for our viewing pleasure," he explained. "The video team has assembled a closeup of everyone's face when I spoke the Keats clue. With the number of cameras in this room, it wasn't hard to capture everyone's expression at the exact moment. Remember, other than Hathaway and myself, only the murderer knew Wilson Croker's last words, and it is my belief that the killer has given himself away tonight. Let's watch."

Of course, they had to start with me. Even with Fleet's preface, I still felt myself shifting uncomfortably in my seat as the montage played. The camera drifted up and down on the still shot of my mug. Ken Burns couldn't have done it better. Finally, they moved on to Claude Croker. Nothing special there. Just a fatheaded face gazing out at the table.

Next was Jack Lockhart. Nothing. Stolid, unmoved. The perfect poker face.

Then Dean Driskill. Very stubbly. I had been looking at his face when Fleet stated his Keats clue. It didn't repay inspection.

After Dean was Ronald. The skinny beard didn't look any better on the big screen.

I was beginning to think that Fleet's clever scheme had come a cropper.

Then we got to the last face. A goofy face, crowned in frizzy hair and made all the more ridiculous with its goggle-like glasses. As with every other depiction, we heard Fleet's voice state the riddle in the background. Then the camera froze. But unlike every other depiction, this face changed. The eyes looked shifty behind the goggles. The lips had parted and twisted into a slight frown at the side. Tiny beads of perspiration had appeared on the brow in HD quality. He had reacted.

"Oh, that one's obvious," said Claude Croker.

"No doubt about it," said Jack Lockhart.

"Perfect match," remarked Sheriff Greene.

The face that had stirred belonged to Todd Parnell.

35 — The Fourth Man

"It was an unexpected treat," said Fleet, "your taking Claude's place tonight. It has allowed me to study your reactions at very close quarters. Tell me, Mr. Croker"—he turned Claude's way—"has Mr. Parnell asked you anything about your uncle's estate since you two met this weekend?"

Claude sat up in his seat. "Um, yeah. I mean, yeah. He did."

"Perhaps something about his papers, papers that would pass to you as his only heir?"

"That's exactly right," said Claude. "He said they had been working on something together, and there were some documents, documents that wouldn't mean anything to anyone else, but might otherwise get lost in the shuffle."

"Documents pertaining to *Sophia*, no doubt," said Fleet, resting his gaze back on Parnell. "I seriously doubt there are any such papers. Wilson was too careful for that. He's hidden them, and only he and the poet know where." Another smile. "I see you still don't appreciate the meaning of your victim's last words, Todd. It's no matter. When it comes down to it, nor do I."

Todd Parnell responded with a chilling, high-pitched laugh. It startled me.

"Do you really think any of this would stand up in court?" he asked. "Hearsay, startled looks?"

"Don't forget the limp."

"What?"

"Last night, someone broke into our cabin and fought with Hathaway. The assailant must have been looking for something *Sophia* related. It was as good a place to look as any. During his escape, the assailant injured his ankle. I've noticed that you've been very careful not to do any heavy walking in our presence. Since that evening, I have never actually seen you arrive in a room. You are always here first. And you never move. I even tried to get you to show some activity by faking a broken buzzer in the studio. You were heated up about it, but still you didn't move. It was odd. Leg playing you up?"

Parnell sniffed. "You have nothing, and you know it."

"You are correct. We have very little. And I will admit, since my retirement, I have become more laid-back. In my youth, I would have collected every detail to present to the police. Now, I will gladly leave the detail work to them. The assembly of tiny clues, the search for chance witnesses, let them at it, I say. I'm sure they will unearth something, now that they have a good starting point. As a celebrated peer of mine was fond of saying, the police are good at that sort of thing."

Parnell did not reply.

"In fact, they can begin with your only living partner. Oh, Mr. Becker."

Ronald Becker had already left his seat. He had made it all the way across the dimly lit room to the door. Fleet's voice arrested him mid-step.

"There's no point in running, Ron. The police are good at tracking petty fugitives too. You confirm that Todd Parnell was the fourth man in the *Sophia* conspiracy, in which you also took part?"

It was Ronald's turn not to reply.

"You don't have to speak, of course. But I will say this to you, beneath your ridiculous exterior, I believe you have a conscience, a conscience that has already begun to rebel against the nefarious deeds surrounding *Sophia*. Know this. Not only did Todd kill Wilson Croker, albeit accidentally, he also murdered in cold blood one of the actors from the show. I refer to poor Nick, whose only crime was agreeing to pose as Wilson to win a bet. That was your explanation, was it not, Todd? A little bet? A bet to fool the great detective Fleet?"

The great detective Fleet, receiving no answer, turned back to the room.

"You see, with Croker dead, Todd found himself in a quandary. He needed time, time enough to think, time to figure out where the dead man had hidden his secret formula. No doubt he had already formulated an idea of his own regarding one of the actors from the game show. He had noticed that the man had a build like Croker, and he was a performer. He could imitate his employer's traits easily. It's a pity he couldn't mimic a good education. As I told the sheriff, it was because of this that I saw through the deception. I don't know if you really thought the police would be fooled by our witness accounts of the false Croker, Todd. You probably thought there was a chance, but whether they were or not, that was all gravy. You bought yourself time. Once your recruit had played his part, he became a liability, and you saw to that. With another accomplice lured away and killed, there was one last item to be done, an item you couldn't do alone—move Croker's body. No easy task that. You had to have help, someone to help carry, someone to make sure you went unobserved. You were the help, Ron."

The illusionist bridled. "I never was!"

"I didn't say you did it consciously. I noticed the morning after you fell prey to my hypnotism, you appeared exhausted. This was strange. Hathaway had also fallen under my spell, but he awoke feeling fresh and revived. Why should you experience the opposite effect? The answer—you had labored. It was cruel of me to leave you in that state, I see that now. Nonetheless, I never would have dreamt that anyone else would use it to their advantage. But someone did. Todd did. Discovering you in your trance, he only had to throw out his own suggestion, that you help him with a little heavy lifting, and you complied. You returned to your dressing room an hour later, none the wiser that you had just helped shift a corpse."

I was astonished. Poor old Ron. Had everyone hypnotized the hypnotist?

The Remarkable seemed to be appreciating this as well. "You bastard!"

Parnell growled, "Shut up, Becker. He's playing you. Just shut up!"

Ron repeated his observation on Todd Parnell's heredity. He swung around to the rest of the room. "Everything Fleet said is right on. Parnell was the so-called fourth man. He's the one who tested the drug. On himself. Your game-show champion was juiced."

"I suspected something of the sort," said Fleet, shaking his head dolefully. I thought he could have shown a bit more sensitivity. Not everyone can come about their knowledge of trivia the old-fashioned way: studying it on a desert island.

Todd Parnell was up on his feet, wobbling. Ronald Becker came at him.

"You knew how I felt about Trev's death, about killing! For you to use me that way—"

"I didn't!" Parnell snapped. "You think I'm stupid? I never went near your dressing room. I didn't need any help with the body! He played you, dummy, so you'd admit my involvement."

"Uh?"

"He knew I couldn't deny it without implicating myself, and you couldn't know he was lying without anyone else to confirm I wasn't there!"

Ron said oh. "Well—uh."

Parnell no longer had anything to say to the Remarkable Ronald. "Well played," he said to Fleet. "It's too bad you won't get the *Sophia* now."

He was staring at me when he said this. And that hideous laugh accompanied the stare. It gave me the willies.

Fleet nodded. "Yes, the clue. I had rather hoped that between your drugged-up intellect and my natural genius, one of us would have spotted the solution. But no."

He followed Parnell's stare to me, and I saw a look on the old man's face that I hadn't seen too often. It was a kind, sympathetic look, completely devoid of its characteristic twinkle. The flippancy was also absent, replaced by a sort of soulful wisdom.

I had made Enescu Fleet sad.

36 — All Together Now

I felt a warmth at my side. Peering to my left, I found myself gazing into the sparkling green eyes of the woman Lesley. She took my hand. I couldn't believe this lovely creature was my girlfriend. And I couldn't remember it!

"Pardon me," said a voice.

It was young E. F. He had insinuated himself into our little gathering with what I would have guessed was a pretty characteristic aplomb.

"First of all," he remarked, addressing himself to Fleet, "bravo on the solving. I'm not saying that my spadework didn't lay the foundation, but I doubt anyone else could have brought it all together as you have. You are, indeed, the king of all storytelling detectives."

"Much obliged," said Fleet gruffly.

"On one point, however, you've hit the wall. The Keats. Still no inkling there?"

Fleet scowled. "There is always the chance that the answer lies somewhere in this room. *Sophia* was written on the blueprints. But I'm not holding out a lot of hope. Wilson wouldn't have left anything in the open, and I'm sure Todd has been all over the place."

The now-quintessential Parnell giggle indicated that he had.

"You may be right about the Nightingale," agreed E. F., "but I think you've missed a step. The clue says more than you think."

"Does it?" Fleet spoke quite tartly now. "I suppose you know the solution?"

"As a matter of fact, I do," said his junior.

That held us. The assembly paused in their exit. Claude and Lockhart ambled back toward us. Sheriff Greene ceased giving orders to his deputes, while Dean gave the new speaker his attention. The floor belonged to the young.

My peer seemed to be enjoying himself.

"The clue was really quite ingenious," he said, drawing the thing out. "I wonder if he thought of it on the spot."

"Out with it, boy," said Fleet. He did not enjoy sharing the PI's spotlight. "If you have something, spill it."

"Assuredly." He paused. "It all comes down to the Keats. I wonder if you recall the poet's famous epitaph?"

" 'Here lies one whose name was writ in water.' "

I could have told them that. I had seen it in the Keats book.

"What about it?" Fleet asked.

"There's your answer."

He strolled over to Ate Fleet. He took her hand in his and smiled into her elegant, perfectly round face.

"Don't you see? The answer lies with *Ate*."

Nobody seemed to get it. Fleet Jr. explained, "Her employer must have slipped her some kind of clue to the *Sophia*, probably just prior to his rendezvous with me."

"How do you figure?" I asked.

" 'Whose name was *writ* in water,' " he replied. "A-t-e, a name literally *written* in water. W-Ate-r."

We got it. There was a cascade of appreciative hums from those assembled, none more astounded than Ate Fleet's.

"I've had the clue all along? But where? How? I would have seen it!"

"Not necessarily. If it's small enough. He could have slipped it on your person anytime. Perhaps if you wouldn't mind submitting to a quick strip-search."

"That will not be a necessity," replied her father. "Where's your purse?"

She pointed to a small leather bag. Moments later, its contents were dumped out on the poker table for all to see.

"Careful," said Ate.

Fleet Sr. sorted through the bric-a-brac. He picked up her key ring. "When looking for a key to a mystery," he said, "always start with actual keys. Can you identify all these?"

"I doubt it. Can anyone identify all their keys?"

Fleet asked her to try.

She took the ring. With a roll of the eyes, she rattled off labels for each key. Cabin, office, storage. She paused. "Hey, I don't recognize this one."

Both Fleets reached for the ring. There was a bustle of tweed, and the older gentleman emerged, having withdrawn the tiny Excalibur from the loop. It had a weird shape. "Did Wilson have an office in this room?" he asked.

Ate was still gazing at the key. "Uh, yeah. Not his personally, it's an employee room. Really more of a cubby anyone from the casino can use."

She led the way behind the audience chairs to a small office tucked away in the corner. The door was unlocked.

She was right. Just a cubby—a desk, a window, a couple of chairs and a plant desperately in need of more sunlight. Fleet went straight to the closet. (There was also a closet.)

He opened this to reveal an even slimmer cubby within the cubby. More of a broom closet than anything, about two-feet deep.

It was empty. He examined the door, the wall, and an exceptionally thin seam between the two. He shut the door and asked for the key again.

We went back out into the Nightingale Room. He peered at the two fireplaces and headed for the one on the same wall as the office.

"Find me a keyhole," he said.

We searched the brick. Here, there and everywhere, we looked, and the sheriff found it. The police are good at such details.

"This could be a keyhole." He pointed at a tiny seam behind the bricks. It was a big night for seams.

It was a little too uniform to be a mortar mistake. Fleet slid the key in. It fit perfectly, just like my checkered shirt. He turned the lock, and we heard a loud clicking noise from the direction of the office.

"Cool beans," he whispered.

Back to the cubby and the closet door. He pulled the knob. The closet had vanished. In its place, a secret passage had appeared. (Yes, I know, an actual secret passage.)

Beyond this passage was a set of stairs. We all crammed down these, and presently we found ourselves in a large room beneath the Nightingale. It looked like a lab.

"Remember," said Fleet, "Wilson Croker was present for the construction of the casino. He must have had this room commissioned. I think we shall find everything we need to know about *Sophia* down here." He picked up a bottle. "Wilson even thought ahead to make up some of his potion. Conscientious." He put this back on the table and smiled at E. F. "Well done, son," he said, and the young man smiled back at him. I think he said shucks.

"You did good, alright," spoke up someone from the assembly. It was Todd Parnell, and if he sounded smugly confident, there was a good reason for this. He had a gun—relieved, it would seem, from the holster of one of the less aware deputies.

"Sister's kid," said the sheriff, shaking his head.

Parnell motioned everyone into the back of the room. All the Fleets, Claude, Jack Lockhart, Dean, Fleet's scientist friend Judith, Ron, the sheriff and deputies and, of course, me and Lesley. The rest of the Nightingale participants had wandered off or hadn't seen us leave.

Parnell appeared to delight in that most of all. "It will be weeks before they find your bodies down here. Maybe more. Now give me the rest of the guns. You too, old man."

My spirits sank when I heard this. How did he know Fleet had a gun? He was a gentleman detective! And Fleet just gave it to him! Him and everybody else! I liked to think that, if I had a gun, I would have put up more of a fight.

E. F. showed some initiative anyway (I was proud he was my friend, a friend I had no recollection of having). He said he didn't have a gun, prompting Parnell to poke and prod him until the junior detective disgorged a small Sig from his underpants. Hey, he tried.

"Not counting that one, of course," he remarked.

This was it. Here would lie a half dozen people who had died for some stupid brain 'roid.

Todd was glaring at the Sig. Tossing the weapon on the table behind him, he waved the deputy's pistol in a menacing fashion. "I should shoot you for trying that."

"You'd know best. Personally, I would go with shooting no one, but I'm sure you've thought it through."

"If you're going to shoot an Enescu Fleet," said Enescu Fleet (the original Enescu Fleet), "then shoot me."

"If you insist," replied Todd Parnell, twirling around to face him. He glared at the rest of the crowd. "Everyone back up! Don't make me ask again!"

We backed up.

Fleet alone did not move. "Have you really thought this through?" he asked.

"I'll figure it out," said Parnell. "That's the beauty of *Sophia*. What I don't see now will become abundantly clear with its help."

"It's that good, is it?"

"It's amazing. Even the small dosage left in Croker's elephant allowed me to work out every last angle to conceal his murder. And fast too. The canoe, the boathouse—"

"You left the light on inside there, you know."

"I was running short on *Sophia* when I got there," sneered Parnell. "Still, the clock trick worked perfectly. The brilliance there was making Dean think he broke it. All it took was bumping him at the strategic moment. I could do everything except solve that damn clue."

"Some things cannot be gotten at from knowledge alone."

"Maybe not, but you can accomplish a lot trying. Now hand me the formula."

Fleet handed him the formula. Parnell goggled at me and Lesley.

"All you wanted to do is get your memories back. Why? What good are memories? Only what lies ahead matters. You would have wasted it all. It takes ten times as much to return memories as it does to enhance. Wasters, both of you!"

I might have said something stinging in reply to this, but he was the man with the gun. I kept silent.

"You must have missed it so," said Fleet.

"Shut up."

"I mean, all this time, having to think. Having to use the brain that God gave you."

"I said shut up!"

"You must have pulled a mental fetlock competing in our match. Maybe you should take a load off for a while. Put your feet up in that chair and rest yourself."

Parnell had had it. He whisked back across the room and shoved the pistol in the older man's face.

I've often wondered if he would have squeezed the trigger. Fleet has probably wondered this himself, although he's such a manly man, maybe not.

At any rate, it never really got around to triggers. Goaded into movement, Todd Parnell had barely time to raise the gun, when he cried out.

I think the best view was mine. From the shadows of the stairwell, an arrow had shot forth, piercing his palm. It couldn't have felt too good, for he immediately dropped the gun and tumbled back against the table, screeching over his wound. An instant later, Neptune emerged with bow (one of his own, I should think).

I knew Pixie couldn't hold him. No Maltese alive could detain a full-grown Penobscot chauffeur for long. And thank God for that.

I suppose I should have felt relief, but honestly, at the moment, I didn't. All I could think was an inch or two to the right or left and that arrow would have missed Parnell's hand completely and gone straight into my forehead.

I'm all for the gentlemanly approach, but I think this was one of those times when you shoot the guy in the back.

37 — Five Star Recollection

Fleet confirmed his collusion with Neptune shortly thereafter. He had never really entertained any suspicion of Lockhart, so there was no reason to suspect his Penobscot chauffeur. After I had been sent away, they had talked, and it was agreed that Neptune would hover outside the Nightingale Room, should the murderer try to make a run for it. The weapon, evidently, had been Neptune's idea.

"It just shows how in the right hands the bow can spare life as well as take it," said Fleet.

I wasn't much in the mood for philosophizing. We were in the secret lab, just me, Fleet, Fleet, Lesley and scientist Judith. Judith had most of my attention. She was using Wilson's notes, putting together a mixture of *Sophia* that would restore our memories.

"It's an amazing substance, really," she remarked, treating us to a fifteen-minute lecture on the *Sophia* and the thin line between total knowledge and utter ignorance. "It's fascinating, fascinating."

"But is it anywhere near done?" I asked her.

"Oh, I finished ten minutes ago," she said.

As she handed it to me, I heard a little huff of remorse behind me. I turned around and saw Lesley, her face twisted in concern.

I suddenly realized how unchivalrous it looked, my taking the first dose.

That wasn't it, however.

"Oh, Johnny," she said.

I stared back at her.

"Do you really think we should?" she asked.

I couldn't understand her. "Don't you want our lives back? Our relationship back?"

"I don't know that I do!"

I continued to stare at her. "Why?"

"Oh, Johnny," she repeated, "we were miserable!"

"Miserable?"

"He told me," she said, pointing a finger at E. F.

My old school friend looked chagrined. "She got it out of me. All those long hours holed up in the hotel room, I had to tell her something. I was only repeating what you told me. I should have made something up."

I still couldn't understand it. "But why? I mean, how?"

"We argued all the time," said Lesley. "We couldn't resolve to call it quits, and we couldn't bring ourselves to stay together. In short, we were miserable."

She crossed to me and grasped my hand. The hand holding the *Sophia*.

"Why don't we forget about it?" she asked. "Forget everything, literally. E. F. was telling me that we have nothing going on in our lives. No families, crappy friends—no offense, E. F. We're in a rut, both of us. Let's start all over; totally over, together. I'm willing to forsake everything that came before if you are. I'm rather used to it now, in fact."

So was I. What a weird couple of days. For a moment, a long moment, what she offered appealed to me. If restoring my memory meant losing her, I was more than willing to start afresh and toss my previous life by the wayside. What did it matter, really?

But then I hesitated. "It's no good," I said.

She released my hand. "I see. Just like a man, isn't it, always needing to know what he might be missing. They say women are overly curious. I say it's men."

I gave her a wry smile. "It's not that. All I care about is you. That much I do know. I knew it from the moment I first saw you two days ago, or what I thought was the first moment. I knew it when I saw you smile, the way you look when you're worried, when you're thinking. The way you play with your hair. I must have noticed these things a thousand times before, and maybe I took them for granted. I must have. That's why this has all been a gift."

"Then let's keep it!"

I shook my head. "I want us to be happy. Forgetting everything might spare some pain now, but it will also deny us everything we've learned. We would end up right back where we were, only worse, because we would already be living a lie."

She sighed. "So it's back to normal or nothing?" she asked.

"I think so."

She stood there, frowning. She played with her hair. "I'm willing to take a chance on us if you are."

I poured out the *Sophia* into two beakers. Handing her hers, I tipped the glasses together and nodded. We drank.

"It might cause drowsiness," said Dr. Judith at the last moment.

It was too late. The curtain came down, and I knew no more.

I lifted my head and looked around the Nightingale Room. We were upstairs again. I was lying supinely across the felt of the poker table, Lesley lying in the opposite direction so our heads came together in the pot. I suppose our noggins were the prize, after all.

I leaned up. "How long were we out?"

Fleet said not too long. "Twenty minutes at the most. We thought it best to move you up here to rest. You're heavier than you look, Johnny."

I continued to look around. My eyes fell on E. F., and suddenly the memories of our friendship came rushing back. It was true, up until a month ago, I hadn't seen him for years, but who could forget my closest friend from English boarding school?

"Hutton!" I exclaimed.

The so-named nodded. "There's the boy! I see the brain is coming back on line."

It was. I knew him well. E. F., I recalled, had started out going by his initials at school, refusing to tell any of us what they stood for. We eventually took to calling him "Hutton" from the E. F. Hutton brokerage firm. It fit well too, for when he talked, we all listened.

"Now I know what the *E. F.* stands for."

"Now you know."

"Good old Hutton," I said, relishing the remembered label. I was getting tired of mentally tacking on the *Younger* or *Older* to their names. "This makes things a lot easier, especially if we're all going to associate with one another."

I fancied I saw a momentary spasm from the older Fleet. Like his daughter, he enjoyed his family in small doses.

E. F. was pondering. "*Hutton.* I had gotten so accustomed to going by Fleet, I almost forgot how much I like that name."

"Don't forget the break you had going as John Hathaway," I reminded him.

"You bet. That was a nice respite. Although, I gotta say, the trickiest part of playing you, Hath, was the accent."

"Yeah—about that? I don't speak with an American accent."

"I know that. But think about it. You have a distinct British accent, picked up from your years of schooling in England. I, too, have a British accent—because, well, I'm British. And there was the rub. When I adopted the role of John Hathaway, American congressman's nephew, I had to make the decision to cover my accent. It would have just confused people if I played it English. Sometimes a lie is more believable than the truth."

I must have nodded, but to be honest I was no longer all that concerned with Hutton and his methods of speech. I had just observed the most beautiful woman I had ever seen sitting up at the far end of the table.

She tossed her head back and said, "Hi."

"Hi," I agreed.

I bounded off the felt. I took her by the hand and led her over to the window where we could talk alone.

I remembered everything now. I remembered our troubles; I remembered telling Hutton all about it at the class reunion in England. I remembered playing the injured man with him, the typical male blockhead who couldn't understand women and never would.

I told him how happy I had been with how things were, how I wanted everything to stay the same. Lesley was perfect; why change anything? But she didn't see it that way. She felt we weren't going anywhere. There were times, she said, when she didn't know who she was.

I could see it so clearly now. Her attempts to get some commitment out of me, and my refusal to notice these overtures. I recalled our arguments, all the petty disagreements that were about so much more. I remembered how hurt I was when she dyed her hair blonde on this trip. I loved her as a brunette. But she had to do it. She was showing me that she had to change herself. I might have been able to hold things in aspic forever, but she couldn't.

That was the last thing we argued about. Shortly after that, slightly drunk and annoyed, I bumped into a guy at the ice machine outside our room. We started talking (about women), and I introduced myself. He told me about meeting another John Hathaway at the casino this weekend, and slowly it dawned on me that someone had assumed my identity here.

I suspected Hutton at once. We had been talking about the Wolf Valley at the reunion, and coming here under my name was just the sort of idiotic thing he would do. I had to confront him about it.

I hardly paused to explain anything to Lesley. That's why we didn't have any identification on us. In my haste, we left it all behind in our room, including my phone, which I now remembered I use as a watch. All we had was our room key, which Lesley had with her. We got Hutton's cabin key from the reception desk (in much the same fashion as I would get my own room key back later on). We went, we waited, and as described, we drank the coffee.

It all came back to me. What I had been denied all weekend in flashback was more than made up for in the gush of memories now.

I might not know everything, but I knew enough. I knew what I had failed to give Lesley for so long. Me.

"Marry me," I said.

"What?"

"I want to marry you."

"I thought you wanted everything to stay the same. You made it perfectly clear that married people lose their identities."

"Not lose. Get assigned new ones. I'm ready for that new assignment. You?"

She didn't keep me waiting long. Not as long as she could have. "Does your Uncle George have to come to the wedding?"

"Not if we don't tell him about it."

"Then I accept."

I hugged her. "And when we have kids," I said, "I think we should name our first girl Emilia."

"You mean like Earhart?"

"Maybe we'll just call her Sarah," I remarked.

We slowly pulled away from our kiss to see Enescu Fleet beaming at us. "I see you two youngsters have found yourselves, after all. Excellent. Judith has something to tell you."

Dr. Judy gave us a cursory glance. "Go easy on the alcohol for the next few days, kids. You'll be as good as new in no time."

"We already are," I said, shaking her hand. "I guess Claude will make several billion off the *Sophia* formula?"

I could picture Claude distinctly from elementary school now. It was just before I was sent to England and met Hutton. Old Claude. What an ass.

"Not Claude," Judy replied. "He's not the rightful beneficiary, remember?"

"Oh right. Then Jack Lockhart will make a few billion."

Again, Judy shook her head. "As a beneficial memory drug, *Sophia* has a ways to go before it will be ready for market. For one thing, the ingredients are incredibly rare. I don't know where that Trevor guy found them. It will take a lot of work to get it smoothed out."

"Maybe you can help with that," said Fleet. "You're the *Sophia* expert now."

Judy supposed she was.

"Do you think Claude will contest the will?" I asked.

Fleet didn't think he would. "Claude has enough problems now that he lost all those bets."

"But you won."

"Nobody won, Johnny. The match never finished. Besides which, the casino is no longer advancing him the credit he bet with. Claude has made a run for it."

I sighed. Poor old Claude. Always running from his problems.

"Looks like everything worked out for the best for everyone," I started to say, as the voice of Ate Fleet floated in over my words.

"Just drop it," she said, storming into view. "There's nothing more to discuss."

My pal Hutton was following her closely, obviously applying the old charm.

"Oh, but I think there is," he said. "You owe me a date, agreed upon and notarized two days ago. I would like to collect on it sometime."

"That was before I knew we were cousins. I mean, we're related. Yuk!"

"First of all, we're second cousins. The child of your father's cousin is—just take my word for it. Secondly, second cousin, we're not technically related, remember? I was adopted."

"Still. You have the same name as my dad. It's icky."

"Call me Hutton, then. That's what everybody called me at school. I only went by Enescu Fleet to get better business. You have no idea the weight that name carries. Now then, if there are no other objections—"

"It's not only that. What about the girls? When I came to meet you for our date, the clerk at reception said she had seen you with girls, girls and more girls."

"There weren't girls, girls and more girls. There was one girl, singular. Lesley. I met her on the path. Once I figured out what had happened, I took her back to her room to protect her. She had a key, but she didn't know where her room was, or even what name it was under. Meanwhile, I needed some time to think what to do about her and Johnny and my client attempting to erase my brain. Then the body was discovered, and I didn't know what to do or think. You agree that all that took precedence?"

"I guess."

"And if you believe I was anything but a complete gentleman with my friend's girl, then you don't know what the Enescu Fleet name means."

"See, there you go again. You're a Fleet. Ew!"

"Slip of the tongue. I should have said the Hutton name."

"Doesn't matter. What about the evening before that?"

"What about it?"

"Girl One is explained. Fine. Great. But another clerk—"

"More clerks," sighed Hutton. "When will this parade of hotel staff end?"

"Another clerk," she went on, "told the clerk I was talking to that she, the first clerk, had seen you with some other slut the night before. Explain that."

Hutton frowned. He seemed to be counting sluts. "That was you."

"What?"

"It must have been you. How could I have hooked up with anyone else?—not that I would have tried. You and I had just parted, right? Consider that."

Ate considered it. "You mean, I was the slut?" she asked.

The arrival of Dean Driskill gave her time to absorb this. He looked troubled.

"Trouble, Dean?" asked Fleet, drawing himself away from his daughter's spat.

"A little. I was talking to the guys in video, and they say the match came out great. We might have to edit down the denouement, but otherwise, it's perfect."

"Then what's the problem?"

"The network is still expecting Trebek's name to be plastered all over the thing, and I—"

"Don't really know him?"

Dean heaved a sigh. "No. His people never called me back."

Fleet put his arm around Dean's shoulder. "Would you like me to talk to him?"

"Who—Trebek? You know him?"

"I do."

"And you will put in a good word for me?"

"Assuredly. I will put in several."

Dean didn't know how to thank him. He skipped off to tell video that they could proceed with the headers. He was even toying with using a bold serif font. The sky was the limit.

Fleet noticed me shaking my head. "Don't tell me you want to meet Trebek too?"

"No, no. I was just asking myself if you know *everybody*, that's all."

"Not everybody. Just those who matter. That's why it's such a pleasure to finally know you, John Hathaway. And, of course, your lovely fiancée." He kissed Lesley's hand.

"You're not going to read her palm, are you?" I asked. "Like you did mine at the cabin?"

He looked momentarily baffled, but only for a moment.

"I wasn't reading your palm; I was looking for ink. Whoever completed that morning's crossword had smudged the ink with their left hand. I could see you had no ink on yours and later noticed you weren't left-handed. That told me that someone else had completed the puzzle, either someone staying with you or the actual occupant of the cabin. The latter proved to be the answer."

"And that detail told you I could be trusted?"

"It set me along a path of inquiry. The coffee, the gazebo, Lesley telling you that she was looking up at the cabin when she awoke—she had to have been in the gazebo to look up at it—little things that would in time bring us to the solution. None of it told me that I could trust you. That I knew instinctively."

I was glad.

"Last thing," I said. "Speaking of trust, how did you get Neptune to play along? When I left, he wouldn't even agree to speak to anyone, let alone lie in wait outside the poker room, sniping for assassins. How'd you win him over?"

"Oh, that was easy. It turns out that he is a devoted fan of the composer Enescu. Apparently, someone gave him a CD of the Romanian Rhapsody when he was a kid, and he's listened to it a million times. It's his favorite piece of music, and Enescu is his favorite composer. When I told him I was a descendant on my mother's side, he was delighted to help."

I frowned. "But *are* you a descendant of the composer Enescu?"

Fleet considered the question a moment before replying. "You know," he said, "I really don't remember."

Further Reading

If you enjoyed *Fleeting Memory*, don't forget to check out John and Lesley's first adventure in *Five Star Detour*. And if you want to match wits with the trivia experts you just read about, don't miss the ebook *Deadly Allusions.*

www.ingramcontent.com/pod-product-compliance
Lightning Source LLC
Chambersburg PA
CBHW020610310726
48979CB00008B/1419/J

* 9 7 8 0 9 9 1 2 3 2 4 3 7 *